A GANGSTER STOLE MY TRUNKS

A GANGSTER STOLE MY TRUNKS

TOM VAUGHAN

Illustrated by NATHAN REED

■SCHOLASTIC

Published in the UK by Scholastic, 2022
Euston House, 24 Eversholt Street, London, NW1 1DB
Scholastic Ireland, 89E Lagan Road, Dublin Industrial Estate,
Glasnevin, Dublin, D11 HP5F

ISBN 978 0702 30529 0

A CIP catalogue record for this book is available from the British
Library.

Printed by CPI Group (UK) Ltd, Croydon, CR0 4YY
Paper made from wood grown in sustainable forests and other
controlled sources.

1 3 5 7 9 10 8 6 4 2

www.scholastic.co.uk

To Issy

ONE WEEK BEFORE THE CRUISE

CHAPTER 1

The Old Man with the Golden Gun

We sat in that kind of awkward silence you only get when surrounded by old people or farts. The clock on the wall above Gramp's armchair ticked in loud, slow tocks. *Tick. Tock. Tick. Tock.* I glanced up from the grey rock in my hand and looked at Mum. Mum looked at Dad. Dad looked at Gramp.

Gramp smiled and shrugged. "What?"

Dad squeezed the bridge of his nose. I desperately wished someone *had* farted. It'd be less awkward than this.

"What?" repeated Gramp, still smiling.

Dad drew in a deep breath and said, "Pops, you never lived on the moon."

Gramp waved his hand dismissively, his moustache bristling. "Course I didn't!" Dad breathed a sigh of relief. "I only visited! Top secret mission in sixty-nine. On the trail of an evil robot."

Dad screwed his eyes shut and pinched his nose harder.

Mum flashed me daggers and hissed, "Jesse Hall, I told you not to touch *anything* in Gramp's house."

I gingerly put the grey rock back in the big cardboard box. I knew I'd get in trouble for picking it up. It's just sometimes I can't help myself – it's almost like I get an itch that I *have* to scratch. It looked so … weird. I had to get a closer look at it. How was I to know that Gramp would claim it was from the *moon*?

"Pops, you came back with that rock after a trip to Lyme Regis. I remember it!" said Dad.

Gramp shook his head – gently ruffling the neat side-parting in his white hair – and levered himself out of his armchair. "That's just what I *told* you, son. I really used it to bash in the robot's head after

3

it grabbed me in its pincers. It almost had me, the fiend..." He straightened his bright orange cardigan and stood upright – very upright for an old man – then fixed me with his piercing blue eyes. "It was a great day! Fought an evil robot in a crater, then had corn-beef hash for supper!" He clicked his fingers, then clapped his hands. "Absolute winner! Now, who's for a cuppa?"

He didn't wait for an answer before weaving between his packing boxes and out of the room.

Dad called after him, "I'll have a coffee." Then he put his head in his hands. I could see visiting Gramp was getting to him – he looked even more dishevelled than usual and his crumpled shirt had come untucked from his trousers.

Mum waited for Gramp to leave the room, then turned to Dad. "I don't remember him always being like this. Not quite so" – she searched for a diplomatic word – "fantastical."

"Is that a good thing?" asked Dad. "Like the Fantastical Four?"

Mum's eyebrows lowered. "It's not."

"It's the *Fantastic* Four," I whispered.

"Oh, right," said Dad, then let out a big sigh. "Why's he behaving like this? He's always been difficult to figure out. Is he making up these stories about visiting the moon because he's bored? Because he wants attention? Or because he really believes it?"

I didn't know what he was so bothered about. Old people always have fruity stories. And even though I didn't know Gramp very well, it was clear from the last hour we'd spent in his new house that he was no different. You've just got to smile and say "Wow" at the right times, and you get free biscuits in return.

Mum rubbed Dad's back with all the tenderness of someone buffing a scratch from a car bonnet. I could see that she wasn't nearly as bothered as him. "It's just old age. He probably watched *Moonraker* last week and started dreaming he was James Bond."

I gazed around Gramp's new living room and its piles of boxes. This was the first time I'd ever visited him at home. Which is weird considering I'm eleven years old and he is my granddad. But since my granny died, before I was born, he'd lived in Virginia in America and he hadn't exactly been a big part of my life. Here's the sum total of what I know about him:

1. He's only visited us once a year since I was born.
2. He's always been friendly but a bit odd.
3. He's just decided to move back to England and Dad's rented him this little bungalow.
4. He used to be a dishcloth salesman.
5. He almost certainly never visited the moon.

"He could have visited the moon if he had some sort

of pressurized moon shelter and his own spaceship," I joked.

Mum fixed me with eyes that were way too serious. "Jesse, he never had a pressurized moon shelter."

"Or a spaceship," Dad added. "I'd have seen it in the garage. What's he playing at? When I told him we were coming over he said I needed to get off the phone because he was expecting a call from an international cat burglar."

I narrowed my eyes. "Is that someone who burgles cats or a cat that burgles?"

Dad chose to ignore me. "Maybe I should bring up the possibility of a care home. I'm not sure it's a good idea for him to be living on his own with his imagination going into overdrive."

Mum reached across and took his hand in hers. It shocked him. In fact, it shocked me. I think it even shocked Mum. It was the most affection they'd shown each other for ... I couldn't remember how long. Mum dropped it pretty quickly, trying to disguise her embarrassed look by picking biscuit crumbs from Gramp's sofa while tutting.

I looked down at the moon rock box and pretended I hadn't seen the whole awkward moment.

Pushing it to the back of my mind, I studied the contents of the box – a jumble of trinkets and knick-knacks: seashells, snow globes and ceramic ducks, with a miniature Eiffel Tower sticking up in the middle. Something else caught my eye. Stuffed in the corner, there was a gold pistol. It looked SO cool. What was it? A toy? A paperweight? An *actual* gun?

I knew I had to find out. Just like that moon rock, it was like an itch that I *had* to scratch. I *knew* I shouldn't pick it up. I'd almost certainly get in trouble.

I glanced over at Mum and Dad. They were turned away from me.

I definitely shouldn't pick it up.

I gave Mum and Dad one last glance, then…

I picked it up. It felt cool and heavy like I imagined a real gun would.

I shouldn't pull the trigger, I told myself. Like, I REALLY shouldn't pull the trigger.

I pointed it at the empty armchair next to me, pulled the trigger and…

With a click and a thud the gun broke into three pieces: the chamber fell on to the carpet with a soft thud, the barrel landed next to it before rolling under the sofa, the handle remained in my palm.

I scrambled to put the handle back in the box but Mum was too fast. She spun round.

"What are you doing?" she snapped.

"Erm … polishing this for Gramp…" I offered with a wince.

"Honestly," she huffed, her nostrils flaring. "Everywhere we go you break something! You'd better not play any of your usual tricks at Maths Camp next week."

I bit my lip and slumped back into the chair. Maths Camp. Urgh. I did *not* want to go to Maths Camp. I didn't want to go to Maths Camp because I hated Maths Camp. But I also didn't want to go to Maths Camp because I knew *why* my parents wanted me to go to Maths Camp. And I felt sick in the pit of my tummy just thinking about it.

It was one secret I wished I hadn't found out. About three weeks ago – just after they'd had a blazing argument over something stupid like milk or Dad not having a job – I overheard Mum telling Dad that they needed a chat after I'd gone to bed. So I snuck down and eavesdropped as Mum told Dad that she wanted a D.I.V.O.R.C.E. She wasn't happy, she said. He wasn't happy, she said. And they should send me to Maths Camp for a week so they could discuss the D.I.V.O.R.C.E. properly with me safely out of the way.

It had knocked the wind out of me. Every time I thought of it was like a jab of sadness digging into my brain. I didn't even want to say the word properly in my head. As though saying it would make it real. And I knew that going to Maths Camp would *definitely* make it real. Mum's a D.I.V.O.R.C.E. lawyer, you see. And she always says a good D.I.V.O.R.C.E. is just a long conversation. And that's why they want me out of the way – so they can have The Conversation. The sadness jabbed deeper into my brain, turning it numb. Mum and Dad together was … well, it was my life. Me, Mum, Dad and our cat, Purrito. We'd always been together. And I'd assumed we always *would* be together.

I tried to shake the numbness out of my head, and reminded myself that I could still change things. And luckily, I had an ace up my sleeve when it came to Maths Camp. An ace that would delay The Conversation, hopefully long enough for me to figure out a way to cancel it altogether.

Gramp strolled back in holding a tray laden with cups and immediately spotted the shiny barrel poking out from under my armchair.

"What happened to my golden gun?" he said, raising an eyebrow. "I got that when I tracked down an evil assassin to his tropical island. I've got to give it to the old fiend, he made a mean piña colada!"

"Pops!" snapped Dad. "You got that from a car boot sale in Winnersh, on your way back from your annual dishcloth sales conference!"

Mum flashed me a dirty look, clearly feeling I was responsible for this latest flight of fancy. "It was Jesse who broke your toy gun, Sid. I'm sorry."

I reached under the sofa and groped for the barrel. When I found it, Gramp was standing over me, his eyes twinkling. "You didn't disengage the secret safety catch," he said, taking the barrel and reassembling the gun. Then Gramp chuckled to himself and handed it back to me. "Guns were never my thing of course. But you had to know how to use one."

"I KNOW GUNS WERE NEVER YOUR THING, POPS!" yelled Dad. "YOU WERE A DISHCLOTH SALESMAN! WHY DID YOU HAVE TO KNOW HOW TO USE ONE? TO EXECUTE A KITCHEN SPILL?"

With the flickering of a smirk, Gramp poured the tea and handed out mugs. Mum shook her head at Dad, who looked embarrassed at his outburst.

"I think it's cool, Gramp," I said, quietly.

He flashed me a grin.

"Look, Pops," said Dad, "all this make-believe..." He stood up and paced over to the mantelpiece with his coffee. "Robots. Assassins. Going to the moon..." He tailed off as he groped for what to say next, then squeezed his eyes shut, took a sip and...

"BLLLEURRRGHHHHHHHH!"

"Mike!" snapped Mum.

"Pops, you just made me a mug of gravy!" cried Dad,

looking at the brown gravy stains he'd just sprayed all over the carpet.

"Did I?" said Gramp. And then, while Dad dabbed at the stains and Mum flared her nostrils, I could *swear* Gramp gave me the briefest little wink. Had he made a mug of gravy … *on purpose?*

Dad held up the mug like it was a piece of evidence, and said, "Do you really think you can cope living on your own?" He pulled a leaflet for a local care home from his pocket and placed it on the coffee table. "I think we should look at this together next week," he said, trying to sound firm. "Scout it out. You might like it."

Gramp took another slurp of tea. *Or was it gravy?* Silence.

Mum coughed.

Finally Gramp replied, matter-of-factly: "Well, I can't go next week. I'm going on a cruise."

Dad's eyebrows shot up. "Cruise? What cruise? You've only just arrived in England."

Gramp pushed himself out of his armchair and picked up an envelope from the mantelpiece. "A week in the Norwegian Fjords. I won it in a competition! We're going to see whales, mountains, the Northern Lights!"

"But we were going to take you to dinner – it's your eightieth birthday," said Dad.

"How very kind of you. But we'll have to do it when I get back," said Gramp. Then, clocking the distrust in Dad's eyes, handed him the envelope and added: "I'm not making it up!"

Before he could open it, Dad's mobile phone rang. He looked at the number and muttered: "I should get this ... it could be about one of my job applications."

I could hear the voice on the other end as he slipped out of the room: "Mr Hall?"

Mum opened the envelope and slid out the card. Sure as homework, there was a big picture of a cruise liner with some mountains in the background.

"Sid, there are two tickets in here," she said, slightly surprised. "Who are you taking?"

Gramp frowned. "I, erm..." He floundered. "I wanted to..." He mumbled something inaudible that was drowned out by Dad shouting into his phone.

"No... I was not having a joke..." Dad's voice was raised. "Yes, I am aware who Albert Einstein is! Yes, I know he is dead. And yes, I KNOW he would not need to go to Maths Camp. And no, I do not think Maths Camp is worth 200 wet willies…" The tinny voice on the other end shouted some more and I heard Dad say, "Well, it's clear what has happened: *someone* has sabotaged our application form."

I suppressed a smile. Someone had INDEED sabotaged the Maths Camp application form when they found it sitting in Dad's outbox. Me!

Dad was growing exasperated. "But if there is still any space left at Maths Camp we'd love Jesse…" A pause. "Fine!" snapped Dad. "Well, I hope you get those 200 wet willies … and more!"

He stormed back into the room and glowered at me.

"Jesse Hall! This is UN-FOR-GIVABLE!" Mum said.

I wasn't sorry. Not one bit. I'd stalled The Conversation.

Mum stared at the two tickets in her hand and I saw a look pass across her face. "So, if you haven't invited anyone on this cruise yet…" She didn't give Gramp a chance to reply. "Why don't you take Jesse? Part of the reason you came back from the States was to spend time with your family, right?"

Oh no, no, no. "I… I… I…" My brain groped for an excuse, any excuse.

Dad looked unsure. "Do you think that's a good idea?"

Mum had switched into lawyer mode. She had made a decision, and I could see that no one was going to talk her out of it. "It's a pensioner cruise, what trouble could he *possibly* get up to?"

"Well, I'm not sure…" Gramp mumbled. I felt a little pang of relief.

Mum butted in. "Then who else were you going to take?" She raised her eyebrows like she was questioning someone in court.

Gramp looked briefly at Dad, then at the care home leaflet, then said, not that convincingly: "Sure, why not?"

"Then it's settled!" declared Mum. "You'll both have a chance to get to know each other properly!"

I sank into my chair. Instead of going to a Maths Camp with a load of friends from school, I was now going on a cruise with an average age of one hundred and sixty. And, what's worse, stuck on a ship a million miles away, I had even less chance of halting The Conversation. I squeezed my eyes shut and let out a silent moan. That golden gun might have been a toy, but I had still somehow shot myself in the foot.

CRUISE DAY 1: DEPARTURE

CHAPTER 2

The *Tom Cruise*

Mum, Dad, Gramp and I stood by the gangway, the air filled with the hum of engines and the smell of diesel. Behind us sat the grey, concrete Newcastle dock. In front of us floated a rusty old ship with a cloud of squawking seagulls circling it. The cruise would set sail in just over an hour and I was still hopeful that I might be able to wriggle out of it.

I had tried everything not to be here: feigned illness, sprained ankle, temporary blindness, phobia of water, phobia of ships, phobia of old people, turning invisible. But Mum had seen through all of them, even the invisibility (but obviously not like I wanted her to). And here I was, suitcase by my feet, ready to board.

A long line of grannies and granddads tottered along the gangway, gazing up at the cruise liner that towered over us like a big rusty monster. I'd been expecting something like you see on those daytime TV adverts for cruises: a brand-new ship that looked like a shopping mall and was as big as an island. Instead we were about to board what appeared to be a battered old cross-channel ferry. Brown rust stains dribbled down its faded hull and its funnel spluttered and spewed out dirty black clouds.

Dad leaned in and whispered in my ear, "Just checking ... but have you seen *Titanic*?"

"Nope," I lied, just to ease his mind. Those disaster movies terrify him. I could sense he was already scared on my behalf.

He relaxed a little. "Good."

Gramp – dressed in grey chinos, a checked shirt and a bright orange cardigan – gazed at the ship like she was a monument to the wonders of human engineering. "So, what do you think of the old girl?" he asked.

I shrugged. "Well, it's definitely not one of those

uber-modern liners you see on daytime TV," I observed.

"Or even a glamorous old one like the *Titanic*," I replied, before quickly reassuring Dad, "even though I've never heard of that ship and definitely not seen the movie."

Giant strips of paint hung off the ship like patches of dead skin. Dad pointed at her name, painted in peeling letters on her bow: *TOM CRUISE*.

He scowled at it. "Are they allowed to call it that?"

Mum stared. "I think this ship was around before Tom Cruise was famous. Maybe even before he was born."

But Gramp clearly thought she was the pinnacle of luxury cruising. "She can clock up to twenty knots on a calm sea."

"How quick is that?" I whispered to Dad.

"About the speed of a scooter," he replied. Then he

sucked in a long breath and said: "Well, I guess this is goodbye." Before adding, clumsily: "Just for seven days, I mean. Goodbye for seven days."

Mum gave him a withering look, then said to me: "Best behaviour. Don't break anything."

Then I asked the thing that had been eating away at me. "Everything will be the same when I get back, won't it?" There was an unexpected lump in my throat when I said it.

Dad went red and looked at Mum. Mum disguised a startled frown.

Dad looked like his tongue had turned into an inflatable lilo as he tried to get the

words out. "You know … it's normal … when you go away … that…"

"You just enjoy your cruise," said Mum, with courtroom cool. Then she reached in and gave me a hug. Normally Mum's hugs were short and sharp. But she lingered. I squeezed back tightly, not wanting it to end when…

"PICK THAT UP!" she shouted, springing up straight. I felt a pang of sadness as my arms dropped to my sides. "Put it in a rubbish bin!" She'd stood up to berate a dopey-looking teenager in a yellow cruise liner uniform who'd dropped a crisp packet. I let out a silent sigh and turned away. I couldn't even get a proper goodbye hug.

I stared instead at the line of grannies and granddads – my cruise mates for the next seven days – shuffling up the gangway. Among the sea of white hair, I spotted a kid my age. He had a brown bowl cut, a square red backpack and a massive smile. He saw me and gave an energetic wave. I lifted a hand half-heartedly as he disappeared into the ship.

Dad ruffled my hair. "You're going to have a great

time. Whales, fjords, the Northern Lights. I wish we'd done this when I was a kid," he said, with a wistful sigh.

Gramp didn't hear. He was too busy snapping pictures of the ship with a disposable camera, like it was an Egyptian pyramid.

Out of nowhere, a burly old man with shoulders the size of a delivery van appeared and slapped him on the back.

"Sid Hall! I never!" he boomed in a Cockney accent. "I don't Adam and Eve it!"

I gaped at him.

The man had a round belly, a brown sheepskin coat and slicked-back, thinning white hair under a black trilby. He smiled with his whole face, which was red, cratered and worn. I was sure I recognized him from somewhere.

"Fists Harris!" replied Gramp in delight, spinning around and disappearing in the big man's embrace. "What a lovely surprise. Don't tell me you're coming on this cruise?"

Fists whistled in delight. "Ain't that the Babe Ruth!" he chimed.

"What a marvellous coincidence!" replied Gramp. "Meet my grandson, Jesse, he'll be joining us too."

Then he tipped his hat to me. "A pleasure to meet you, young Jesse." Then he set off up the gangway.

Dad looked at Gramp incredulously. "How do you know Fists Harris?"

Gramp watched Fists heave his vast bulk up the gangway, then said breezily: "Oh, I brought down his East End crime racket in the nineteen-sixties. We made up and became chums in the late eighties."

Dad looked flustered. "Pops, he's a TV presenter. He presents that home makeover show on the telly."

That's where I knew him from!

"What language was he speaking?" I asked.

"Cockney rhyming slang. 'Adam and Eve' – believe. 'Babe Ruth' – truth," replied Gramp. "I told you. He used to be an East End gangster. Before he was a TV presenter, that is."

Mum and Dad exchanged doubtful looks. And suddenly, I could see a chink in their armour. Especially Dad's. The rusty ship, the wacky stories... Was this *really* a good idea? My heart leapt – maybe I could wriggle out of the cruise and delay The Conversation after all.

But before I could seize my moment, Mum put a hand on Dad's arm to stop him saying anything and plastered a big smile on her face. "You're going to have a wonderful time, Jesse," she said.

And that was that. No point arguing. My last little bit of hope evaporated.

"Bye. I'll miss you," I said, with a little lump in my throat, and headed up the gangway after Gramp. As I reached the top, I looked over my shoulder to see the two of them standing together, just like they always had. Then I swallowed the lump and stepped on to the liner.

CHAPTER 3
Inspector ... Gramp?

Going inside the *Tom Cruise* was like stepping inside something from a history lesson. I entered through a square door into a packed metal staircase; a queue of frail figures snaked up it, coiling around the spiral stairs in a twisting line of grey hair. The ship creaked and groaned like we were deep in the belly of some enormous whale. I felt my stomach twisting in horror as the reality of the next week sank in: holed up here, completely unable to stop Mum and Dad talking about the D.I.V.O.R.C.E., with only old people for company ... old people who seemed to sense there was a young person on board, and who had all turned around and started smiling at me.

There must have been hundreds of gummy smiles pointed in my direction. I forced my face into a sort of grimace-grin and nodded at them. Their smiles got bigger and my heart sank out of my shoes, through the deck and to the bottom of the harbour. How was I going to get through the next week?

Desperate to look away, my eyes wandered over to an itinerary pinned on the wall. It was for the week's activities. I scanned it, hoping there might be something I could get excited about.

DAY 1 – DEPARTURE

DAY 2 – WATER AEROBICS, DECK GAMES, CAPTAIN'S DRINKS RECEPTION

DAY 3 – BINGO, NATURE-SPOTTING, FJORDS

DAY 4 – NORTHERN LIGHTS

And so it went on until day seven, which ended with yet more water aerobics. I'd been realistic enough to know there wasn't going to be a paintball course on board, but I was hoping for something a bit more exciting than water aerobics and bingo. At least seeing the Northern Lights would be cool.

Gramp stood on the step above me, saying nothing.

I took a deep breath, steeling myself to break the ice a bit, but I couldn't think of a single thing to say. I gazed at his back, trying to conjure up some small talk. Gramp wasn't like the other old people around us. He stood dead upright, for a start, unlike the other hunched frames clutching on to the handrail. Along with his moustache, it gave him a vague military air. But then I thought of him swapping Dad's coffee for gravy like he was some practical joker. He was a hard person to get a handle on.

After a while, he seemed to remember I was there. He looked over his shoulder and smiled his Cheshire Cat smile. "Have you seen *Titanic*?"

That again. "Nope." Didn't want Gramp worrying about me being scared either.

"Shame," he said. "Great movie. Absolute bloodbath. Thing sinks. Everyone dies. Let's hope this old girl doesn't bump into an iceberg." He knocked the inside of the hull and it gave out a bong so loud that an old lady spat out her false teeth. I couldn't help but laugh.

We shuffled upwards, one step at a time. As we turned a corner, Gramp did a double take at the sight of a tall, thin man standing about twenty steps further up. "I don't believe it! Perkins! Perkins!"

"Sid?" replied the man, turning around with a big smile on his face. "I'll wait here!" He stepped aside, letting other passengers past. As we approached, I could make him out more clearly. He was perhaps a bit younger than Gramp – with faded streaks of brown still in his neatly combed grey side-parting. He had a grey goatee beard, glasses, a pale linen suit and seemed delighted to see Gramp.

"You're here as well, old boy?" asked Gramp, excited but slightly disbelieving.

Perkins's head bobbed to the side, then he let out a hearty laugh. "Erm … yes! I won a ticket in a competition!"

"Me too! How extraordinary!" said Gramp, before remembering that I was standing next to him. He put a hand on my back and stepped aside. "Perkins, this is my grandson, Jesse."

A flash of surprise crossed Perkins's face. "I didn't know you had a grandson!" He smiled. "A pleasure," he said, shaking my hand and beaming at me.

Gramp looked around suspiciously and lowered his voice. "Perkins, don't you think this is all a bit odd? Fists, you, me – all on one cruise together? It seems like a *huge* coincidence."

Perkins nodded. "I was thinking the very same thing." Then he put a friendly hand on Gramp's shoulder. "But I'm sure there is a simple explanation."

We continued to climb the stairs. "Perkins and I worked together for years," explained Gramp. "I think you were fourteen when we first teamed up."

"Eighteen," laughed Perkins. "You can't do what we did when you're fourteen, Sid!"

"Did you sell dishcloths too?" I asked.

Perkins let out a tiny little chuckle, then bit his bottom lip. He exchanged the briefest of glances with Gramp, before Perkins quickly switched to a serious face. "That's right. Selling dishcloths."

I glanced up at him. I had the teeniest sense, deep down in my tummy, that he wasn't completely telling the truth. That they were *both* hiding something. Gramp *was* a dishcloth salesman … right? That's what Dad had always told me…

We reached a landing and Gramp pulled out our tickets. "Looks like this is us, Jesse. Let's meet on deck once we've unpacked, Perkins, my boy, and we can see if we can get to the bottom of this coincidence," he said.

We left Perkins behind and ducked through the door into a long, grey corridor that had an overpowering smell of old cigarettes and cleaning product. "Room 1099 and 1098," said Gramp, heading left, brandishing our room keys.

Just then, I was startled by a CLOMP CLOMP CLOMP coming down the corridor.

I swung around to see an immaculately dressed old man who was perhaps just an inch taller than me. His face was sunbed-orange and he wore a purple double-breasted suit, a keyboard tie; he had a thin, curled moustache and combed-back grey hair with a shock of white rippling through it.

"Inspector!" he said, in a thick Latin American accent. "What a very large coincidence."

Inspector? Why was this man calling my dishcloth-selling grandfather "*Inspector*"?

Gramp spun around and raised a single eyebrow. "The Silver Slipper?" The happy surprise he'd shown Fists and then Perkins had gone – replaced by something a lot more suspicious.

"At your service," the elegant man said, with a dramatic bow.

Gramp muttered under his breath, "Something is *definitely* going on here." He introduced me: "Jesse. This is the cat burglar I told your dad about: Felix 'the Silver Slipper' Felipe."

Inspector? Cat burglar?! Just WHAT was going on?

"If you had a valuable cat, no matter where you lived, this man would break in and steal it!" said Gramp. Well, I

34

guess that answered the whole burglar-who-is-a-cat vs burglar-who-steals-cats question. "The two of us have something of a chequered past. But that was all a long time ago."

Felix held his hands up modestly, although his face radiated smugness. "And I am, of course, retired. May your cat sleep in peace."

Something was up. Something was *definitely* up. And I HAD to find out what. "Hello," I said, through a clenched jaw.

It was then that I noticed what the noise had been.

"Are you wearing … silver shoes?" I asked.

He looked down at the shiny metal objects on his feet. "My signature shoes," he said, clearly impressed by what looked like a hideously uncomfy choice of footwear. "They are … silver slippers." He raised one eyebrow and fixed me with a smug glare. Then he added: "Like my name."

I nodded. "I got it."

"You are smart," he said, his eyebrow still raised. "You will perhaps be a detective, like your grandpapa here."

The words knocked me for six. *What?* "Gramp

wasn't a detective…" I said, my head spinning. "He was a dishcloth salesman."

I looked bewildered at Gramp, whose face gave nothing away.

Felix tittered and put a hand over his mouth as if he had been naughty. "I have said too much." He mimed zipping his mouth shut, padlocking it and swallowing the key.

"You, er, can't swallow the key if your mouth is zipped shut," I pointed out.

He raised an eyebrow again, even higher than the first time. "Very good, very good. Most excellent deduction. Maybe being a detective, it runs in the blood?"

He walked backwards to leave us – CLOMP CLOMP CLOMP – still watching us both intently, clearly pleased with himself for revealing a secret. Then he bowed, spun on his incredibly heavy heels and shuffled off down the corridor – CLOMP CLOMP CLOMP – as stealthy as a combine harvester.

I looked at Gramp and I couldn't stop my suspicions from bubbling over. "What was he talking about? Were you really a detective? I thought you were a dishcloth salesman?" I said, the words streaming out at lightning speed.

Gramp coughed and a flickering of a smile passed beneath his moustache. "I *was* a dishcloth salesman. Of sorts. I spent a lot of time cleaning up other people's mess, put it that way."

"But…"

"Here's your ticket," he said, cutting me short. "Room…" He looked around as he tried to remember it.

"1099," I said.

"That's it!" Then he hurriedly turned to his cabin, the one opposite mine. I watched his retreating back, wondering if he was trying to escape me.

"Gramp, can you just…" I called after him.

He didn't let me finish, but gave me a smile and a wink, pushed his key card into his door and said: "Meet on deck at 12.30, OK?" before disappearing inside.

I stood in the corridor for a second, my head spinning. I debated whether to knock on his door and demand to know what was going on. Was he *really* a detective, like that Felix bloke had said? Then why had he always told us he was a dishcloth salesman? And had all these shady people he knew *really* won tickets to the cruise? That seemed far too much of a coincidence.

I tried to ignore the itch – the itch I'd got when I *had* to pick up Gramp's moon rock, or that golden gun … the one that told me I *had* to find out these secrets. Trying to distract myself, I pushed open my cabin door, to be hit with a strong smell of damp. It was a dingy room with a faded red carpet, a dank little bathroom and no windows or natural light. But, right now, I couldn't care less if I had to sleep in a bottle bank for the next week. I had bigger things to deal with. I stepped inside and closed the door. But I just couldn't ignore the itch. It was all I could think about. The thought that Gramp was keeping secrets from me was driving me bananas. But at the same, I realized that I hadn't thought of The Conversation *once* since we'd met Perkins. And if scratching that itch meant finding out the truth *and* taking my mind off Mum and Dad, then I was going to scratch like hell.

I pressed my eye to the little spyhole in the door. A

bulging, frog-eye view of the corridor came into sight. I wasn't quite sure what my plan was, but I thought perhaps I could follow Gramp at a safe distance and see if I could find out what was really happening...

Sure enough, within a couple of minutes, Gramp casually sauntered back out and headed down the corridor. I waited thirty seconds, then slunk out, ready to follow him. But as I closed my door with a soft click, my eyes fell on Gramp's. He'd accidentally left it ajar.

My pulse quickened.

I shouldn't go in there, I thought. But I was feeling all itchy just looking at that open door.

I looked at him sauntering down the corridor...

I really shouldn't go in there...

I glanced down the corridor one last time to make sure he had gone. Then I pushed his door open and slipped inside.

CHAPTER 4
The Secret Scrapbook

I stood in Gramp's cabin, my heart beating and my palms sweaty, not entirely sure what I was doing in here. It felt *very* naughty. I told myself that I was simply helping Gramp close his door. I was just doing it … from the inside. And seeing as I was already in here, I *might as well* take the opportunity to have a snoop around, see if I could get any answers about this "Inspector" business. I'd already *tried* asking Gramp about it. And if he wasn't going to give me a straight answer, I'd have to find one myself. It was definitely the kind of thing Mum would go bananas about if she found out, but thankfully she wasn't going to.

I moved quickly, looking around, trying to see if I

could spot anything out of the ordinary. The room was as damp and tired as mine. The only difference was that it had a large window overlooking the sea that cast a square of light on his bed, on top of which lay his brown leather suitcase. He hadn't unpacked a thing. I hurried over to it, clasped hold of the cold little locks and pushed them sideways. The latches sprung upwards with a satisfying POP and revealed two stacks of neatly folded clothes.

There had to be *something* in here that'd tell me who Gramp really was. Was he the dishcloth salesman he'd always told us, or some kind of *inspector*?

I began to remove the clothes layer by layer, like I was on an archaeological dig, lifting them gently from the case and placing them on the bed.

Shirt

Shirt

Trousers

Trousers

Pants

Pants

And so it went on until the last item. A wool cardigan.

I lifted it out and my heart did a little flutter as the corners of a large hardback notebook began to appear, tucked into the bottom of the suitcase. I threw the cardigan aside, snatched it up and immediately felt the hope drain out of me. Printed on the front cover were the words DISHCLOTH SAMPLES, and poking out from the sides, the edges of multicoloured cloths. I let it fall from my fingers and back into the suitcase. I couldn't believe that I'd thought snooping around in here might dig up something interesting. What was I hoping for? An inspector's badge and magnifying glass? A tell-all diary? No, this was a stupid idea. Maybe he *was* a dishcloth salesman after all.

I reached down for the cardigan to repack everything. And that's when my eyes fell on the SAMPLES book, now lying open at the bottom of the suitcase, and my heart nearly exploded out of my ribcage. There, on the open page, someone had glued a picture of a very young Gramp. He was holding a gold medal and beaming. Next to him stood a baby-faced Perkins. And on the opposite page was a yellowing, typewriter-written letter with the words TOP SECRET MEMO stamped on it.

I snatched it up and read, my heart pounding.

RE: LUNAR ROBOT CASE

DATE: 3 NOVEMBER 1969

The lunar robot case is now closed.
Inspector Sidney Hall yesterday
successfully executed Operation
Metalania, to capture the robot and
return it to Earth. The operatives were
initially outmanoeuvred by the target,
but Detective Chief Inspector Hall single-
handedly apprehended the robot, using
just a moon rock as a weapon. For bravery
and initiative, he receives a Distinguished
Service Medal.

My head spun. I could hardly process the information.
Gramp *had* been to the moon to kill an evil robot!!
And he *was* a detective? As was Perkins? *What the what?*
I almost couldn't believe it. Was it some kind of joke?

I reached up a trembling hand and turned over to another page.

There was the same combination of yellowing memo and faded photo of Gramp and Perkins, both glued on to the spread.

I read on, my head swimming.

RE: THE SILVER SLIPPER CASE

DATE: 16 JULY 1972

Fugitive cat burglar Felix "The Silver Slipper" Felipe has been detained in Rio de Janiero, Brazil. Detective Chief Inspector Sidney Hall and Assistant Chief Inspector Clarence Perkins apprehended him during the heist of a luxury cattery. No cats were harmed during the raid. Felipe is now cooperating with operatives to identify the current whereabouts of the 300+ felines he has stolen during the last five years.

I furiously leafed through the other pages – there were dozens of them the same, with pictures of Gramp and Perkins through the years, alongside the yellowing TOP SECRET memos. I could hear the blood rushing through my ears as I tried to make sense of what I was reading. This wasn't a DISHCLOTH SAMPLES book at all! There was the odd cloth glued in to make it look like it was. But in reality it was some sort of scrapbook of Gramp's memories. Memories … from his time with MI6?!

RE: THE HARRIS GANG INFILTRATED
BY CHIEF DETECTIVE INSPECTOR
SIDNEY HALL

RE: INTERNATIONAL ARMS RING
TERMINATED BY DETECTIVE CHIEF
INSPECTOR SIDNEY HALL

RE: CONMAN'S CROWN JEWELS
THEFT HALTED BY DETECTIVE CHIEF
INSPECTOR SIDNEY HALL

I felt like my brain might explode. The room was spinning. I couldn't believe it. My gramp – the same guy who served my dad a mug of gravy and used to give us dishcloths for Christmas – was a secret MI6 detective? This was unbelievably COOL!

Questions began to stack up inside my brain like a pancake tower. How come Dad didn't seem to know ANY of this? Would Gramp be angry that I'd found out? And WHY was he now on a cruise with two of the criminals he'd arrested? As well as his old assistant? I'd come in here looking for answers and ended up with more questions. I shut the scrapbook and instinctively stuffed it up my jumper. Now I'd found it, I wasn't going to be satisfied until I'd read every single page.

I stood up to leave when something else caught my eye – an opened envelope lying half under the bed with the word SID on it. I snatched it up and pulled it open, wondering if there could be *more* secrets lurking here. After finding out that Gramp was a secret detective who had visited the moon, nothing would surprise me now. I lifted the flap but felt my excitement deflate. It was empty. I thought for a nanosecond, and then grabbed for the bin. My tummy did a cartwheel. There, at the bottom, was a little white postcard! I fished it out.

I have booked for eight at Davy Jones's Bar at noon. Please join us.

It was unsigned.

A table for eight? Who were the other four people aside from Gramp, Perkins, Fists and Felix? Could *more* shady characters from his past be on board? The thought made me excited and anxious and even more determined to find out the truth.

All I knew was that something fishy was DEFINITELY going on. And either Gramp knew all about it and was pretending otherwise, or he was as in the dark as I was. And both those scenarios sent my suspicion-o-metre soaring. I *had* to find out what they were all doing here. I *had* to spy on that meeting at Davy Jones's Bar. After that, I'd decide when and if I was to confront Gramp with the truth about his past. I didn't know him well enough to have a handle on how he'd react to me snooping around like this. I needed to choose my moment carefully. Perhaps, I was thinking, I wouldn't tell him at all. Maybe I'd just spy on things from afar.

That was *one* way to stay occupied over the next seven days and keep my mind off The Conversation.

I checked my watch. Noon was in thirty minutes. I sprang up and, as carefully as I could, placed his clothes back in his suitcase. Then I closed it and, with the scrapbook still stuffed up my jumper, let myself out.

I'd scratched one itch. But, like a skin rash or a mosquito bite, it was just getting itchier. Because one thing was apparent – there was a lot more happening on this cruise than bingo and water aerobics.

CHAPTER 5
Wendall

I stood on the top deck, Gramp's scrapbook gripped tight under my jumper, soaking in the bombshell: I wasn't on holiday with a retired dishcloth salesman, but a **secret government detective**. *And* he was my grandpa.

It was mind-blowing. And, I was starting to suspect, just the tip of the iceberg. Why was Gramp *really* on this cruise alongside his old assistant, two former criminals and heaven knows who else? There was no way they'd all simply won tickets in a competition. That was *far* too convenient.

The *Tom Cruise*'s horn blasted – a deep, reedy noise

that seemed to rip the sky apart and sent a cloud of gulls screeching into the air. Clouds of diesel spewed out from the dirty funnel behind me and, with a soft lurch, I felt the liner pull away from the shore. This was it. No turning back now. I was stuck here with Gramp and his secrets. I had to get to the bottom of it all – even if it took me the whole week. Which I was starting to hope it might. I'd barely thought of The Conversation since boarding.

I pushed off the railing. Behind me was a tired old mini-golf course that looked like it hadn't been used for decades. It was full of dirty fibreglass sea creatures as big as me: with flaking paint and a coating of black soot from the diesel fumes. I idly stepped on to the course, wandering through it, thinking hard. Just *how* could I try and spy on that meeting at noon?

I picked my pace up, heading for the exit, but then I spotted an old golf ball wedged in the mouth of an eel-shaped tunnel. I prodded it free with my toe and it rolled out in front of me. I stared at it and started feeling itchy.

I knew I shouldn't kick it.

Like, I really shouldn't kick it.

I looked left and right, then…

I booted it hard with my toe.

It shot off through the forest of mini-golf obstacles and I was overcome by an immediate wave of regret. If it rolled off the deck and landed on one of the passengers below I'd be in so much trouble. I sprang after it, weaving between a large fibreglass cod and a mossy lobster and out the back of the golf course. The ball sped across the wooden floorboards, heading straight for a set of railings. I sprinted after it, lunged across the floor and … grabbed a fistful of thin air as it plopped off the end of the deck.

Oh. No.

I screwed my eyes shut as I heard it hit the deck below with a loud crack. I gingerly stuck my head between the railings and opened my eyes, expecting a baying crowd to be staring back. Instead, I was greeted by the sight of a dirty, deserted deck with an outdoor pool in the middle. Or rather, an *ex*-outdoor-pool. Now it was just a square blue hole with a miserable brown puddle at the bottom. The golf ball bounced once, twice, three times, then landed with a splosh in the shallow brown water.

"They drained it," said a sing-song voice behind me.

I stood up and swung around to be greeted by the rosy-cheeked boy I'd seen on the gangway.

"I'm gutted as well," he said. "I LOVE swimming. In pools, mind, not out there!" He pointed at the sea and laughed like he'd said a really funny joke. I forced a weak smile.

He scampered over and offered his hand. "I'm Wendall," he said, out of breath just from running the three paces between us.

I eyed him up cautiously. He had a moon-shaped face, a bowl cut and big brown eyes like a milk cow. He was still wearing his boxy red backpack. No offence meant, but he looked like the kind of kid who it'd be social suicide to hang around with at school. Don't get me wrong, I'm no cool kid myself. But this guy, he'd drag me down six rungs just if I shared a bag of Wotsits with him.

"Jesse," I said, tentatively shaking his hand.

"It's always been empty," he said, pointing at the pool. "At least as long as I've been coming."

I stared at him in horror. "You mean you've been on this ship before and you've … come back?"

He smiled and nodded, thinking I was impressed. "This is my eighth cruise on it with my nan!"

"Right," I replied, narrowing my eyes. "And do you … enjoy them?"

"Do I?" he answered, his eyes springing wide open. "I love them! I spend time with my nan… I get to see the world! Plus, it's mega fun on board."

I stared out at the depressing grey sea and thought of the bingo and water aerobics. I began to suspect he was out of his mind. I'm not sure what the opposite of cool is – hot, warm? Whatever it is, this guy was roasting. He was like an excitable five-year-old. And I had bigger fish to fry than chatting O.A.P. cruise activities with him.

"Look," I said, putting on a fake smile. "It was nice meeting you, but…"

He sensed I was about to leave and his voice dropped to a hurried, conspiratorial whisper. "Here … did you know there's a haunted flume ride called the Black Hole in the indoor pool? It's out-of-bounds. It's supposed to be so scary it killed four pensioners last time it was open. Do you want to go and see it with me?"

I rocked on my heels, momentarily torn. In any normal circumstances, I'd have been there in a heartbeat. Even with this excitable gnome. But I couldn't get distracted – I had to find out what was going on with Gramp.

"Maybe another time..." I said, turning away with a pursed smile.

"Any time you want!" he said, stepping towards me eagerly. "We've got all week together and I can show you around whenever you want! I know every bit of this ship! Every nook and cranny!"

I turned back to him. "Every nook and cranny?"

He nodded, like one of those wobbly toy dogs you see in the back of cars.

"Do you know where the Davy Jones's Bar is?"

He beamed, clearly overjoyed that he'd finally got my attention. "Of course I do!" he replied, unfurling a map of the ship from his back pocket and holding it between us. "It's here, on Deck 2!"

There it was indeed, right below us, beside the empty outdoor pool.

"*Anddddd*...." I said, steepling my fingers and putting them to my lips. "What if someone wanted to spy on someone there? Where would be the best place to hide?"

He looked up at the sky. "Well, I suppose they could go by one of the windows beside the old outdoor pool there and..."

I grabbed him by the arm. "Wendall, you're coming with me."

CHAPTER 6

A Small Gathering of Criminal Masterminds in a Nautically Themed Bar

Wendall and I wove down a flight of rusty stairs, along the promenade deck and towards the drained pool at the back of the ship.

Wendall led the way and I followed, crouching below each window so I wasn't seen. There was a stack of old, dirty sunloungers between the bar and the drained pool. Wendall wedged himself behind them, right next to a window into Davy Jones's.

"This is where I'd probably go," he said, scanning my face and looking delighted at my nod of approval.

Then a thought hit him and his face fell into a confused frown. "Say … what exactly are we doing here?"

"I told you," I said, pulling him down so we were both sitting on the floor beneath the window. "Spying."

"Like, *really*?" he asked, suddenly nervous. "Cos I don't want to get in any trouble."

I smiled and shrugged. "Then let's not get caught."

He pushed his mouth to the side and let out a nervous noise that sounded like a tyre deflating.

I reached up and peeked over the window ledge and into the bar. It was a square space decorated in a nautical blue-and-white theme, its ceiling strung with old fishing nets. Gramp was sitting near our window, deep in conversation with Perkins, Fists and Felix, as well as an old lady I didn't recognize.

I pushed my fingernails into the bottom of the cold metal window frame and wiggled it upwards. To my delight, it slid open an inch. I moved my ear to the gap and found I could hear everything inside perfectly.

"Perkins, mate, I 'ear you're still a private detective?" said Fists.

Perkins wiggled his eyebrows and laughed

disarmingly. "Certainly am," he chuckled. "Still in the game, somehow!"

Fists lifted his hat and slicked back his hair with his palm. "What's it like still snooping about in your seventies? You're getting too old for that lark."

Perkins shrugged an easy shrug. "I wish I could afford to retire, Fists, old friend!" he smiled.

Wendall was now next to me, peeking through the window gap. I could sense his nerves ratcheting up. "Please, Jesse – can you tell me what we're spying on?"

I pushed my mouth to the side and stared into his big brown, worried eyes. I took a deep breath and decided to hit him with the truth, the whole truth and nothing but the truth. There was nothing to lose. "So…" I sucked in a lungful of air and launched straight into it: "I've thought my entire life that my Gramp was just a boring dishcloth salesman but recently he's been making ridiculous claims like he fought a robot on the moon and caught a cat burglar. I thought he was making it all up. But when we got here it turns out he knows loads of people on board and they are all calling him Inspector. So, I broke into his room and found a secret file saying he really *did* go on all these secret missions to the moon and stuff – as a secret MI6 detective. What's more, some of those people are actually old criminals he once arrested. Except he doesn't *seem* to know why they're all here or who invited them. So that's what we're doing here – spying on their meeting so we can find out what on earth is going on." I finished and took a big gulp of air. I looked at Wendall with utter seriousness. It didn't really matter if he believed me or not. But I thought that, after helping me out with a spy place, he deserved a straight answer.

Wendall looked at me dumbfounded for a second. Then his face creased. "Hahahaha. You nearly had me there! That's a good one, that is!"

"Here, don't believe me? Then look at this!" I pulled the scrapbook out of my jumper and handed it to him.

Wendall gingerly took the scrapbook, opened it and his eyes immediately enlarged to the size of pizzas. "Should I be looking at this?" he asked, still looking at the file. He didn't wait for an answer before turning a page, then another, then another.

I peeked over the window sill again. The old lady

was showing Gramp and co. her walking stick. She looked a bit more normal than the rest – like a run-of the-mill granny in a brown cardigan, buttoned white blouse and long grey skirt. Her hair was in short little curls and she had horn-rimmed glasses perched on her nose.

"I made it myself," I could hear her say, in a deep throaty croak.

Then she raised the walking stick to the ceiling and suddenly a blinding light and violent

ROOOOAAARRRRRRRRRRRRR

ripped the room in two as a pillar of fire burst out of its end. Gramp and Perkins's hair blew backwards like they were on a rollercoaster.

My eyes nearly popped out of my sockets. I could feel the heat through the windowpane, as the flame melted a load of plastic fish placed in the ceiling's fishing nets. Then finally, with a splutter, it died back down. Gramp, Perkins, Fists and Felix sat there speechless, their eyebrows lightly smoking, their cheeks covered in soot.

"Very, erm, nice, Eileen," said Gramp.

Drops of molten plastic dripped down from the

ceiling. Thank goodness there was no one else in the bar.

"Who. On. Earth. Is. She?" I said, looking across at Wendall. Surely she must be *another* shady character from Gramp's past?

"Here, wait. I think I saw a picture of her in here," said Wendall, opening the scrapbook. I watched him as he leafed from page to page, his tongue sticking out of his mouth as he concentrated. Going on first impressions, I'd thought he was the kind of kid who'd get scared by all of this. But I was wrong. He seemed as intrigued as me. He turned another page, then thrust the book at me triumphantly. "Ms Eileen Ho-Renton! Arms dealer!"

Sure enough, there was a picture of her in combat fatigues, holding a bazooka in what looked like the jungle. The caption talked about her supplying weapons to Vietnamese rebels and Gramp later busting her international arms ring.

"You haven't changed, Eileen!" laughed Perkins.

"Shall we get some tiddly winks?" said Fists, before offering a translation: "Drinks?"

"Here, I know that bloke," whispered Wendall. "He

presents *Changing Changing Rooms* on telly. You know, when they do makeovers on changing rooms. I once saw him knock through two rugby locker rooms with his bare fists. It was awesome telly. Building collapsed of course, but that's not the point. Who are the other two that your gramp is with?"

"That's Perkins, Gramp's old assistant," I replied. "And Felix 'The Silver Slipper' Felipe. Apparently he was an international cat burglar who Gramp arrested."

"But they are all … friends now?" asked Wendall, tentatively.

"I *think* so," I whispered. "I haven't quite worked it out yet. But they're all being very friendly to Gramp – considering he arrested most of them."

A loud voice erupted from close to the table: "Drinks orders, please, homies!"

Whoever was speaking – or rather, shouting – was hidden behind a pillar. But they had a voice like someone acting in a bad play.

"Scotch on the rocks," croaked Ms Ho-Renton.

"I'll have a Rosy Lee – a cuppa tea," said Fists. "Cream. Twelve sugars."

"Right you are," boomed the waiter. "Any more drinks, rude dawgs?"

Who *was* this guy? And why did he sound like a cartoon character? He stepped out from behind the pillar and I got a proper glimpse of him for the first time. He was an old man about Gramp's age, but he was dressed up like a skater – baggy shirt, back-to-front cap, shaggy, long hair that looked a LOT like a wig.

Gramp and Perkins gave their drinks orders and the waiter nodded without writing them down. "Finally, dudes," he bellowed. "Can I interest anyone in a nice refreshing slice of…" He left a pause, then said: "Squid."

Gramp spun around and gave a gasp.

"Sonny, you fiend!" he declared.

The weirdly dressed waiter pulled off his hat and wig and did a theatrical bow. "At your service!"

"Who is *that*?" I whispered, pulling a face.

Wendall leafed through the scrapbook and thrust it to me, open on another page. "It says here he is called Sonny 'The Squid' Smith. He's a conman. A fraudster. Apparently a master of disguise. Responsible for stealing some of the most valuable items in the whole world. Famous jewels, priceless artworks, that sort of thing. Your gramp arrested him in 1975 for stealing the Crown Jewels."

"*Another* of Gramp's old enemies?" I muttered. "Just *what* is going on?"

Sonny dropped into a chair, pleased as punch. "Still got it!" he purred, smugly. He had a thin face like a weasel and a messy shock of silver hair swept back over his head. "And..." he said, lifting a wallet.

"Why, you sly devil!" said Gramp, shaking his head.

As Sonny handed it back to him, I noticed he was missing a little finger.

"Am I still one of the best pickpockets you ever arrested?" he asked with a smug chuckle.

Perkins laughed. "*The* best, Sonny."

I counted the attendees. Six.

Just then, there was a loud cough and the noise of someone hawking phlegm. It came from the entrance to the bar, where a bulky man with long white hair stood. He had a square chin and wore a leather jacket with tassels and cowboy boots.

A silence fell over the group. They all seemed

desperate to look *anywhere* except at the man. Like a prowling tiger, he made his way towards their table.

I whispered to Wendall, "Who is *he*?"

Wendall leafed frantically to the end of the book, and then back again. "Ivan Django. Says here that he ran an international criminal operation called G.E.M.I.N.I. … but that your gramp never managed to catch him!"

I shook my head. This was all becoming far too bizarre.

The silence hung over the group as Ivan arrived. He didn't say hello. He simply lowered himself into a chair with a soft grunt. From my position peeking over the window ledge, I could see his eyes closer-up. One was black, the other one bright green, and together they had the intensity of two death rays. He gave me the shivers.

Suddenly, the lights dimmed and a spotlight lit up, casting a yellow circle on the stage curtains. Oldy-worldy gramophone music sounded over the speakers. The curtains pulled back to reveal a tall, stunning black lady. She was dressed in black-and-white and had a huge beehive hairdo. Everyone broke into spontaneous applause at her appearance.

"Well I never!" declared Gramp. "It's Bridget Bouffant!"

Bridget stood motionless, her chin on her chest, her shoulders hunched, her hands hanging limp. The music picked up in intensity and her two gloved hands flew up, palms towards us, moving along as if pressed against an invisible piece of glass. The hands explored left and right, then down, then up. Her fingers curled over a pretend ledge, pulled down an invisible window and her face sprang up in mock shock at the sight of everyone. All seven of them clapped sensationally.

"Who's she?" I whispered to Wendall, not taking my eyes off the stage.

Wendall flicked some pages, then whispered back: "Bridget Bouffant. Femme fatale. Apparently she used to seduce rich men, then rob them. Made off with millions before your gramp caught her. Says here that later on she became a silent-movie star and mime."

"That makes eight of them," I muttered under my breath.

Bridget finished by dropping into a sweeping bow and Gramp's table gave a standing ovation. She sashayed her way across the room to them.

"Madame Bouffant!" exclaimed Gramp, still clapping.

"Sid!" She beamed, giving him two big air kisses before going around the chairs one by one. There was something hypnotic about her. Even though she must have been Gramp's age, she was still beautiful, and moved with a cat-like grace.

Finally, she came to Felix but he refused to even look at her. She lingered for a second, clearly disappointed by his reaction, then sat down.

Her bum had barely hit the seat before Gramp was standing up. His face looked like it had switched to inspector mode. He was looking from person to person, his eyebrow ever so slightly raised. "Why are we all here?"

The answer rang out in unison. "I won a ticket!"

They looked at each other, shaking their heads in puzzlement. I thought I saw a couple of them exchange side glances, but I couldn't be sure.

"Me too," muttered Gramp. "This is too much of a coincidence."

"*Too* much of a coincidence," echoed Sonny. He

was smirking, but I couldn't be sure if that was just his normal resting expression.

"Darlings, what a peculiar little mystery!" said Bridget. "I hope we're not in danger!"

"*Oh dios!*" said Felix, making the sign of the cross.

"Well," said Fists, sombrely removing his trilby and scratching his head. "If there is one person I know who can solve a mystery, it's you, Sid."

"Yes!" croaked Ms Ho-Renton. "Find out what the heavens is going on, will you?"

A quiet fell over the group. Some of them glanced fleetingly at one another. Was there something knowing in their looks? Or was I just imagining it?

Finally, Felix broke the silence. "I fear that we are perhaps in for a very big *surprise*." Then he smirked.

I stared hard at them all. I may be new to the detective game, but there was one thing I was certain about – some of the people around that table *definitely* knew more than they were letting on.

CHAPTER 7
Busted!

I slipped back under the window ledge, stared out to sea and soaked in everything I'd just heard.

Next to me, Wendall was processing it all himself. "So, let me get this right: your gramp, who used to be a master detective or something, has mysteriously been invited on a holiday with *six* of his former enemies, as well as his former assistant? And none of them claim to know why?"

I nodded. "It's very odd, isn't it? Emphasis on the *claim* to know."

"Do you think one of them is up to something?"

I nodded again. "One of them. Or all of them."

"Golly." He sucked his teeth. "What do you plan to do about it?"

I dragged my eyes away from the rolling grey waves and looked at Wendall. He stared back at me with brown eyes.

"I dunno," I said, pushing my lips to one side in thought. "But I know I've got to find out."

He stared back. I could see he wanted to know too – that he had that same need as me to scratch the itch.

"How do you think we do that?" he said. The word "we" seemed to slip out and he immediately looked embarrassed. "If you want some help, that is."

I felt a smile unfold across my face. Some kids would be scared of spying on a bunch of strangers. Others would be too wrapped up in themselves to care about someone else's problems. Wendall was neither. He was up for stuff: up for riding the Black Hole, up for spying on my gramp, and – so it seemed – up for solving this mystery. I'd judged him too quickly and felt a bit ashamed. Despite the bowl cut and the over-excitedness, there was something I liked about him.

"Wendall, you know what?" He looked up at me

eagerly. "I think you and I are going to become good buddies this week."

A smile as bright as a supernova spread across his own face, only for it to freeze halfway as a voice boomed from the other side of the sunloungers.

"Jesse!"

My limbs turned to ice. It was Gramp. He was peering over the sunloungers, frowning at Wendall and me.

"What are you doing there? Were you spying on me?" he asked, calmly but directly. Then he clocked the scrapbook in my hand and raised an eyebrow. "And *how* did you get that?"

Wendall bought me some time by turning bright red and blabbering. "I'm sorry, sir, it weren't my idea, sir, I don't usually go spying on people, I just…"

Gramp held up a cool hand to cut him off. "It's OK, young man. I think perhaps I need to have a chat with my grandson. Why don't you run along…"

"Wendall, my name's Wendall, sir," he said, getting up and scampering past me. "Thank you, sir. Sorry, sir."

Gramp stood there, his hands in his pockets, his

orange cardigan bright against the grey sea. "New friend?" he asked.

I looked down at the scrapbook on my lap, nerves sloshing inside me with every wave the boat rode over. Was he angry? Would he tell Mum and Dad? I didn't know Gramp well enough to be sure. I probably shouldn't incriminate myself any further, but...

"It's all true, isn't it? Everything you've been saying about the moon and stuff." The words blurted out of my mouth before I had a chance to stop them. I pushed my head into my shoulders and winced as I asked: "Are you cross?"

Gramp's vivid blue eyes blazed. "Let's go for a walk." Was there a little smile beneath his moustache? Or was I imagining it?

He turned on his heels and started walking down the promenade. I scampered after him, still clasping the scrapbook.

"How much did you see back there?" he asked.

This was no time to lie. "Everything."

"Right ho," he said, merrily.

A sea breeze whipped past my cheeks, the salt

catching on my tongue. England was gone now, and there was nothing in view but choppy waves and a line where grey sea met grey sky. The boat rocked back and forth gently, and I could feel the sway becoming part of me, altering my every movement.

An itch gnawed at me. I had to confront Gramp with the secrets I'd found. There was no way I could pretend otherwise. I took a deep breath and plucked up the courage.

"Were you a … secret agent?" I asked, as we headed up the steps and back on to the top deck.

Gramp laughed, the smile bursting forth from under his moustache. "Lordy, no! I was a detective for MI6. I did all the boring stuff – chasing down leads, following clues, piecing together witness statements. Building a case, really. All with Perkins as my assistant. It was the secret agents who did the fun stuff – apprehending the bad guys."

"Like Felix, Fists, Sonny, Ivan, Bridget and Ms Ho-Renton?" I asked.

He laughed. "Well, actually, *I* ended up arresting all of them."

"But … you're all friends now?" I asked, tentatively.

He nodded a nod that said, "I guess so". "Fifty years ago we were enemies. But we became acquaintances – friends, in some cases – once they came out of prison. They are reformed characters. There's no animosity any more. At least, none that I know of."

Now that I'd started, I decided to go for it – to not hold back with the questions. "Why does Dad think you were a dishcloth salesman?"

He chuckled. "Why, it was my cover. For years this was all top-secret stuff." Gramp didn't seem to have anything to hide. And, more importantly, he didn't seem cross with me. In fact, if I was reading him right, he almost seemed *pleased* that I had spied on him. He gestured at the scrapbook clutched against my chest. "This has all only recently been declassified. But now when I try and tell your dad about it, he won't believe me!" He sucked his moustache pensively. "I've spent a lifetime hiding the truth from your father. Now I'm finally revealing it, he thinks I'm going senile!" He laughed at the irony of it.

"So, er, why don't you show him this?" I asked,

holding up the scrapbook. Dad would have to believe him then. I tried to imagine how he'd react. He hates risk. And danger. And being away from home for long periods. Maybe he wouldn't be so impressed after all.

We came to the back of the deck, the Union Jack flapping wildly from a flagpole and an angry white trail of foam snaking through the waves behind us. He gripped the railings and looked to the horizon, his little side-parting fluttering in the wind. "Your dad and I are a bit like chalk and cheese," he said, without answering my question.

I sucked the side of my cheek. "You really don't mind me stealing it?" I asked.

He carried on looking out to sea distractedly and frowned. "Stealing what?"

I pulled a face. "The scrapbook?"

He blinked hard, as if scolding himself. "Sorry. No, of course not!"

"Or me breaking into your cabin?"

"My cabin?" He looked confused by the word, which I thought was odd.

"Your bedroom," I added.

"Oh. Of course." He blinked again. "Certainly not! That was sterling detective work."

It was *good detective work!* I thought. Normally, when I did something like that, I'd end up in huge trouble with Mum and Dad. But Gramp ... Gramp seemed genuinely impressed! Impressed by me! I stared at the sea and felt the happiest I had for months. For the first time, I was glad I was stuck on this mouldy cruise for the next week. And, what's more, I had something to take my mind off The Conversation.

"So you *really* haven't got a clue who's invited you all?"

He shook his head. "No. But someone's up to something. That much I can tell."

"You must know them better than anyone, right? You're the one that tracked them all down and arrested them? If anyone can work out what's going on, surely it's you – the master detective?" I blurted excitedly.

I began to daydream that he might let me help, that he might teach *me* how to be a master detective.

Gramp continued to stare out to sea and looked like he was thinking about what to say next. Finally, he said: "I don't know if I'm still up to it. I can't trust my memory these days. It's … it's…" He groped for the right word. "Unreliable."

"Really?" I asked, circling back to how he'd forgotten little details like what a cabin was.

He bristled his moustache. "I remember some things from back in the day," he sighed. "Landing on the moon. Felix in handcuffs in a celebrity cattery. Fists trying to punch my head off when I arrested him after a race around Rome in Mini cars. But the in-between bits are gone. It's like it's someone else's life. I find it hard to believe it was me. And what's worse, the *feeling* is gone as well. I struggle to remember what it *feels* like to be a detective any more." He gripped the rails and stared out to sea, a look of pain in his normally sparkly eyes. "A lifetime of adventures slowly disappearing like a fading radio signal. That's old age for you. It's a stinker."

My feeling of brief happiness evaporated. It curdled with the sadness I felt about the D.I.V.O.R.C.E. *Everyone* in my family was having it rough. I didn't know what to say to make him feel better, so I said: "Sometimes I wish I could forget stuff. You know, not have to think about things at home."

Gramp's ears pricked up. "What's going on at home?" he asked softly, tilting his head to the side.

We stared at each other in silence. Now wasn't the time to tell Gramp about the D.I.V.O.R.C.E. It'd only make him sadder. I felt my cheeks go tight as I squeezed out the lie: "We've got an ant infestation."

He looked at me down the end of his nose with a wry smile, then burst out laughing. "Jesse Hall, you know what, you remind me of a younger me! Stubborn and sneaky, but certainly not without your charm."

I grinned in reply. I liked how he seemed to *get* me. More than Dad and Mum did, these days.

The downbeat mood changed with Gramp's laughter. I could see he wasn't someone who liked to dwell on sad things. There was a spring back in his step. "We've got a whole week together, let's not get all down about my old age and your ant infestation. Let's have some fun!" Then he put his hand around my shoulder, lowered his voice conspiratorially and looked around. "Do you know, I saw where they keep the golf balls and clubs. Are you thinking what I'm thinking?"

"Game of mini-golf?" I asked.

His blue eyes twinkled. "Oh, no. *Much* more fun than that."

CHAPTER 8
Bridget Bouffant

Gramp emptied the wire basket of golf balls next to the giant faded lighthouse on the mini-golf course. They rolled off chaotically in all directions and he used his club to bring one under control.

"Ready?" he asked.

"Ready!" I said.

Then he shuffled his hips, arced the club back over his shoulders and swung at the ball, connecting with an almighty THWACK. I burst out laughing as the ball launched off out to sea like a rocket, disappearing into the rolling grey waves beneath.

I couldn't believe Gramp had suggested this; it was

AWESOME! I tried to imagine Mum or Dad teeing up beside us and shook my head. They'd *never* do this with me! They'd go bananas at the thought of it!

Gramp tossed the club one hundred and eighty degrees, catching it by the head and offering me the grip. "Fancy a go?"

"Do I?" I replied, practically snatching it out of his hand. I tried to copy his pose, but the scrapbook dug into my ribs. I slipped it out from under my jumper and placed it on the ground.

He folded his arms and chuckled as I swung wildly at a golf ball, which sliced off into the open ocean.

"Don't rush it!" he replied. I handed him back the club, and he set himself up and drove another ball off deck, straight as an arrow.

I prepared myself for another shot when I spotted Perkins out of the corner of my eye. He was standing between the fibreglass shark and a pirate ship, watching us with his hands in his pockets, shaking his head and tutting.

"You two!" he said, his shoulders heaving as he chuckled. "Is your gramp leading you astray, young Jesse?"

Gramp laughed heartily, saluting his friend's arrival with the golf club. "Fancy a shot, Perkins old boy?"

Perkins held his hands up, palm towards us, and shook his head. Then he looked down at the scrapbook and raised his eyebrows. I went to snatch it up, but it was far too late for that.

"He knows," said Gramp, matter-of-factly.

"Everything?" asked Perkins.

"Everything," replied Gramp. "*And* he spied on our meeting."

Perkins's eyes widened in surprise. "Did you now?

A chip off the old block, I see." He looked me up and down. "I suppose you must have lots of questions?"

I had THOUSANDS. But for some or other reason, the first that came out was: "Why did you never catch Ivan Django?"

"Ah! Our old friend Ivan," said Perkins. "Sid, do you want to field that one?"

Gramp nodded unconvincingly. "Sure. Ivan was our old nemesis. And he ran G.E.M.I.N.I., which was a global criminal operation and … and…" I could see him looking at Perkins, willing him to take over, as if he was struggling with one of those memory gaps he'd mentioned.

Perkins obliged. "He was 'the one that got away'. However hard Sid and I tried, we could never bring him down. He was just too cunning. Too slippery."

A *nemesis*? That sounded pretty serious. "Why is he on this cruise with you, then?" I asked.

"Why are any of us on this cruise, hey?" replied Perkins, pursing his lips and studying Gramp's face for any indication that he might have a clue or answer.

"Beats me," replied Gramp.

Just then, a loud cry came from across the golf course and I saw a giant bouffant weaving its way towards us. "Siiiiiiiid, my dahling! I don't feel like we had a chance to properly say hello down there!"

It was Bridget Bouffant, still in her mime costume, gliding across the mossy tarmac towards us. "And Clarence, you too, of course," she said, with less conviction.

Then she draped a hand affectionately down Gramp's cheek.

"Meet my grandson, Jesse," he said.

She barely acknowledged my presence. "It's been, what, ten years since we last saw each other properly?" she continued, staring into Gramp's face.

Gramp squinted and replied vaguely: "Something like that."

She stared deep into his face, holding him affectionately in her gaze with two huge mascara-ed eyes, as if Perkins and I didn't even exist. They might have been enemies once upon a time, but it was clear she now held him in a lot of affection. Affection that perhaps Gramp wasn't completely reciprocating.

Perkins broke in gently: "Are you looking forward to seeing the Northern Lights, Bridget?" he asked. Gramp looked at him gratefully as Bridget turned his way.

She flicked her wrist at the horizon. "Pah! I've got something *much* more beautiful than the Northern Lights. Just you wait and see!"

I cocked my head to the side. *What*, exactly, could be more beautiful than the Northern Lights?

She drew a breath deep into her lungs, then spun around and wove her way through some of the obstacles, trailing a gloved hand on them as she reminisced out loud. "Why, Sid, can you remember the first time we met?"

She didn't give him a chance to answer. "I was dining in my revolving penthouse atop that Swiss mountain," she continued, staring out to sea. "Caviar and chips – my favourite. Felix was there, although I think he'd slunk off by the time you led that SWAT team through the floor-to-ceiling window, shattering my world."

Gramp stared at her and smiled, as if the event had

fleetingly revealed itself to him. "Great times," he said, quietly.

She moved cat-like over to Perkins, draped an arm on his shoulder and said with a mischievous smile, "And Perkins, you were somewhere else completely – remind me where again?"

He went red and looked embarrassed – exactly the reaction I could see Bridget wanted. "Ah! Well, Bridget. I think you know..." He coughed. "I was hiking up Ben Nevis because..."

"Because you read the clues all wrong and thought I was in Scotland!" she cut in, roaring with laughter.

Perkins turned even redder and tried to mask his embarrassment with a laugh. "Sometimes hunches can be wrong, yes." Gramp looked at him with a mix of sympathy and compassion. It felt like cruel sport from Bridget – like teasing a Labrador.

"Now, Bridget – behave," said Gramp, reprimanding her with a little smile.

"Clarence, my dear. I'm only joshing," she said to Perkins, letting go of him like a banana peel, and moving back to Gramp. She extended a white-gloved hand on to his cheek and turned his face towards her. He tensed his neck but let it happen. "Sid, I did fifteen years in prison because of you. But I came out a reformed woman! Why, I'd never have made it into Hollywood if you hadn't arrested me and put me on the straight and narrow. I owe it all to you! You can't complain when you're caught by the best, can you?"

She let go and glided over to a giant faded cod, leaning her elbows on it and placing her chin in her hands. "And we *were* the best, you and I! The best criminal. The best detective. After all these years, you're still as refreshing as an early morning swim and sauna. We're both so much … classier than those crooks downstairs. Why would you want to come away with them?"

My ears pricked up. But Gramp didn't *know* he was coming away with them. What was she talking about? Was she getting confused? Or letting something slip?

Gramp pursed his lips. "Well, I won my tickets in a competition, I…"

"Of course, of course … What I meant to say was … the way they look at me…" Her voice had turned deadly serious. "Some of them have still got it in for me, despite all these years."

I looked at Gramp. Behind those smiling eyes, I could tell his brain was whirling, trying to figure things out. What was she talking about? Did she know who'd invited them all on this cruise? I *really* wanted to help him get to the bottom of it – to be a detective just like Gramp was. I put on the same face as he does when he's being a detective, slightly raising an eyebrow. "Excuse me, Ms Bouffant, do *you* know why we are all here?" I felt pleased as punch with myself. Then clocked her cold gaze and dissolved like an ice cream in the sun.

She studied me, like an owl studies a little rabbit, her face icy but beautiful. "And if I did, young man, would you expect me to tell you now? Up here on deck? Where anyone could be listening?" She waved a hand around theatrically. "I'm afraid what little I know cannot be divulged in such a public setting." Then, she lowered her face and the corners of her mouth curled into a grin. "But whatever *is* going on, I'd be damned if one of us isn't in for a BIG surprise. One they *thoroughly* deserve."

CHAPTER 9

The Case of the Missing Peppa Pig Swimming Trunks

After Bridget and Perkins left us, Gramp and I spent all afternoon hitting golf balls into the sea. Then we headed downstairs and collapsed in the On-board Board Games room, my arms sore, my cheeks red from the sea breeze and my chest aching from laughing so much. Whatever secrets Gramp had up his sleeve, I'd worked out one thing: he was FUN to hang around with.

I sank into my tatty armchair and asked, with a big, happy sigh: "Why haven't you visited us more, Gramp?" It was meant as a compliment – that I wished I'd got to know him sooner – but I winced as it came out more like a complaint.

Gramp pursed his lips and stared across the games room – a dingy space with grey walls, dotted with a few round portholes looking out on to the dusky seascape. "I'll be honest with you, Jesse – your father and I don't have the easiest relationship," he replied. "I think when you came along, it reminded him how little I was around when he was a boy – what with work taking up so much of my life."

"Oh," I said. "Did you fall out?"

"We didn't fall out, as such," Gramp replied. "We just never sorted out some stuff that perhaps we should have long ago."

"It's never too late," I said, with a chipper shrug.

He smiled. "It never is." He had a real knack of sounding non-committal about things.

For a brief second, my brain threatened to gravitate back to The Conversation and dwell on things at home. I desperately looked around the rest of the Games Room for something to distract it. It was hardly the most riveting of settings, with its faded pictures of old sailing ships and clusters of tables populated by a few elderly couples playing Monopoly. At the front, there was a small stage, no more than a foot off the ground, and a table with a big clear plastic contraption on it that I think was a bingo machine.

And then, beyond it, I saw Perkins and Sonny sitting with an open bottle of wine and playing cards, seemingly oblivious to our presence at the other side of the room. Perfect, I thought – I'll watch them for a bit, see if I could spot *any* sort of odd behaviour, anything at all that might hint why we were there. But pretty soon I realized how boring that was. Perkins was showing Sonny his watch. Sonny inspected it like it was some amazing piece of art at a museum, then he took a sip of wine and put his hand on his stomach, as if he was queasy. "Seasickness?" I heard Perkins say. He rooted around in his jacket pocket and pulled out a green box of tablets, pressing one out of its tin foil and handing it to Sonny, who popped it in his mouth and swallowed. I was trying to convince myself that they might say or do *something* incriminating when…

The lights flickered and the room plunged into

darkness. There were gasps and little breathless murmurs of surprise – not just coming from our room but through the walls, from all over the ship. Then, in no more than a second or two, the lights blinked and sprang back on.

Gramp looked up at the ceiling lights. "Just a power cut. Guess that's another quirk of the *Tom Cruise*." Then he stood up and stretched. "What do you say we get some dinner?"

Feeling a tiny bit sketchy at the sudden lack of power, I pulled my eyes from Sonny and Perkins and headed through with him to the busy restaurant, where a smell of school meals hit me like a greasy tsunami. I grabbed a tray and inspected the hotplate – it was a choice between spag bol and some very grey-looking chicken nuggets. The spag bol looked least likely to kill me.

"Nuggets!" chimed Gramp, grabbing a plate and helping himself to a dozen revolting chicken bits.

I gripped my tray and searched the packed restaurant, looking for a table. Pretty much the whole cruise – all three hundred or so passengers – seemed to be in there, a sea of white hair and a heavy smell of lavender perfume. At the far end sat Wendall and a lady I assumed was his nan – a short, smiley granny with the same round face as him. He spotted us and waved, pulling two spare chairs out from under the table.

"Jesse, Mr Hall! Come sit with us!" he called. "Meet my nan!"

We wove through the dining room. Gramp lowered himself into the chair with a big smile and I popped myself next to him.

"Nan – meet Jesse and Mr Hall!" said Wendall, beaming at us.

She nodded. Now I was up close I could see she was the spitting image of Wendall. She had a round, kind face and big brown eyes, alongside a black bowl cut.

"Mr Hall here used to be a detect…" Wendall began to say, then checked himself and went red. "I mean a dishcloth salesman."

Gramp flashed an amused smile. I pulled a face and said, under my breath, "Sorry."

Wendall's nan leaned in, fixing me in her big brown eyes as she said, in a Welsh accent thicker than leek soup: "Are you going to keep my Wendall out of trouble, Jesse? He's a naughty one!"

Then she ruffled Wendall's bowl cut affectionately. "Stop it, Nan! You're embarrassing me!" he said, leaning over and slicing up her spag bol with his knife and fork. She spooned some into her wrinkled mouth and wagged her eyebrows.

Gramp watched the two of them with a wry smile. "What sort of trouble do you get up to, Wendall?"

"Yeah!" I said, shovelling my own forkful of spaghetti into my mouth. "What sort of stuff *are* you into?" I asked. I was hoping maybe he'd say football or computer games, and that'd be another thing we'd have in common.

Wendall looked up to the ceiling and thought. "I'd probably say my favourite three hobbies are … Drama Club, Science Club and Murder Mystery club." He nodded and looked at me with a big smile.

I narrowed my eyes. "That's not naughty."

He looked surprised. "Nan says it is."

Wendall's nan nodded. "Murder Mystery Club! Have you ever 'eard of anything so naughty!" Then she shovelled more sliced spag bol into her mouth.

Wendall nodded enthusiastically. "That's probably my favourite, that one. It's not real murders, mind!" He laughed. "They're just pretend ones we have to solve. Sometimes they're not even murders at all. They can be crimes or mysteries or anything we need to work out."

It brought my mind back to the mystery of why we were here. The itch to find the truth was getting itchier and itchier. I *had* to scratch it. But I couldn't do it alone.

Wendall's nan finished her last bit of bolognese and declared it was time for pudding. So, as Wendall helped her up and over towards the dessert trolley, I took my opportunity. I sucked in a deep breath, turned to Gramp and blurted out something that had been pressing at me ever since we'd found the scrapbook: "I want to help you crack a case!"

"I beg your pardon?" he replied, a little smile under his moustache.

"You said earlier that you had forgotten what it feels like to work a case. Well, I want to help you remember! I LOVE finding secrets out. Love it. And I'm good at it. I found your scrapbook and spied on your meeting. I mean, I'm not as good as you, but I could learn." I looked at Gramp hopefully.

He had that half-inquisitive, half-amused look on his face again. "And what case do you propose we crack?"

"The mystery of why you're all here, on this cruise! We can work it out together!" My mind raced ahead, to the two of us solving the mystery together. How cool would that be?

Gramp sucked his moustache. "Perhaps. But that's not a crime. A real case needs a crime."

I opened my mouth to argue, but was halted in my tracks by Wendall returning to our table, leaving his nan inspecting the dessert stand. He scurried over to me, speaking quickly and quietly: "Jesse, I've been meaning to tell you something. I've got some bad news about the..." He glanced guiltily at Gramp and lowered his voice even more. "... Black Hole."

I frowned, trying to work out what he meant. And then I had it – the Black Hole, the haunted flume he'd been talking about.

"I heard that that thing's haunted?" interjected Gramp.

Wendall took a sad breath and said: "I'll never know cos I won't be able to ride it with you."

"What?" I said. "Why not?"

He sighed. "My trunks have been stolen."

"Stolen?" I said. "When?"

"This afternoon. And it wasn't just my trunks, it was my whole swim bag – mask and towel and everything. After I left you, I took it out of my room to go scout out the Black Hole. I put it down to grab a fizzy drink and before I knew it, it had gone."

"Gone?" I repeated.

"Gone."

"Can't you just go in your pants?" I asked.

"Jesse Hall!" He went bright red, like I'd suggested he do a school show and tell in the nude. "I've never heard anything so rude!"

And then it hit me: *this* was a crime we could build our case around! The Case of the Missing Trunks! It would give us the perfect ruse for sneaking around and investigating the *real* mystery – why we were all here.

I looked at Gramp and I could tell he was thinking the same thing. He had a little sparkle in his eye. OK, it was hardly busting an international arms ring like he used to do, but it was *something* to get our teeth into. It was more than enough to help Gramp remember what it felt like to be a detective. More than enough to distract me from The Conversation. And lots of opportunity for me to learn Gramp's detective skills.

"Gramp, what's our first move?"

"Wait," said Wendall. "You're gonna try and find them?"

"No," I said, gesturing at all three of us. *"We're* going to try and find them. Up for it?"

He couldn't have looked more excited by the question if I'd painted it in fireworks across the sky. "Am I?" he chimed. "That sounds a billion times more fun than bingo!"

"So, Wendall. What do your trunks look like?" asked Gramp.

"Well," said Wendall. "They're blue, and they've got a pig on the side of them."

"A pig?" I asked.

"Any type of pig in particular?" asked Gramp.

Wendall looked at his feet and mumbled: "Peppa Pig."

I let out an involuntary laugh. "Peppa Pig?"

"Shhhh," he said, frowning and looking around in case anyone heard. "Please, don't tell anyone."

"Why do you have Peppa Pig swimming trunks?" I asked, trying not to laugh again.

"Nan bought 'em for me. She said Peppa's a good role model."

"She's a pre-school pig," I replied, still struggling against the grin that threatened to spread across my face.

"PLEASE don't tell anyone I have Peppa Pig trunks! I'll never live it down. I usually wear them inside out so no one knows." I put on my best serious face. "Your secret is safe with us." And then I turned to Gramp. "What do you think, Gramp? Why would someone want to steal Wendall's trunks?"

He thought for a second. "There's only one reason I can think of."

"Because they love Peppa Pig?" whispered Wendall.

"I was thinking more: to go swimming," said Gramp.

Wendall hit his palm against his forehead. "Yes, yes, of course, Mr Hall. That makes more sense."

"What we need is an old-fashioned stake-out," he said. "We need to watch everyone coming into the swimming pool and see if they're wearing your trunks. Let's meet there first thing tomorrow morning – 6 a.m. – and we'll start the surveillance."

"It's a plan," I said.

"Thank you both so much!" said Wendall. "Nan'll be so sad if she thinks I've lost those trunks."

A buzz rippled up my spine. We were going to be detectives – the three of us together. I was excited. *Dead* excited.

CRUISE DAY 2: WATER AEROBICS, DECK GAMES, CAPTAIN'S DRINKS RECEPTION

CHAPTER 10

The Body in the Sunroom

It was 6.10 a.m. when Wendall and I pushed open the heavy glass doors and a waft of chlorine smacked us in the face.

We'd both struggled to get out of bed and were running ten minutes late. I'd knocked on Gramp's door but got no reply. I was expecting to see him at the pool, but it was eerily quiet and he was nowhere to be seen. There was the dopey-looking teenager who had been told off by Mum for dropping a crisp packet on the dock. He had long black hair and a baggy T-shirt, and slowly dragged around a mop as he rubbed his eyes. He must be the lifeguard, I thought.

We walked past a sign that said: WATER AEROBICS, 7.00 A.M., then settled on to a couple of yellowing sunloungers.

Where is Gramp? I thought, gazing all around the pool. It was a tired space decked out in beige tiles. In the middle lay the kidney-shaped pool. At the far end sat a separate area with a sign over the door saying SUNROOM AND SAUNA. But it was the flume that really grabbed my attention: the Black Hole itself. It burst in from the wall like a dark python gently supping the blue water. Beside it, there was a little spiral metal staircase covered in red-and-white DO NOT ENTER tape. I tried to picture where, exactly, the flume went and I realized it must have snaked out of the side of the ship – so that it was suspended above the sea – before entering back in. That was SO cool. If it wasn't for the presence of the

lifeguard, I'd have ridden it there and then.

Out of the window, the pink dawn framed a rugged, jagged coastline, like chunks of Toblerone arranged on the horizon. I guessed we were crossing the North Sea and approaching Norway.

Wendall was wearing jeans and a T-shirt, which was a bit odd, but what choice did he have, seeing as someone had nicked his trunks? He leaned forward in his lounger, his neck craning left and right, scouring the pool with unblinking eyes. "How long do you reckon this could take?" he asked, his eyes beginning to water.

"Dunno. A few hours? All day?" I clocked him and his quivering eyelids. "You *can* blink, you know. You won't miss anything."

"Thanks. Gosh, stake-outs are hard, aren't they? They look so easy on the telly." He rubbed his eyes, blinked furiously then frowned as he refocused on something over my shoulder. "Look in there! It's Bridget Bouffant!"

I spun around and, sure enough, there was Bridget. She was in the sunroom, which was a bright, white, little room with a big window, a load of sunloungers and a door into the sauna. She was dressed in a black-and-white striped swimsuit and was standing in a little glass booth under the bucket shower (which is basically a bucket of freezing water hanging from the ceiling that people tip on themselves once they get out of the sauna). She was staring down at the ground, hands limp by her sides, just like she had when she'd appeared on stage yesterday.

Wendall rubbed his hands. "She's so classy, isn't she? Do you think she's about to do a bit of mime? I'd love that."

Still, she didn't move. She was as still as the pool was quiet. Was she practising her routine? I didn't know. Actually, to be blunt – I didn't care. Because this was the *perfect* opportunity to ask her what she was talking about on deck yesterday. She definitely knew more than she was letting on – of that I was sure. She'd made out like she couldn't say it in public. Now, however, she was alone. There was no one to eavesdrop. It was a perfect chance for her to spill the beans. What I really wanted to know was why she thought they were all on this cruise. Wendall's Peppa Pig trunks would have to wait.

I was up and moving around the pool before I could think about whether it was a bad idea. She was definitely scary but ... well, my mind went racing ahead to how impressed Gramp would be if I found the first clue. Maybe even if I cracked the case. Wendall scurried anxiously in my wake as I hurried into the sunroom and approached the shower booth.

Bridget remained still, staring at the floor like a wound-down clockwork doll. It was amazing *just* how still she could be.

Wendall gazed on in awe. "I just think she's *so* captivating," he whispered. Then shouted so loudly it made me jump: "Madame Bouffant, you don't know me, but I think you're wonderful. My nan's a big fan of the Magic Circle!"

I spoke out of the side of my mouth: "She's a mime, not a magician."

Wendall shouted again: "Although I just remembered, it's Magic Mike my nan likes, not the Magic Circle."

It was about this moment that I began to feel uneasy.

It wasn't that she was just standing still – she wasn't standing up completely of her own accord either. She was leaning forward, the top of her head pressed against the glass screen so that it supported her weight.

Wendall pointed to something on the shower floor. "Look at that smashed glass. She wants to be careful she doesn't cut her feet." Sure enough, there was what looked like a smashed glass vial on the floor, leaking a strange green liquid down the drain. I looked from the vial up to Bridget, her glassy eyes staring down at the floor, and started to feel panicky at *just* how still she was.

"Do you think she is … OK?" I murmured, a terrible unease growing in the pit of my belly.

"I dunno…" muttered Wendall.

We had clearly grabbed the lifeguard's attention because he stumbled dozily into the sunroom.

"Whoa! Is she … all right?" he asked, hugging his mop handle for comfort.

"I dunno. Maybe you should go check on her?" I said, my heart beating faster and faster. I started to desperately wish Gramp was here.

"Hey!" the teenager said, pushing his hair over his

forehead. "Why's it up to me? Why do I have to be the one that makes sure she's alive?"

"You're a lifeguard!" I replied. "Your job description is *literally* that you have to make sure people are alive."

The panic rose up in me. Wendall began muttering nervously under his breath, "I'm sure she's fine, I'm sure she's fine, I'm sure she's fine," in a way that you definitely don't do when someone is *actually* fine.

"All right!" huffed the lifeguard. "Here, take this and … I dunno … wait out there." He handed me his mop and pointed us back towards the loungers.

We retreated, pacing backwards to the pool as the lifeguard tiptoed towards Bridget. "Hi!" he said, with a weak wave. "Are you, like, OK, miss?"

The door into the sunroom swung shut so that we couldn't see anything except the plain tiles framed by its little round window.

There was a horrible silence. My heart was in my throat. And then the door swung open. The lifeguard was staring at us, white as a sheet, eyes as wide as a cave entrance. "She's … she's … she's … dead!"

And just like that, Wendall and I were running,

sprinting, fleeing the swimming pool, every limb pounding with adrenaline as we barrelled down corridors past oblivious old people, leaving the dead body behind us.

CHAPTER 11

The Case of the Almost Murdered Mime

The next moments were a blur. We sprinted to Gramp's room, my heartbeat thumping in my ears, and pounded on his door. He appeared in his pyjamas, looking tired and queasy. But before he could open his mouth, we were unloading the terrible news about Bridget. He snapped to and a grave look passed over his face.

"Give me a moment to get changed," he replied. "And, quick – go find Perkins. He's in room 1120."

Wendall hurried off to do just that and ten minutes later all four of us were hurtling through the pool room, my head still spinning with the thought of

Bridget's death. We burst into
the sunroom and the first
thing I noticed was that
Bridget was nowhere to be
seen. In her place stood the
dopey lifeguard and, going off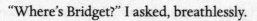
his hat and uniform, what looked to
be the ship's captain.

"Where's Bridget?" I asked, breathlessly.

"Being choppered off to hospital!" said the captain.

"Choppered off?" I repeated. "To hospital? So she's
not…"

"Dead? No, no!" replied the captain, with a chortle.
"She's alive, all right. Injured, mind, but very much
alive. Last you'll be seeing of her on this cruise."

The lifeguard looked sheepish at his misdiagnosis.

"Thank heavens," I said, a wave of relief washing
over me.

The captain half-heartedly inspected the shower.
He was an older man, but not as old as Gramp. He had
thick, wiry hair that was probably once blonde but was
now a pale straw colour, bushy eyebrows like two hairy

caterpillars and buck teeth.

He glanced back at us and seemed surprised we were still there. "Can I help? Do you chaps know her, or something?"

"I know her very well, as it happens," replied Perkins.

"These are the little dudes who were with me when she collapsed," said the lifeguard.

"Well! Lucky this young man…" The captain waved in the lifeguard's direction.

"Ax … Akshay…" he interjected.

"Yes, lucky this Ax … Akshay acted so quickly, otherwise we might have lost a passenger. And I hate losing passengers, absolutely hate it." He took in a sharp intake of breath and looked at the horizon. "Once lost eight passengers on one cruise!"

"Eight passengers died on one cruise?" asked Wendall.

"No," he replied, chortling. "Genuinely lost them! Couldn't find them anywhere. Turns out they'd got off in Corfu and no one had noticed."

He chuckled some more, then remembered the

gravity of Bridget's accident and forced his bushy eyebrows into a concerned frown. "Still, we do get the odd death." He looked over his shoulder at Gramp and spoke out of the side of his mouth. "To be expected when passengers are this old. Heart attacks. Slips and falls. That sort of thing."

The captain pulled out a notebook and pen and started scribbling. "Always got to log all such incidents. Time of injury..." He checked his watch. "Six-ish. Cause: slipped and fell."

"Slipped and fell? That's rubbish!" I cried. "There was no way that she slipped and fell! She was already unconscious and standing up when we found her! Someone did this to her!"

The captain looked up from his notebook, in shock that I'd dare question him. "What are you talking about? I've never heard anything so pre..."

"There was a smashed vial beside her!" I cried, not letting him finish. "With a bright green liquid flowing out! It was on the floor of the shower, by her feet. I think it was poison! I think someone was trying to kill her."

The captain blew his lips out like a shire horse and

said: "Poison? What is this nonsense?"

Perkins scoured the floor. "Where did you say the vial was, Jesse?"

"Just there on the floor!" The words caught in my throat. The vial had gone. And the trail of green liquid had been washed away.

"I was first on the scene and it wasn't here when I arrived," said the captain, shaking his head.

"It was here, just here," I said, frantically gesturing at the floor. I looked desperately at Wendall. "Back me up!"

"It was right there, where he says. Swear on me nan's life," he said. Then I swung around at Gramp and it hit me why he hadn't said anything so far. He looked terrible. He was grey and shivering. I was about to ask him what was up when the captain laughed that shire horse laugh again.

"That's what I love about kids. Such wonderful imaginations!" He ruffled my hair while he spoke to Perkins: "A poison vial, indeed! What does that make me? Hercule Poirot?" He did a really bad Belgian accent, brayed hysterically, and then when he realized that no one else was laughing, rearranged his eyebrows back into a concerned frown and coughed awkwardly.

"No!" I said, refusing to let it go. "It was there! I swear on my life, it was there! She was poisoned! You have to tell the police!"

The captain straightened up. The casual disinterest he'd shown earlier had morphed into something more serious. "Listen here. No one gets poisoned on the *Tom Cruise*, you hear me?" He blew his cheeks out. "Oof. If the public got wind of this accusation...! Why, it'd be terrible for business. This was a simple slip in the shower!" He nodded, like the decision was final. "And if I hear anything more about it, you will be making your own way back from Norway. Understood?" He pointed his pen at each of us in turn.

"As you wish, Captain," said Perkins.

I looked at Gramp – he had plopped himself down on a sunlounger and didn't seem to have the energy to speak, let alone argue with the captain.

"Good chaps," said the captain, exhaling his anger and looking, once again, far too chipper considering the circumstances. "Golly! Better be heading off, I'm calling the bingo numbers in ten minutes!" He popped his cap on and gave a big grin. "Ball ninety nine! Badly injured mime!" Then he laughed heartily at his own joke, before realizing its distastefulness and disguising it with a cough. He lingered awkwardly as he thought for a second what to do next, made a clumsy sign of the cross on his chest then, looking pleased with himself, headed off through the pool.

I looked desperately at Perkins. "That can't just be it, can it? He can't just brush it under the carpet? Someone tried to kill her, I saw the evidence with my own eyes! There is a killer on board!"

Perkins shook his head. "I'm sorry, Jesse, but without any evidence, what can we do?"

I looked pleadingly at Gramp. "You believe me, don't you, Gramp?"

He placed his hand over his stomach and said, weakly, "Probably. Maybe. I'm not sure. I just... I just think I might be sick."

I looked desperately back at Perkins's genial face, his eyebrows slanting down apologetically. I wasn't going to give up that easily. "Well, if you don't believe me, I'll prove it wasn't an accident! Something fishy is going on aboard this ship and we're going to get to the bottom of it."

"Really?" said Perkins, taken aback by my determination.

"Yes! This is *exactly* the kind of detective work Gramp and I were talking about last night: a proper crime to solve! And one that really matters – no offence to your Peppa Pig trunks, Wendall... This attempted murderer is stuck on the ship with us. They could strike again. Any one of us could be next! Isn't that right?"

Perkins pushed his chin into his neck and blinked heavily, as if he was struggling to get to grips with the suggestion. He looked nervous for us. "But boys, you have no idea *how* to conduct an investigation!"

Wendall's voice cut through the room: "Check alibis. Establish motive. Identify suspects."

We spun around to look at him.

He shrugged. "I told you, I do Murder Mystery Club after school."

Perkins stared at us. Underneath the wrinkles and the grey hair, there was still a boyishness about his face. With Gramp clearly feeling unwell, it had fallen on him to act as a surrogate grandfather. "You two really shouldn't be getting tangled up in all this. You're just kids."

"Exactly!" I said, clapping my hands. "And who would *ever* suspect two kids? The captain won't know a thing!"

He let out a long sigh, a sigh that seemed to say: *I couldn't stop you if I wanted to.* He pushed his side-parting back and thrust his hands in his pockets. "I suppose I only have one question: why? Why do you want to put yourself in danger like this?"

I pressed my palms together and put them to my lips. Which answer to pick: to let Gramp remember what it feels like to be a great inspector? To help me momentarily forget about the D.I.V.O.R.C.E.? To learn detective skills off the best in the business? I opened my mouth to speak, but Wendall got in there first and answered for me.

"There's a murderer on board, sir – at least, an attempted murderer – and we're the only ones who know about it. We can't go letting them get away with it. What if they try to murder my nan next?"

Reluctantly, Perkins said: "Fine. Well, I suppose if you are determined to do it, I will help where I can. Just" – he paused, looking down at Gramp's sweaty face – "keep me regularly updated."

I rubbed my hands. The Case of the Almost-Murdered Mime was OPEN. And then it struck me like a free-falling hippo: things had got serious. We weren't dealing with stolen swimwear any more. Whoever had invited Gramp and company on this cruise had *much* more devious plans. Plans that involved murder. And we were thrusting ourselves right into the middle of it.

CHAPTER 12
The Investigation Begins

Gramp let out a little burp and brought his fist up to his mouth, like he might be sick. What was wrong with him? Was he seasick? Had he been poisoned as well? The thought sent a shiver down my spine. And then a much simpler answer popped into my brain. The memory of those grey chicken nuggets came swimming back. "Gramp, I think you have food poisoning," I said, placing my hand on his shoulder. He said nothing, just gripped it and squeezed.

Perkins helped him to his feet. "You need a lie-down, Sid. I'll take you to your cabin."

"Let me help," I said, moving towards him.

Gramp summoned up his last bits of energy and said: "You stay here, Jesse. Look for any clues at the crime scene."

I felt a little surge of excitement that Gramp was trusting me like that. "Of course!"

Then he drew a breath and looked at Wendall and me. "Be careful. Whoever did this, did it for a reason. And if they find out that you are sniffing around..." His voice trailed off.

I thought about that for a second and decided it was best not to dwell on it. "We'll be careful," I said.

"Get better soon, Mr Hall," said Wendall.

Perkins guided Gramp out of the exit and they were gone, leaving us in the empty swimming pool.

I ran the circumstances through my head, turning to Wendall. "Not only has someone tried to kill Bridget, they've done it in a calculated way: they've smuggled a vial of poison on board and somehow smashed it near her, making it look like an accident."

Wendall nodded. "That's pretty scheming."

Slowly, the first sign-ups for water aerobics tottered through the door. I stared at them and found it impossible to believe that any one of the normal passengers on board could be behind this. Then my mind wandered to those old criminals: Fists, Felix, Sonny … Ivan. "This *has* to be the work of one of Gramp's crew, right?"

"They're right up the top of my suspect list," Wendall replied. "They all knew her. And you normally get murdered by someone you know. At least you do on the telly."

I nodded. "But why? Why would one of them want to kill her?"

Wendall fished his notebook and a pencil case out of his red backpack, opening it up to reveal a selection of immaculate stationery – a ruler, pens, scissors – each with his name embossed on them: WENDALL.

"Whoa," I said. "Do you carry that everywhere?"

He looked at it affectionately. "You like it, do you? It's pretty smart. Nan gave it to me last birthday."

He pulled out an embossed biro and perched on a pool-side lounger. Then he turned to a fresh page of his notebook and wrote at the top:

ESTABLISH TIME OF ATTEMPTED MURDER
CHECK ALIBIS
ESTABLISH MOTIVE
IDENTIFY SUSPECTS

"Gosh, it's *just* like *Midsomer Murders* this," he said. Then he drew a big circle around the list and moved his pen down the page. "Shall we write down everything we know so far?"

"Sure."

He said the words out loud as he spoke: "2 p.m. yesterday: Wendall's trunks and mask reported as stolen..."

"Hang on!" I said, cutting him off. "All due respect to your swimwear, but I think the investigation has moved on from that."

He looked at me with his milk-cow eyes. "I know, but they could be tied to this case. You never know..."

I pulled a face. "How? A Peppa Pig mega-fan is on board and a pair of swim trunks is the missing piece of their collection?"

Wendall pushed his lip out. "Not a bad one. Shall I write that down?"

"I was joking," I replied, deadpan.

"Oh," he said. "Well, I'm gonna keep it in 'ere just in case." He carried on scribbling:

2 p.m. Sunday: Wendall's trunks and mask reported as stolen.

6.10 a.m. Monday: Bridget Bouffant found poisoned in swimming pool sunroom.

He did a big full stop, then sucked his pen. "What else can we put down here?"

I thought for a second. "I guess we should find out who else came into the pool this morning."

"No one else came in..." The voice came from behind me, making me jump. I spun around to see Akshay the lifeguard sitting on the floor behind a sunlounger, his chin on his chest and his back against the wall. I'd completely forgotten about him!

"Golly, hello again," said Wendall.

The lifeguard let out a long sigh and stared at the floor as more people filtered in; taking off their robes and descending slowly into the pool, oblivious to the grisly scene that had taken place here just minutes ago. "This is heavy, man. Like, *really* heavy. This is only my second day as a lifeguard. I thought it'd be all hot girls and beaches. Instead, it's old ladies and water aerobics. I never thought anyone would get hurt. Do you get me?"

He looked seriously depressed and I felt sorry for him. I wasn't completely sure if a lifeguard's employability was determined on how many people died on their watch. But so far, his CV read: Full days: 1. Hospitalizations: 1. Not a great ratio.

There was also a more sensitive issue we needed to get out of the way. "Um, Akshay … how much of that did you hear?" I asked, referring to the whole chat with Gramp and Perkins.

"Don't worry," he replied, looking up and pushing his long hair back over his forehead. "I won't tell the captain about your investigation. I saw that vial, man. No jokes. I don't want anyone thinking it was my fault. So if you can prove it was attempted murder – knock yourself out. And call me Ax."

"Great, thanks, Ax!" I said. Then thought for a second before adding: "Maybe you could help the investigation?"

He pushed his bottom lip out. "Like, how?"

I glanced at Wendall's notebook and the words: *establish time of attempted murder.*

"You are certain no one else came into the pool this morning?" I asked.

He didn't even need to think. "Stone cold certain," he replied, getting up and joining us on our lounger. "I unlocked it at 5.50 a.m. That lady…"

"Bridget," I said.

"Yeah, that Bridget lady came in at 6 a.m. on the dot, and went straight for the sauna. She was the only person through that door until you two."

I creased my forehead and thought out loud. "Then how did someone manage to smash the poison vial and get away?"

Wendall's head sprang up from his notebook. "Maybe the attempted murderer left the vial in the bucket shower, so that when she poured the water over her head, the vial fell on the floor and smashed?"

"No dice, Sherlock," said Ax. "I cleaned the sunroom this morning. I emptied and refilled the bucket shower, just like I did yesterday. If it had been anywhere in that sunroom, I'd have seen it."

"Hmmmm," I said, feeling a bit deflated. "So between 5.50 a.m. and 6.10 a.m. someone managed to smuggle in and smash a poison vial ... without actually being there?"

"That's a tough one, that is," said Wendall. "Perhaps they got in another way? Like, not through the front door, so that you wouldn't have seen them?"

Ax shook his head again. "Uh-uh. The only other way in is through the window, and that has a catch on it. And anyway" – he laughed at the thought – "they'd have to scale the side of the ship to climb in through it."

"Can you show us the window?" I asked.

He shrugged – "Sure" – and heaved himself on to his feet. He skirted the outside of the pool in a sort of dazed, mopey stroll, his T-shirt hanging off his skinny frame. We followed as he opened the glass door and went into the sunroom. Out of the window, I could see the sun had risen into a cloudless sky, casting a bright, long square on the tiled floor.

"Here it is..." The lifeguard stopped in his tracks and stared down at the window. "Whoooooa!"

"What is it?" I asked, rushing over.

"The latch…" he said. "It's, like, broken." Then he pushed the window wide open – wide enough for a person to fit through.

"This must be how they got in!" I exclaimed, gesturing frantically for Wendall to write it down.

Wendall scribbled in his notebook, then popped his little round head out of the window. "Cheese on toast," he said, peering round at the sides of the ship. "I wouldn't want to climb in through here…"

I stuck my head out, the chill wind whipping past my cheeks as the *Tom Cruise* cut through the dark blue sea. I saw what he meant. Left, right, up, down: every direction I looked there was a sheer, featureless side of the ship with barely a hand or foot hold to grab on to. It would be almost impossible to climb along it. And if you slipped… I looked down at the dark, foaming waves spraying out from the sides of the hull. Well, there would be no second chances, put it that way.

"Whoever managed to get in through here must be a pretty amazing climber," muttered Wendall, pulling his head back in.

"Not your average passenger on this ship," muttered

the lifeguard dozily. I stared at the two dozen pensioners now up to their chest in pool water. The aerobics instructor blew her whistle and they slowly moved their arms above their heads, every single face wincing with effort. I had to agree: the average cruise member could barely put their own socks on, let alone scale the sheer, featureless side of the ship. But for now, it was the only reasonable explanation we had as to how the attempted murderer *might* have got in.

"So," I said, peering over Wendall's notebook. "We have a time of almost-death – between 5.50 a.m. and 6.10 a.m. What's next?"

"Alibis," he replied. "We need to find out who was busy at the time of the attempted murder and who wasn't."

"Hmmmm…" I said, pushing my mouth to the side. "How can we do that? If only we had some way of seeing where they all were this morning…"

"Hey…" said the lifeguard, pushing his hair back and coming to life. "I might have an idea!"

CHAPTER 13
Alibis

Wendall and I hovered cagily outside a brown door in some dingy corridor on Deck 1.

"I'll get in, like, *soooooo* much trouble if I'm caught," said the lifeguard, pushing his long hair back over his forehead again and shuffling nervously. "It's one thing me closing the pool to secretly help you. But if I'm caught doing … this…" Despite *"this"* having been his idea, I could see he was getting cold feet.

"Come on, Ax!" I said. "It's kind of in your interests. There's an attempted murderer on board and, to be blunt, you were the only possible witness." He looked at me and squinted, not quite catching my drift. "And murderers don't tend to like witnesses…" I added.

He narrowed his eyes even more.

"They usually try to murder them," I added.

His eyes sprang open as he realized what I was spelling out.

"All right, all right," he said, and pulled out a key card. "You don't have to scare me. Lifeguards have feelings, too. We're not just heroic hunks of meat, you know." I took in his skinny frame. If he *was* a hunk of meat, it'd be a Peperami. "Just cos people have watched *Baywatch*, they think I'm all muscle and no brain, you get me? But I've got smarts."

Wendall put a reassuring hand on his shoulder. "I think you're great, Ax."

Ax looked at Wendall's earnest face and nodded slowly in appreciation. "Thanks, Windmill."

"My name's Wendall."

"Right on," said Ax, not really listening.

He slid his key card into the door handle. It clicked.

"How come you've got a key card if you're not allowed in?" I asked.

"Emergency skeleton key," he replied, eyes darting

up and down the corridor to check the coast was clear. "Only to be used in a real emergency. That's what they say when they give it to you."

"A real emergency?" asked Wendall.

"Yeah," said Ax. "Like … like … like…" He thought as hard as he could to imagine what an emergency on a ship might look like.

"Like the ship sinking?" I offered.

He gave a big dopey smile. "Yeah! Like the ship sinking! Nice one!"

Then he checked the corridor one last time, pushed the handle down and ushered us inside.

It was a small, dark room with four old, boxy TV monitors displaying grainy footage of the ship's corridors. This is what Ax had told us about: the ship's CCTV cameras.

Ax slipped in after and closed the door softly behind him.

"Where's the one by the pool?" I asked, excitedly. "I want to see who went in and out this morning." I couldn't believe we were about to crack the case *this* quickly. It looked like I had a real knack for this inspectoring business. Gramp would be proud as punch.

Ax shook his head. "Afraid there isn't one, dude. They're only installed on the cabin corridors. To make sure no one steals stuff from rooms."

"Ach," I said, with a pang of frustration. "When you said CCTV I thought…"

Wendall raised a knowing finger and wagged it. "We might not be able to find the culprit … but we can *rule out* culprits."

"Oh yeah?" I replied. "How?"

"Well," he said, rolling his shoulders as he settled into the investigation. "If we rewind the footage to last night when everyone went to bed, and then spool through to this morning, we can see who was still in their cabins at the time of the attempted murder … and who wasn't. We'll catch anyone who left their rooms!"

I looked at him in wonder. He might look like a garden gnome in chunky knitwear, but Wendall was spot on. That was *exactly* what we could do.

"You're a genius," I said. "Let's start going through them!"

I pulled out my phone and started to film the screen

as Ax pulled up the footage for each of the twenty cameras on board. First, we found Perkins. I talked his movements through as Wendall wrote in his notebook and Ax spooled: "He goes into his room straight after dinner but then immediately leaves in his coat." Ax spooled on. "Stop there! He returns at 8 p.m. and stays in his room all night." Ax spooled on through the night. "He stays there and stays there and – stop there." I could see Perkins leaving his room. I checked the clock in the corner. "He leaves his room at 6.20 a.m., shortly before you found him so he could help us with Bridget."

"Got it!" said Wendall, scribbling furiously.

It must have taken us a good hour, working quietly and quickly, identifying every one of Gramp's friends and former enemies and their cabin numbers while Wendall furiously scribbled in his notebook.

By the end of it, we had a grid that looked like this:

NAME	BEDTIME	GETTING UP TIME	IN CABIN AT TIME OF ATTEMPTED MURDER?
PERKINS	8.15 p.m.	6.20 a.m.	YES
MS HO-RENTON	8 p.m.	6.30 a.m.	YES
FELIX	8.15 p.m.	5.30 a.m.	NO
FISTS	8 p.m.	7 a.m.	YES
SONNY THE SQUID	DID NOT GO TO BED	N/A	NO
IVAN DJANGO	6.30 p.m.	4 a.m.	NO
GRAMP	8 p.m.	6.20 a.m.	YES

I cast my eye over it. "That means Felix, Sonny and Ivan are our main suspects," I said. There was also one other factor we needed to be aware of: the killer *might* have climbed in through the sunroom window. "And add Fists to that list. He's the only one who has a cabin facing the sea. So he *could* have maybe climbed out of his window."

We all stared at the grid approvingly. It was a great start. I got a little fluttering of excitement in my tummy. OK, we hadn't cracked the case, but we'd definitely made a good start. Gramp would definitely be impressed.

"What do we do next?"

"Have a lie-down?" said Ax, clearly exhausted by detective work.

"I guess we need to find out what our suspects were up to," said Wendall, tapping his pen on his notebook.

"OK, how do we do that?" I asked. Wendall continued tapping as he thought long and hard. "What would the bloke in *Midsomer Murders* do?"

"He'd probably just ask them," said Wendall.

"OK," I replied. "Then let's do that."

Ax's shoulders shook with a little guffaw. "Good luck with that, guys. Asking a murderer if they murdered someone? Better you than me."

Then I looked at him, with his shaggy long hair and dozy eyes, and a thought popped into my head. "No, better *you* than us."

CHAPTER 14
Deck Games

"Do I really have to do this?" asked Ax, shuffling nervously, his long hair now slicked into a nice side-parting.

We were, once again, standing by a door. But this time, the door to the ship's On-board Board Games Room. A sign on it read DECK GAMES, 11 A.M. I checked my watch, bang on. Then I peeked through its window: at one of the room's tables, I could make out Ivan, Sonny, Fists and Ms Ho-Renton all sitting together.

Wendall put a hand on Ax's shoulder. "Do you know what I do when I'm scared, Ax?"

"What's that, little Windmill?" he asked.

"I'm sick."

Ax took an involuntary step backwards.

"But once I'm sick," continued Wendall, "that's it, I'm not scared any more."

Ax narrowed his eyes. "Okaaaaaaaay…"

"What I mean to say is: being scared is just a feeling in your tummy and you can get rid of it, easy as." He looked at Ax like a nurse and asked, softly, "Would you like to do a sick, Ax? Even just a little one?"

Ax pulled a face. "I'm OK, dude. Let's just get it over and done with." Then he turned to me and said: "Talk me through the plan again."

"Right," I said, "you are going to go in here, pretending like you are conducting an investigation into Wendall's missing swimming trunks…"

"Why me though?" interjected Ax. "I mean, why am I investigating that? Why can't you do it?"

"You heard what the captain said – we can't be seen investigating the crime," I replied. "Even us asking after a pair of swimming trunks might arouse his suspicion."

He pushed his mouth to the side. "But, why will it

make sense to those old people that I'm asking about a pair of trunks?"

I shrugged. "Cos you're the lifeguard and that's the kind of thing lifeguards do."

He thought long and hard. I could see he wasn't quite buying it.

Wendall chimed in and saved the day: "Just think about *Baywatch*! They spend their whole time investigating loooooads of pointless stuff. Like this one time, a whale ate someone's wallet and Mitch went inside it to get it out."

I gave Wendall a look. "Is that true?" I whispered.

He looked to the ceiling in thought. "Now I'm thinking about it, it might have been a robber who stole the wallet and a bowling alley that Mitch went inside..."

It didn't matter. The mention of *Baywatch* had done the trick. "Yeah," said Ax, turning the corners of his mouth down as he reflected favourably on the comparison. "I guess this *is* a bit like *Baywatch*."

Not giving him any more time to dwell on it, I continued explaining the plan: "You ask everyone in this room whether they can account for their activities between 5.50 a.m. and 6.10 a.m. this morning – and whether they have alibis. Although, the only ones we *really* care about are that guy with long hair and a leather jacket – Ivan Django – and the bloke over there who looks like he's asleep in his chair, Sonny the Squid. And maybe that big guy with the slicked-back hair and cratered face, Fists Harris."

Ax began to limber up. "And where will you guys be?"

"Right behind you," I said. "It was Wendall who had his trunks stolen, so he'll be around to answer any questions. And I'm just a friend lending moral support."

"You've got this, Ax," said Wendall. "Just think: what would the guy from *Baywatch* do?"

Ax stood up straighter. "He'd go in there!" he said, suddenly energized. "Probably on a quad bike!"

"That's the spirit!" I said, slapping him on the back. "Although we haven't got a quad bike."

Ax grabbed the door handle, then pushed his shoulders back and opened the door confidently.

The perfumed waft of freshly talc-ed pensioners hit us like a lavender tsunami. An employee of the

Tom Cruise flitted between the packed tables, smiling pleasantly and explaining the rules to the different games.

After what felt like a lifetime, we eventually reached Fists and co.'s table. Sonny was slumped back in his chair, dozing; Fists was completing a word search from his puzzle book with Ms Ho-Renton's help; and Ivan was silently, broodingly filling in a dolphin jigsaw puzzle.

Ax approached them and Fists looked up from his puzzle book. "Wotcha, Jesse!" he said, his whole cratered face turning into a smile as he spotted me. He still had his sheepskin coat and trilby on. "Ms Ho-Renton, have you met Sid's grandson?"

She peered over her horn-rimmed glasses like a friendly librarian, her purple-tinted curls immaculately coiffured and her floral blouse and cardigan perfectly ironed. Then she opened her mouth and out came a voice that sounded like it had been dipped in tar and fed through a mangle: "Hello, my dear!" she croaked. "How delightful to meet you."

I gave them both a winning smile and she looked

back down at Fists's puzzle book.

"So, erm, this little dude has lost his trunks," said Ax, "and I'm conducting an investigation."

"CLAPTRAP!" shouted Ms Ho-Renton.

All three of us looked at her, shocked at the outburst. I could feel Ax's body tense beside me. Then, slowly, she extended a finger to Fists's puzzle book.

"There, diagonal across: C-L-A-P-T-R-A-P," she croaked, then looked back up at Ax. "What was it you were saying, dearie?"

"We're, um … investigating some stolen swimming trunks…" repeated Ax.

"'Ere, you're the lifeguard, ain'tcha?" said Fists, looking him up and down. "Were you there when poor Bridget slipped and fell this morning?"

"I, erm, was, yes."

"COINCIDENCE!" yelled Ms Ho-Renton.

Everyone turned to her again, half-wary.

"C-O-I-N-C-I-D-E-N-C-E! Three across from the top left." She looked up from the puzzle book again. "Sorry, I do love a word search."

"Were you two close?" I asked Fists, gently probing.

"Oooooo, we go back years!" he said, replacing his trilby. "She used to help me sell stolen cars. We became good pals. Robbed Hatton Garden Jewellery Market together in sixty-eight! A great lark." He chuckled fondly at the memory. "But we met our match in your gramp! He caught me in Rome first, then Bridget in her secret hideaway. That's water under the bridge now, though. We all became pals once we got on the straight and narrow. Got a lot of respect for your gramp. So does Bridget."

"WITCH!" shouted Ms Ho-Renton. We all looked at her again, expecting her to point at the letters in the puzzle book. But she wasn't even looking at it. She smiled unapologetically. "I don't like her. But that's another story."

Cogs inside my brain whirled as I tried to make a mental note of who disliked who. Were they really all friends, like Fists said? Because there seemed to be unresolved issues between some of them: first Felix and Bridget, now Ms Ho-Renton and Bridget. Had one or more of them been conspiring against her? Was that why we were all on this ship? Or was it something else, something bigger? Could they be conspiring against Gramp as well, who put them all in jail? The thought made my tummy churn.

"Right," said Ax, the *Baywatch*-inspired energy leaching out of him. "Like I say, we need to find out where you were between 5.50 a.m. and 6.10 a.m. so we can rule you out of our investigation..." He quickly corrected himself: "Our swimming-trunk investigation."

"I was in my room," croaked Ms Ho-Renton. "Asleep."

"As was I," said Fists.

We all looked over to Sonny. When he wasn't in disguise as a bad interpretation of a waiter, he was dressed like a dishevelled lord of the manor: white shirt, battered waistcoat, silk cravat. He was slouched back, hands folded on his waistcoat, snoring.

"Sonny!" shouted Fists. "SONNY!"

He didn't stir.

Fists slowly and shakily rose from his chair. "Oooof," he groaned, his limbs practically creaking. Then he shuffled over to Sonny – having to stop once to steady himself on a table – before shaking him by the shoulder. The way he moved made it hard to imagine him climbing out of a cabin window and along the sheer side of the ship.

"WAKE UP, SONNY!" he yelled. "SOME KID WANTS TO ASK YOU IF YOU STOLE HIS SWIMMING TRUNKS!"

Sonny drowsily came to and tried to sit up, but just slumped back down in his chair. "What is it … who…?"

Ax repeated his question: "Can I, like, ask where you were between 5.50 a.m. and 6.10 a.m. this morning?"

I could see Sonny trying to fight through his slumber. It was like he'd been drugged or something. "I was, erm, in my room asleep," he said.

Wendall and I exchanged an excited glance. *That*, we knew, was a lie. He hadn't gone into his room all night. Was this the first break in the case? I felt a little tingle of excitement.

But before we could press our lead, Sonny's heavy eyelids fell down like weighted blinds, and he slipped back into a deep sleep. There was no use trying to get any more out of him, he was dead to the world. The only person we had left to ask was Ivan. Ax turned his gaze on him and withered in his sinister stare.

"Er, and you, sir, could you, erm, tell me where you were this morning between 5.50 a.m. and 6.10 a.m.?"

Ivan looked back down at his puzzle, his long, greasy white hair hanging over his face like the stalactites in some haunted cave, before slowly lifting a jigsaw piece with a mermaid tail on it. The guy looked bad to the bone. He even managed to make a dolphin puzzle seem menacing.

"Like, hello?" said Ax. "Does he need his hearing aids in or something? I said…"

Ms Ho-Renton interjected. "He heard you. He won't answer. He's grumpy like that." Then she gave him a little warning look that said: *leave it*. "Tell me … why are you taking time out to investigate a pair of stolen swimming trunks?" she croaked, raising a single eyebrow.

Ax pushed his hair to one side nervously. "You know … us lifeguards … we … we never like to leave a good pair of trunks behind … you get me?"

I blurted out a lie: "He's also the ship's lost property officer!"

"Yeah … I'm also the, um, lost property office."

"Officer," I corrected.

"Yup, officer," he said, with a strained smile.

Ms Ho-Renton's raised eyebrow didn't move.

Then she leaned in, her voice now quiet like a frog in a library. "And what if *I* had had something stolen? Something important? Something" – she glanced left and right, then lowered her voice even more – "confidential. Who would I talk to? Someone who could keep it quiet?"

Ax winced. "It's not a swimming costume, is it?"

She shook her head slowly. "No."

I stepped forward, moving Ax out of the way and said in a low voice: "Ax's busy, but we could help and report back to him!"

She looked from me to Ax. Ax shrugged.

She was wavering. I tried to seal the deal: "We're really good at finding things and keeping secrets."

She stared at me, studying my face, which I was fighting to keep breezy and helpful, while really I was desperate to uncover whatever clue she was sitting on. Finally, she croaked quietly, "Meet me at cabin 1019 in five minutes."

We nodded and turned to leave.

"NAKED!" she boomed.

We collectively held our breaths until she followed it up with: "N-A-K-E-D. Diagonally down, top left."

CHAPTER 15
Ms Ho-Renton

We knocked on cabin 1019 exactly five minutes later. The door softly creaked ajar, and the short, squat frame of Ms Ho-Renton appeared, her grey cardigan buttoned up and her long skirt ending just above a pair of chunky ankles and sturdy black boots. She looked every bit the elderly librarian. But one you'd think twice about crossing.

"Hello, again," she croaked.

She opened the door fully and my mouth fell open as I saw the state of her room. I say "room": it looked more like a warehouse. Stacked floor to ceiling on virtually every available surface were towers and towers of hard, black suitcases – the kind people use to transport expensive camera equipment.

"Come in, dears," she said. "Don't just stand there."

Wendall and I squeezed inside as best as we could.

"Wowzers, you've got a lot of stuff," muttered Wendall, mouth ajar.

"Don't mind the clutter," she croaked, closing the door. "Please, take a seat." She ushered us through a gap and towards her bed. We perched on the end as she seated herself on a small mound of suitcases. The black cases loomed over and around us, soaking up the light and leaving us in a sort of dingy twilight.

Wendall craned his neck. "If you, er, don't mind me asking: what is all this stuff?"

Ms Ho-Renton croaked a response: "Just stock. For my business." She looked at it matter-of-factly, like it was completely normal to have a cabin that looked like a completed game of Tetris.

My eyes fell on a half-open suitcase and almost popped out of their sockets. Inside, clear as day, was a long-barrelled rifle next to a half-dozen colourfully plumed darts. I fought the lump in my throat and asked:

"And what business is it that you're in?" Inside, my brain was shouting: *INTERNATIONAL ARMS DEALER!*

Wendall had obviously seen the same thing as me. He tensed up like a breadstick.

Ms Ho-Renton chuckled and said in her hoarse voice: "Well, I'm not an international arms dealer any more, if that's what your gramp has told you?"

"He hasn't said anything…" I replied. It was half true; his scrapbook had told us everything we knew.

"I've been out of that game since Sid caught me in Sierra Leone in seventy-two." She looked to the ceiling and began to reminisce. "I was helping a belligerent group of chimpanzees at the behest of a rogue conservationist so they could overthrow the government. But the thought of monkeys with guns scared the British Secret Service, so Sid and Clarence were sent to track me down. Clarence, as he always did, got things wrong and ended up getting stuck in Freetown Zoo for three days while your gramp's men and my chimps did battle in the jungle." She chuckled at the memory. "It was quite a scene! Sid climbed through the rainforest canopy and arrested me. Great times!"

Wendall and I slowly exchanged a side glance. That was the oddest story I had ever heard. If she wasn't in the arms trading game, what *was* she doing with a giant gun?

"Anyway, I packed in that business when I came out of jail." She coughed and tapped her suitcases. "Of course, I can see how my business inventory might be a little misleading."

She eased herself up, edged over to the suitcase and pulled a gun the size of the Eiffel Tower from the foam padding inside.

I gasped in surprise. It was the biggest gun I'd ever seen! Sitting in the hands of an old lady.

"Say hello to Jemima," she said, holding her megagun across her chest and tenderly stroking it. "I made her myself." She looked up, expecting a response.

"Erm, hello, Jemima," said Wendall, giving the gun a nervous wave.

I was still speechless at the sheer size of it. It looked like the kind of thing you'd use to take down an elephant.

"This is what I use for taking down elephants," she

croaked. Then she added, as an afterthought: "Just to stun them of course, not kill them."

Wendall raised his hand. "Er, why would you need to stun an elephant?"

"I wouldn't, young man," she replied. "But my clients would. I'm in the conservation game now, you see. That scrape in Sierra Leone told me how much we need to look after our wildlife. Every bit of equipment in here" – she tapped on another suitcase – "is to help catch and trap large animals. Poachers are getting more and more sophisticated these days. So game-keepers have to keep up. And that's where I come in."

Wendall and I both sat there and soaked it all in. It was pretty surreal – an old lady sat cradling the kind of weapon you'd find strapped to the side of a tank. She looked like some sort of bizarre, elderly Rambo.

After a moment's pause, I asked: "Why do you need to bring all of this on a cruise?"

She looked at me like the answer was obvious. "Polar bears, of course, dearie! We're going deep into polar bear country. Lots of poachers try to catch polar bears.

Not to mention whales! And orcas! Conservationists want my weapons to help them fight poachers and keep track of their beloved animals." She popped open a nearby suitcase. "I've got explosives to break up ice packs. Stun guns to tranquillize polar bears. Jet thrusters to soup up snow-mobiles. Bulletproof vests to protect yourself against poachers. Everything an Arctic conservationist could want ... at a price, of course!"

A thought started to form in my mind. "And what does that gun fire?"

"Darts," she replied, pulling one out and popping it in the chamber. Then, without warning, she pulled the trigger. I leapt out of my skin as a giant THWACK exploded into the air and a dart flew out of the barrel and embedded itself in her bathroom door with a deafening splinter.

"What the...?" cried Wendall, falling backwards on to the bed in panic.

"Don't worry, dearies!" she shouted over Jemima's decompressing hiss. "I didn't load the vial of elephant anaesthetic in it!" She gave a throaty laugh. Sitting there with her giant gun, chortling, she looked like the scariest granny I'd ever met. I wouldn't want to be a poacher with her on the prowl.

I swapped a glance with Wendall. He looked slightly rattled by the massive dart sticking in the door, but I could see he had latched on to the same word as me: *vial*.

I put on my best detective face and asked: "Exactly *what* was it that was stolen from your room?"

"Yes, yes!" she said, giving Jemima a kiss and slipping her back into her case. "I nearly forgot."

She pulled out a small metal case, popped it open and stared at its contents ruefully. I had a feeling deep down in my tummy that I knew what was inside. "One of these was stolen sometime yesterday," she said with a frown. Then she spun the suitcase around and my knowing feeling did a cartwheel.

Wendall tried his best to sound surprised. "Golly, those are…"

"Vials of elephant anaesthetic," croaked Ms

Ho-Renton. *Green* vials of elephant anaesthetic – the exact type of vial we'd seen lying by Bridget Bouffant's feet. "They are for knocking out your largest mammals. One vial of this could take down a T-Rex."

I tried to contain my swirling thoughts, composed myself and asked: "And what would happen if it was administered to a human?"

She blew her cheeks out. "I wouldn't do that, dearie. Even breathing in its gas fumes could kill you. Especially if you are frail or elderly."

"Wow," muttered Wendall. He was thinking the exact same thing as me: we'd found the attempted murder weapon! Thoughts and questions began to frantically connect inside my brain. Who took it? And when? And could Ms Ho-Renton really be believed when she said it had been stolen?

Wendall scribbled in his notebook and asked: "Did that case ever leave your room yesterday?"

"Only once," she replied. "I took it to afternoon tea after I got a mysterious note asking to purchase some of the anaesthetic. But whoever wrote it never showed up."

I leaned forward, eagerly: "Have you got that note?"

"I certainly have," she said, and pulled it out of her pocket.

It simply read:

I AM INTERESTED IN BUYING YOUR STRONGEST POISON. MEET ME AT AFTERNOON TEA. I'LL BE WEARING A RED CRAVAT. REGARDS, A WEALTHY BUYER

Who could that be? We'd seen Sonny wearing a cravat ... but surely a master criminal wouldn't continue to wear something that obvious if he really was responsible.

"Anyway," she continued, "I popped to the loo after waiting around for an age, and when I got back, a vial was missing." Then she pursed her lips and asked: "Do you think there's a thief about? Same person who stole your trunks? These vials are expensive, you know, about a thousand pounds a pop."

"I think you are right," I replied, a mental image flashing up of that broken green vial lying by Bridget's feet. "It looks like there is a thief on board." And not just any thief, I thought to myself, a thief with murderous plans.

"And you'll ask around, see if you can find it?"

"Sure," I replied, forcing a smile.

She flashed her yellow teeth in gratitude. "You're good kids. I'd love to get it back. That thing could be dangerous in the hands of the wrong person."

I tried as best as I could to read her face. She *looked* genuine, but I couldn't rule out the fact that this might be one big cover story. "I'm sure we'll find it," I said, knowing full well where it had ended up, and that she wasn't getting it back. A thousand pounds down the drain. Literally.

I stood up to leave, but another thought hit me: we shouldn't waste the opportunity of having Ms Ho-Renton's attention. We had complete privacy. She might be able to help us with more clues. "If you don't mind me asking: why don't you like Bridget Bouffant?"

She paused and looked me up and down. I suddenly felt a bit nervous at how blunt I had been. Then she smiled her bullfrog smile and croaked, "You kids are a bit too young to understand properly. But Bridget never treated men the way I think men should be treated."

Wendall chimed in from behind me: "How so?"

"They were just … disposable to her. At least that's the way I saw it. Once upon a time, as a young lady, she was engaged to Sonny. He was something of a criminal celebrity – dashing, handsome, a master of disguise. But when Felix waltzed in with his silver slippers, her head was turned. She broke off her engagement with Sonny and married him instead. It soured poor Sonny something rotten. Then, when your gramp arrested Bridget, then Felix, they both spent years behind bars. Felix got out first. He waited patiently for her. And when she was released, first thing she did? Divorced him! She had her eyes set on Hollywood, and being married to a crook like Felix wasn't going to help that. Way I see it, she liked 'em while they were useful to her. And the minute they weren't, she tossed 'em aside like a crisp packet. Sonny never got over it. Nor did Felix." She sucked in a breath in disapproval. "And don't believe all Fists tells you either. Yes, they had a grand old time robbing Hatton Garden. But he forgot to tell you how she ripped him off straight after – keeping most of the loot! She's a devious one. Made a lot of enemies."

Wowzers! Talk about motives! I couldn't believe it ... it seemed almost *everyone* had a reason to want to kill Bridget.

Next to me, Wendall scribbled in his notebook.

Ms Ho-Renton nudged her chin at his notebook. "'Ere, why are you asking all of this?" She narrowed her eyes and looked at us suspiciously. "What happened to Bridget this morning *was* an accident, wasn't it?"

I got the sudden feeling that it was time to leave. I didn't know who was in cahoots with who on this ship – and the last thing we wanted was for word to get out that we were investigating Bridget's attempted murder. Murderers don't tend to like detectives snooping about. "Erm, thank you for your time, Ms Ho-Renton," I said, standing up and pulling Wendall up by the arm. "We'd better get going." I squeezed through the little suitcase corridor, tugging Wendall after me. "We will do everything in our power to find out who stole your vial."

"You're good kids!" she cried, from somewhere among her towers of black boxes. "And if you ever need to tranquillize a rhino, you know where to find me!"

I squeezed out of the door with Wendall right behind me. We both looked at each other wide-eyed. We'd found the murder weapon. We'd found a motive. We were going to crack this case, I was sure of it.

CHAPTER 16
On Deck with Wendall

Wendall and I headed straight for Gramp's room to see if he was feeling better. It'd been hours since we'd found Bridget and I couldn't wait to tell him everything that we'd learnt. We *had* to tell him about the vial and see what he could remember about Bridget, Sonny and Felix. We hurried along the cabin corridors, dropping down the stairway and on to Deck 1.

I tapped quietly on Gramp's door.

No answer. I pushed the unlocked door and it creaked open. Inside, Gramp was lying under his covers, shivering. Only his grey, sweaty head protruded from his sheets.

"Jeez, Gramp, you're looking even worse."

He let out a little groan, his voice as thin as tissue paper. Boy, those chicken nuggets had really done a number on him. I felt a sudden pang of guilt that I couldn't be two places at once – looking after Gramp *and* chasing leads for our investigation. I tried to reassure myself that he'd have wanted me to be out there, trying to find clues.

I sat at the end of Gramp's bed and told him all about the CCTV, the alibis and the vial. He gave a meek smile, his skin pallid and damp. He opened his dry lips to speak, and a weak voice came out: "Top-rate detective work, Mike."

I exchanged alarmed glances with Wendall. Gramp was utterly confused – completely out of it. "Um, I'm Jesse, Gramp," I said. "Mike is my dad, your son."

His weak eyes looked right through me and whatever he was seeing brought a smile to his face. "Just remember to get as much evidence as you can, Mike, my boy," he continued. "Evidence is everything."

Whatever was wrong with him, it hadn't just made him queasy, it seemed to have transported him back in time thirty years. I could feel the blood in my veins chilling. Could he have been poisoned as well?

"Gramp, I'm going to go and get a nurse."

Gramp squeezed his eyes shut and lifted a hand up to his forehead. As he pressed his palm against it, I saw he had a little green box clasped in his fist. It looked exactly like the box of seasickness tablets I saw Perkins with.

I took them from his grasp, feeling relieved that he at least had *some* medicine to try and help him feel better. "Did Perkins give you this?"

Gramp opened his eyes and focused on the pills. He thought hard for a second, then said: "I took them. From his jacket pocket. While he was in the loo."

Whether it was the chicken nuggets or the rocking of the boat, a couple of seasickness tablets *might* help.

Wendall reached for a glass of water and handed it over. "Here, Mr Hall, take them. They'll help you feel better."

Gramp took the pills off me with a shaky hand and popped them in his mouth. Wendall held the glass up to Gramp's lips and he swallowed a mouthful.

Gramp lifted a weak hand and popped one in his

mouth. "Thank you, Alice," he said, looking at Wendall affectionately.

Then he fixed me with his piercing blue eyes. "I'm sorry, Mike, my boy," he said. "Sorry I haven't been there for you like I should have." Then he put his hand on mine.

Lying there, grey and shivery, for the first time I saw beyond his cool, assured exterior and I saw an old man. What if he *really* wasn't well? What if he was ill for the rest of the cruise – leaving Wendall and me in the midst of all this tangled web of secrets and attempted murder? I put my hand on his as he closed his eyes and drifted off into sleep. A little feeling of fear trickled down from my brain into my tummy.

I turned to Wendall. "I think we should get the nurse."

He nodded.

I stood up and we hurried out. Wendall pulled the cabin door shut behind me and asked, with a confused frown: "Who's Mike?"

"My dad."

"And who's Alice?"

"My gran, who died before I was born."

Wendall left a long pause, then said: "Is he all right, your gramp?"

I chewed my lip and stared into space. "I don't know. But we need to get the nurse quickly." As we ran down the corridor, I said a little prayer to myself – I prayed that this was all down to a dodgy chicken nugget or a bout of seasickness. Because a horrible fear was gnawing away inside of me – a fear that whoever had tried to poison Bridget had done the same to Gramp.

The ship's nurse came and took Gramp's temperature and listened to his heart, all while he snored away. He made me feel a lot better by reassuring us that Gramp wasn't *that* ill – he had a slight fever and a normal heartbeat. Then the nurse promised to keep checking on him through the day and told us not to worry.

Wendall and I stood on deck, a feeling of relief washing over me with the cool sea breeze. Gramp seemed to be OK. And if he was awake and could talk, I knew what he'd tell me: to keep on with the investigation. We had to find out who was behind all of this.

I looked out to sea and wished Gramp was here to

tell us what to do next. The afternoon sky had turned a moody grey and the *Tom Cruise* rolled and rocked in the choppy waves. The jagged mountains were closer than before. England felt a long way behind us.

Nearby, I could overhear a granny telling her husband that we'd be in Norway by tomorrow and how she couldn't wait for the whale spotting, the fjords and the Northern Lights. I'd been so wrapped up in the attempted murder case that I hadn't really given much thought to any of that stuff. Or anything else really, not even the D.I.V.O.R.C.E. I winced as I remembered that Mum and Dad were probably sitting at our kitchen table right now, talking about who was going to get to keep the TV.

I pushed off the railings and tried to drag my mind back on to the case. Wendall was rummaging around in his red backpack and I could see the edge of the scrapbook poking out – we'd been storing it there since yesterday, and I'd almost forgotten it.

"There's got to be more clues in here," I said, reaching over and pulling it out. "Something we've missed."

I started at the back this time. The final page was a

story covering Gramp's retirement – once again looking like it had come from an internal newsletter. The headline read:

LEGENDARY DETECTIVE RETIRES AFTER
FORTY YEARS' SERVICE

It was dated fifteen years ago and, as with so many of the stories, featured a grey, pixelated photo. Gramp's beaming face stared back at me, holding a silver plate that was engraved with a special goodbye message. Perkins stood beside him, looking much more sombre.

MI6's most senior detective, Chief Inspector Sidney Hall, formally retired last night after four decades of service. In a small private ceremony, Chief Inspector Hall received a specially commissioned award to commemorate his remarkable

---

achievements at the agency. Alongside his assistant Clarence Perkins – who is also taking early retirement after twenty-nine years' service – Hall was responsible for apprehending some of the world's most wanted villains.

My eyes flicked back to the photo. If there was a clue there, I was missing it. And that's when my eyes landed on something *very* hard to make out. It was heavily pixelated but if you squinted hard, the long, limp hair and granite face came into view.

"Look!" I said, jamming my finger into the yellow paper. "Right there, standing behind Gramp! It's Ivan Django!"

Wendall moved his nose closer to the paper and narrowed his eyes. "Oh yeah! What's he doing there?"

"I dunno," I said, scanning down the rest of the article. "There's nothing here that mentions him, it's all just boring coverage of Gramp's retirement party."

We turned back a page and found ourselves on a

story we'd already read. Working our way backwards, we scanned every page, looking for hidden clues. But there was nothing.

"Hold on!" said Wendall. "There's one thing we haven't tried. I saw it on *Midsomer Murders* once."

He picked up the scrapbook and shook it. A little folded sheet fell out. It must have been tucked behind another cutting.

"Ta da!" he said, holding it up with a toothy grin. I took it off him gently, its edges as dry as an old bone, and unfolded it, making sure not to damage it.

Once again, it was some sort of news story – but this time it looked like it was cut from a national paper rather than an internal newsletter. It was dated sixteen years ago, shortly before Gramp retired and featured a mugshot of Ivan, his dead eyes staring straight down the camera.

GOVERNMENTS AGREE AMNESTY
WITH "CRIMINAL MASTERMIND" IVAN
DJANGO

The leader of international criminal organization G.E.M.I.N.I. has agreed an amnesty with the United Kingdom and United States governments. Ivan Django, 63, has pledged to disband his criminal network and cooperate with security agencies on both sides of the Atlantic, in exchange for both governments dropping all pending charges against him. In a move that has come out of the blue, considering the size and extent of his operations, commentators have been left wondering what has lured Django to the negotiating table, considering his long history of eluding and double-crossing security agencies. While both governments insist that the amnesty is genuine, there is speculation that it could even be a ploy by Django to get close to his former adversaries.

The last words almost leapt off the page: "Former adversaries ... is that Gramp?" I said, looking at Wendall.

"Or does *Ivan* have beef with Bridget that we don't know about?"

"Maybe..." I replied. "We need to write this all down."

Wendall pulled out his notebook and began to update his suspects grid. When it was finished, it looked like this:

	ALIBI	MOTIVE
FELIX	None (that we know of)	Bridget ended their marriage.
SONNY THE SQUID	None. LIED ABOUT BEING IN CABIN.	Bridget broke off their engagement.
FISTS	In cabin. (Could have climbed along the outside?)	Ripped off by Bridget.
IVAN	None	Revenge?

"In my book those are pretty good reasons to want to kill someone. Scorned love: it's a real zinger. At least, it is on *Midsomer Murders*," he said.

I nodded. Behind me, the couple who'd been talking about the Northern Lights had started to argue. Something about a lost key card.

We both stared at the notebook. There were still so many unanswered questions: how did the attempted murderer get into the sunroom? How did they escape without being seen? And, underpinning everything, there was the mystery of who had invited us on this cruise – and whether there was more to it than simply getting their revenge on Bridget.

Gramp's advice rang in my ears. "More evidence," I muttered. "How can we get more evidence?"

The wife was now shouting at her husband: "No, you had it last! You put it in your wallet after breakfast."

"Look, look," I could hear him say as he tried to defuse things. "We'll just ask at reception. They must have spare keys they can lend us. Or else, how would the maids get into our room to clean it?"

And then it hit me. I knew *exactly* where we could look for more evidence. And I knew how we could do it without getting caught.

CHAPTER 17

Maid Sonny and the Empty Case

I stood next to Wendall and Ax in one of the long cabin corridors. Dim uplighters stretched down the walls, tapering into the distance like streetlights on a motorway. It was now late afternoon – nearly twelve hours since someone had tried to murder Bridget. Outside, the waves had picked up, rolling the boat side to side in long, unsteadying sways that I felt at the very pit of my stomach. Just down the corridor from us sat the door to Bridget's cabin. And behind it, I hoped, clues.

Ax scratched the back of his neck and mumbled: "I

really dunno about this."

It'd taken every ounce of persuasion – plus another *Baywatch* speech – to convince him to close the pool and help us again. And I could see he wanted to back out of it already.

"What if I get, like, caught?" he asked.

"Yeah," said Wendall, as tense as a rice cracker. "He could get fired. We could get thrown off the ship."

"Then…" I tried to think of something inspiring to say, but all I could think of was: "Just don't get caught." It was hardly a stirring speech, but for the record, I was as nervous as them. I just didn't want to show it. Even though there was practically zero chance of anyone being inside, breaking into Bridget's room still felt like the most dangerous thing we'd done. And what if someone *did* catch us in there? Rooting around in a dead woman's room? We would undoubtedly be in a TONNE of trouble. Wendall was right, we might even get kicked off the cruise and then we really would be out at sea. But if we wanted more clues, this was where we should be looking.

"Remember, guys," I continued, digging deep for a

pep talk. "There's an attempted murderer on board, and we are the only people who can catch them."

Ax gave a reluctant sigh, scratched his neck one more time, then pulled out his master key card. "I'm gonna unlock it. Then I'm gonna scram. You guys are on your own."

"You're a real hero, Ax," I said. And he seemed to like that.

I put a hand on Wendall's shoulder. "You ready?" He took a deep breath and gave a single, firm nod. To think, just yesterday, the idea of riding an out-of-bounds water flume was the naughtiest thing he'd ever heard – now he was breaking into someone's room to search her stuff. I felt a bit bad – I'd promised his nan that I'd keep him out of trouble, and I was doing the exact opposite.

I checked the coast was clear and we tiptoed down the corridor, coming to a silent halt by the cabin. I put my ear to the door. Nothing. I nodded at Ax. Softly – almost in slow motion – he inserted the key card into the slot on the door. It gave a gentle click as it unlocked.

Ax scurried off immediately, leaving me there

holding the door handle.

I took a deep breath and pushed it open.

The curtains were drawn and the room was dim. It was also a complete pigsty – bed unmade, mime clothes strewn about the floor, a big make-up box spilling its contents on to the dressing table.

We slipped inside and closed the door behind us.

"What are we looking for?" whispered Wendall.

I shrugged. "Anything suspicious, I guess…"

Wendall began lifting clothes off the floor and looking under them. I did the same, peering under the bed and working my way up to the rumpled bed sheets covered in strewn skirts and blouses. I moved along the bed systematically, lifting clothes up then replacing them exactly as I found them. There was the odd hair curler lying around, a lipstick, a brush. But nothing of any interest to us.

"Anything?" I whispered to Wendall, who was on all fours scouring the carpet.

"Not yet," he replied.

I worked my way to the top of the bed, stuffed my hands down the sides and felt my heart miss a beat. Stuffed down the sides was something square and hard. I pulled it out to reveal a *very* large blue jewellery box. Whatever it contained – a necklace, a tiara maybe – must be enormous. My palms sweaty, I prized it open with a soft creak, only to feel the hope escape from me like a deflating beach ball. It was empty. I peered in closer. Stitched in gold calligraphy on the insides were the words *Le Gâteau Glacé*. What did it mean? And where was it? Probably in this pigsty, I thought. And then a second realization hit me – what if this room had been trashed by someone looking for it? And what if they had taken it? The thought made me sit up straight.

"Wendall!" I hissed. "I think you're gonna want to see this."

Wendall's voice was low and strained, almost quivering with nerves. "Erm, Jesse, I think you're gonna wanna see *this*."

I raised my eyes to see Wendall's white, startled face staring back at me from the carpet. Crouched on all fours, pointed towards the curtain but his face turned to me, he looked like some sort of terrified sniffer dog. "What is it?" I asked.

But he didn't need to answer. My eyes travelled past Wendall to the juncture where the long curtain met the floor. There, poking out, were the ends of two black shoes.

My heartbeat was now thumping – thump, thump, thump – thumping against my ribcage, threatening to break out of it. Someone was in here – hiding!

Wendall, his face taut with panic, whispered, practically sub-sonically: "What do we do?"

I gestured at the door with my head and opened my eyes wide; the international code for LET'S GET OUT OF HERE. Wendall nodded and rose to his feet. But as he did, horror struck. It happened almost in slow motion: as the *Tom Cruise* went over another big wave, he stumbled forwards. Throwing a foot out to steady himself, it landed on an eyeliner, which flung his foot back, launching him forwards, straight into the curtain with an almighty:

"OOF!"

My stomach dropped through the decks.

Wendall sat on the floor, rubbing his head as the curtain doubled over and clutched its groin area – right where Wendall's skull had connected.

I wanted to run, flee, but I was frozen to the spot. Wendall rose a shaky hand and pulled the curtain back to reveal a puce Sonny, bent over and clutching his groin. He was dressed as one of the ship's cleaners, with a knee-length grey dress and a long wig.

He spoke between gritted teeth, his eyes clasped shut in pain: "I was just, erm, cleaning this window." We gawped at him in amazement. He unclasped his hands and lifted one shakily to the window, wiping it with a cloth and saying: "There, all done!"

He straightened himself up, took a calming breath, threw us a fake smile and began to shuffle towards the door. As he passed me he gave a small but unmissable side glance at the jewellery box lying in my lap. Then, without another word, he pulled the door open and left.

CHAPTER 18
Perkins on Deck

We stayed in Bridget's room after Sonny left and looked *everywhere* for the contents of the box – but it was nowhere to be found. Desperate to tell him about the new clue, we then went to check on Gramp in the hope that he might be feeling better. But we found him still asleep, the nurse taking his temperature. The nurse said his fever had passed and he couldn't understand why Gramp was sleeping for so long, but we should let him rest.

Instead, Wendall and I headed to the top deck, trying to make sense of it all. Afternoon had turned into evening. Outside, the sun had set and dark clouds had swallowed the moon. The wind was blowing Wendall's bowl cut about like a cold hairdryer. The boat rolled and rocked over the waves. I grabbed extra tight on to the jewellery box, which I'd taken and stuffed under my jumper, and thought about Bridget's room.

"So do you think Sonny is behind all of this?" I said, raising my voice over the wind.

"He's got to be," said Wendall. "You can take your pick for a motive: scorned love, money, revenge. He's got loads of reasons to want to kill Bridget."

"Plus, we've seen that he is a master pick-pocket who can sneak into places undetected," I added. "If *anyone* could steal Ms Ho-Renton's vial then slip into that sunroom, he could."

The wind battered and bit at my cheeks, grabbing my words and whisking them off into a sea that swelled and churned in rolling black mounds. I could feel the *Tom Cruise* ride over each wave, dip down into its trough, then rear up again. However cold and windy it was, the top deck was still the safest place to talk without being overheard.

Wendall fished his notebook out of his backpack and

opened it to his grid, holding the fluttering pages down as we inspected it:

	ALIBI	MOTIVE
FELIX	None	Bridget ended their marriage.
SONNY THE SQUID	None. LIED ABOUT BEING IN CABIN.	Bridget broke off their engagement. To steal the necklace?
FISTS	In cabin	Ripped off by Bridget.
IVAN	None	Revenge?

As I read it, I had an overwhelming feeling that we were just one more jigsaw piece from an answer. "Everything points to Sonny," I said. "We just need proof."

It felt *so* close. I desperately wanted to solve it before Gramp woke up – he'd be so impressed! Although another part of me wanted it to drag on just a *tiny* bit longer. Just enough for Gramp to feel better, help out the investigation and regain his spark.

I gripped the railing and leaned over the side, staring down at the side of the ship – its sheer wall punctuated only by the yellow glow of cabin windows – and then to the churning black waves far below. Could Sonny really have climbed along there? It seemed hard to believe. But how else could he have got the vial into the sunroom?

Just then, someone on the lower promenade deck caught my eye. They were facing away, towards the back of the ship. They appeared to throw a bit of rubbish off the side, then get annoyed when it got caught in some rigging on the side of the ship. I thought of Mum, telling off Ax for dropping a crisp packet when she should have been saying goodbye to me. Which made me think about The Conversation and how they might already have had it. The thought threatened to suck me into a little hole of sadness when the person on the deck below turned their face towards us and I recognized them immediately.

"Perkins!" I shouted. "Wait! We're coming down! We've got so much to tell you!"

He cupped his eyes and stared up, offering a tentative wave.

I grabbed Wendall's elbow and pulled him after me,

clattering down the metal steps to the lower promenade deck and hurrying over.

"Were you up there the whole time, boys?" he asked.

I nodded.

"Did you, erm, see the wind whip my napkin away?" he said, pushing his side-parting down as it flapped around madly. "It's blowing a gale out here!"

Frankly, I had bigger fish to fry than his napkin. I unloaded everything on him: the alibis, Ms Ho-Renton's stolen vial, Sonny breaking into Bridget's room, us breaking into Bridget's room and, finally, the missing necklace.

He took a moment to soak it all in. "You really have been busy."

I pulled the jewellery box from inside my jumper and showed him.

His eyes widened.

"Do you know what was in it?" I asked.

He stared at it for a second, lost in thought. Then he snapped his eyes away and blew his cheeks out. "I do. It's *Le Gâteau Glacé* – a necklace with a diamond so big that people say it is the size of a cake. Bridget always said she was given it by the Grand Duke of Luxembourg for performing a one-off mime on his wife's birthday. At least that's what she claimed. Your gramp and I always suspected she stole it, but we could never prove it."

"But you were master detectives!" I said. "Surely you could prove anything?"

Perkins allowed himself a laugh as he looked almost embarrassed at the compliment. "I ... well..." He looked out to sea. "Your gramp was the real brains; I just helped where I could and there were always cases that we couldn't crack: Ivan, *Le Gâteau*. . . Some things were just too hard."

"Is it worth a lot of money?" asked Wendall.

Perkins bounced his eyebrows. "Lots."

"Thousands of pounds?" asked Wendall.

Perkins shook his head.

Wendall's eyes bulged. "A million?"

Perkins pursed his lips. "Add a zero."

"Holy macaroni!" exclaimed Wendall. "A billion!"

"Well, ten million, actually."

Wendall shook his head in wonder. "Why would she bring a ten-million-pound necklace on a cruise?"

Perkins shrugged and sighed. "She's Bridget Bouffant. She's a show-off. She likes all eyes to be on her, all the time. She was probably trying to outdo the Northern Lights."

Perkins slipped into thought for a moment, and then, with an angry clap of his hands, burst out with a tirade. "I bet Sonny has stolen it! Of all the crooks your gramp and I arrested, he has been the only one who didn't turn over a new leaf. He kept stealing things, and we kept on catching him. Even now, he's still a suspect in dozens of thefts over the last twenty years!"

I'd been thinking our next move over, and I had an idea. It was riskier than a greasy tightrope walk, but if we pulled it off we could close the case against Sonny. I took a deep breath and said: "I think we should tell the captain."

"Really?" spluttered Wendall.

"Absolutely not!" said Perkins, almost choking on the words. "Madness! He warned us off snooping around Bridget's accident. Do you want us to get thrown off the ship?"

"Look, hear me out," I said. "We're *not* snooping

around her accident. We're just three of Bridget's friends who were packing up her stuff after her unfortunate slip and noticed her favourite diamond was missing. Now, if people find out that a ten-million-pound diamond has been stolen on board – which they definitely will when she wakes up in hospital – it will be terrible press for the *Tom Cruise*. The kind of press the captain would do anything to prevent. Even, say, ordering a search of the ship in order to track it down."

Perkins face switched in an instant. "And if he finds the necklace, we'll find the…"

"Culprit!" exclaimed Wendall.

"This could be the proof we need to arrest Sonny!"

Perkins pulled an impressed face and let out a knowing laugh. "You are one smart cookie, Jesse Hall."

I stifled a little smile and tried to look professional.

"Right then. No time like the present, I suppose!" said Perkins, straightening his tie. "Now tell me, have you ever been to a captain's drinks reception before?"

We both shook our heads in unison.

Perkins gave a sharp inhale. "Then brace yourselves. If these waves aren't making you feel queasy, this *definitely* will."

CHAPTER 19
The Captain's Reception

We wound our way through a deserted *Tom Cruise*. Where was everyone? It was only 8 p.m.; *surely* they couldn't all be in bed? Perkins led us through the viewing room, its lights dimmed; the choppy sea made each step feel like my legs were made of jelly.

He paused, pushed open the door to Davy Jones's Bar and a waft of perfume and aftershave escaped like a toxic cloud. Everyone in the *entire* ship seemed to be crammed around tables and facing the stage.

On stage, spot-lit in his full uniform, stood the captain. He had a microphone in his hand and his buck teeth stuck out in a goofy grin. "What do you call a ship-load of blue paint crashing into a ship-load of red paint," he said, licking his lips and wagging his bushy eyebrows. "Two marooned crews!"

Everyone burst into laughter, even Wendall. I watched on, stony-faced.

Perkins whispered into my ear: "He's got millions of these stinkers. Millions."

"Why couldn't the sailors play cards?" said the captain, his lips so close to the mic that his voice was fuzzy and bass-filled. "Because the captain was standing on the deck!"

Cue more laughter. Perkins was right; these jokes honked like a blue cheese.

Wendall's nan was sitting just a couple of tables away, her big brown eyes crying with laughter. "'Ere, Wendall! Bring me some tissues!" she whisper-shouted, waving him over. "And I 'ope you brought a spare of pants cos you're gonna pee yourself at these jokes!"

Wendall pulled an apologetic face and went over to his nan.

A few tables along from Wendall's nan, I spotted Fists, who was creased over and red in the face from laughing. He sat alongside Ms Ho-Renton, her head tipped back, emitting a long, dry cackle, and Felix, who shook helplessly and wiped a tear from his eye. Alongside them, Ivan: as expressionless as a lump of granite, cradling a small glass of wine in one hand and staring blankly at the stage. I eyed them all in disbelief. It was hard to believe there was a cold-hearted attempted murderer among them.

"When the captain comes off stage, first thing we do is grab his attention," whispered Perkins.

I looked up at the stage. The captain didn't seem to be in a rush to finish.

"Why are pirate ships like discount stores?" he said, scanning the audience in excited anticipation. Suddenly, the room plunged into darkness and the hum of the microphone died. I heard surprised gasps and glasses toppling over as well as the captain swearing through the dark. "Damn generator!" he cried. Then, the lights blinked back on, just as they had that morning, and the mic hummed back to life. The captain blew out his cheeks. "Sorry all!" he said, before carrying on as if nothing had happened: "Anyway, pirate ships are like discount stores … because they always have a sail on!" The crowd laughed hysterically and the power cut was forgotten.

We waited through another agonizing ten minutes of terrible jokes, until finally the captain climbed down off the stage and made his way through the crowd. It was like he was some sort of movie star at a premiere: shaking hands, kissing cheeks, paying compliments. Perkins and I were hot on his heels, weaving our way through the crowd, pushing past the sea of tweed and knitwear until we caught up with him.

"Captain! We need to show you something … urgently," said Perkins.

The captain looked up at Perkins and the genial smile drained from his face. "You two? Remember what I told you in the pool. If this is about…"

"It's got nothing to do with Bridget's slip and fall," said Perkins. "It's about" – he lowered his voice to a whisper – "something we found in her cabin. If we could show you … in private. We think you are going to want to see this."

"Fine, I'm listening. But be quick," he said.

Perkins led us out into the quiet of the viewing room and over to one of the big windows. Rows of empty tables stretched in either direction. Outside, a weak moon broke through the clouds and bounced off the jet-black sea. Beyond it, like dragons' teeth growing on the horizon, the mountains of the Norwegian coastline.

I checked one last time to ensure the coast was clear, then pulled the jewellery box out from under my jumper, taking a deep breath and saying: "We found this while organizing Bridget's possessions. It is the box for an incredibly expensive necklace – one that is missing from her items. We suspect it has been stolen. And the thief is still at large. We thought we should tell you before…"

The captain butted in. "That's right! I'm the man you are looking for!"

Perkins frowned. "Come again, Captain?"

The captain carried on. "I have it in my safe on the bridge. Bridget gave it to me yesterday. She asked me to look after it because she didn't trust it being around her friends." He muttered under his breath: "I think that means you lot."

"And it's still there, in the safe?" asked Perkins.

"Under lock and key!" boomed the captain. "Now, if you don't mind. There's an audience in there desperate for some more jokes…"

And with that he marched back down the corridor.

Perkins and I both stared at each other, dumbfounded. Had Bridget realized that someone was trying to steal it?

I let it all swirl around in my head. That scuppered my plan. If the captain wasn't going to search the ship, we needed another way to catch Sonny. I turned to Perkins. "What are you thinking?"

He was lost in his own thoughts, before blinking and snapping to. "I'm thinking…" he replied. "That we tell *no one* about that necklace. The attempted murderer could still be looking for it. If they find out it is in the safe, there's no knowing what they might do to get it."

He was right. Apart from telling Gramp, we needed to keep this to ourselves while we plotted our next move.

Perkins glanced at the clock on the wall. It was coming up for 9 p.m. – fifteen hours since someone tried to murder Bridget.

"For now, let's get some sleep. We need to be thinking clearly," he said. "There's nothing more we can do tonight. We'll regroup in the morning."

He went to leave and then, as an afterthought, turned back and said: "You've done incredibly well today. You'd make a great detective." He gave me that kindly, disarming smile and it filled me with satisfaction. He may not be as sharp as Gramp, but I could see why he made such a good assistant – it was easy to like him.

"Thank you," I replied, beaming and blushing all at once.

As Perkins disappeared down the stairway, an overwhelming tiredness hit me. I headed into the Captain's Reception to say goodnight to Wendall, but it looked like he'd already left for bed himself. On stage, the captain looked like he was getting ready for another set.

As I headed back towards the exit, something else caught my eye. In the shadows beside the stage, Fists, Felix and Sonny were locked in a furious row.

Fists – normally so friendly – had a face of pure fury and was jabbing his fingers into Sonny's chest. Beside him, Felix glowered silently, while Sonny snarled back at the two of them. I thought for a second about weaving over and eavesdropping, but just as I stepped forward, the captain tapped the mic. A loud burst exploded from the speakers. The three of them stopped and – with faces like thunder – turned to the stage.

"Ladies and gentlemen," called the captain. "What do you call…"

I couldn't handle any more cheesy sea jokes. It'd been a long, long day: a 6 a.m. start, an attempted murder, a rollercoaster investigation. I turned on my heels and headed off to bed, making my way out of the bar and through the dark, deserted ship to my cabin. Being there on my own, knowing an attempted murderer was at large, made me shudder and pick my pace up.

As I passed Gramp's room, I stopped to see if he'd woken yet. I knocked but there was no reply. The door was unlocked so I pushed it ajar and poked my head through. Gramp was fast asleep, snoring loudly. There was some colour back in his cheeks – he no longer looked grey and clammy. I smiled and, under my breath, told him to sleep it off. I needed him to help close the noose on Sonny.

I shut the door with a soft click and crossed the corridor to my cabin. As I went to open it, my phone buzzed. We must be getting close to Norway if I was picking up signal, I thought. I slipped inside and pulled my phone out. It was a message from Dad. My thumb hovered over the notification ... but I suddenly realized I was almost scared to open it. I couldn't face bad news right now. Not about the D.I.V.O.R.C.E.

Instead, I turned the phone off and slipped it back in my pocket. Then, I plonked face down on my bed and fell almost immediately into a long, deep sleep. When I dreamed, I dreamed of Gramp calling me "Mike" over and over again, until I was red in the face trying to convince him otherwise. But still he wouldn't – couldn't – listen.

CRUISE DAY 3:
BINGO,
WHALE WATCHING,
FJORDS

CHAPTER 20

Confession!

The sleep recharged me. I woke up with a ping, sat upright in bed and said out loud the word that had been echoing around my half-asleep brain: "CONFESSION!"

It was genius! What we needed from Sonny was a confession! We knew he had a motive. We'd found him snooping around in her room. And we knew that he – of all people – would have been able to steal the poison vial without Ms Ho-Renton noticing. If we confronted him with all that, perhaps he'd slip up and give the game away.

I lay in bed for a bit just to double-check that it wasn't

one of those really bad ideas you have when you wake up. But after five minutes, I was even more convinced of its genius.

I turned my phone on and checked the time. 8 a.m. My message notification blinked in the top corner of the screen and I remembered Dad's late-night text. I bit my cheek, thought about it for a second, then turned the phone back off. I'd deal with it later. I pulled on my clothes and headed into the corridor with a jaunty skip. I knocked on Gramp's door and shouted for him. No reply. I tried the handle but it was locked. I crossed my fingers hard that he was better and headed to the dining room.

Outside the storm had passed, and the ship felt calm and steady as I hurried down the corridor. When I reached the main staircase, the view from the window stopped me dead in my tracks. Huge, jagged mountains loomed back at me – green and grey and enormous in the bright morning sunshine. They were practically within touching distance as the *Tom Cruise* chugged alongside them. Below them, dotted along the shoreline where the pine-covered feet of the mountains met the still turquoise water, sat little clusters of pretty red and yellow timber houses. We were in Norway. And it was EPIC.

I took a moment longer to drink it in, then set off again: up the stairs, across the dirty blue carpet of the viewing room and into the restaurant. The smell of stewing bacon and eggs filled the room. I scanned the tables and felt a surge of joy and relief when I spotted Gramp seated with Wendall and his nan, enjoying breakfast with the bright mountain-scape framed beyond them. I dashed over.

"Jesse!" chimed Gramp, as I pulled up a chair.

"You're better!" I replied, excited to tell

him everything we'd been up to.

"Right as rain. I tell you, whatever that pill was that I took off Perkins did the trick, I slept right through! Eighteen hours straight!"

I leaned forward on the table, barely able to contain myself at having Gramp back on the case. "So much has happened!" I whispered, glancing furtively at Wendall's nan, who smiled at me, displaying a half-dozen kipper bones poking out of her false teeth.

Wendall read my glance. "Here, nan: let me check if your hearing aids are working

properly this morning."

She pulled them out and Wendall pretended to fiddle with them. "She won't hear a thing now."

I quickly filled Gramp in on everything, right up to the Captain's Reception last night. He nodded, sipping at his coffee as he listened.

"So the necklace is in the captain's safe? It hasn't been stolen at all?" asked Wendall, glancing up in surprise.

"Bridget must have been one step ahead of Sonny," I said, before fixing my gaze squarely on Gramp. "It's got to be him, right?"

Gramp nodded. "Perhaps," he replied, taking another sip of coffee. He squeezed his eyes shut like he was trying to process it all. He was a million times better than yesterday, but he still seemed to be struggling to get up to speed. Finally, he said: "What you have there is circumstantial evidence. It wouldn't be enough to arrest him."

I leaned forward even more, my bum now off my seat. "That's it, I reckon there's one easy way to get more evidence. Maybe even conclusive proof." I paused, triple-checked that no one could hear us, then whispered: "A confession!"

Gramp raised an eyebrow: "A confession? That's a long shot. Why would he confess?"

"Because we're on to him! Because there is no way he can get the diamond necklace now!" I winced. He was right – why *would* he confess? "And, um, we haven't got another plan…"

Gramp took another long slurp of coffee and studied my face, which I could feel draining of confidence. He put his coffee cup down and said: "Sure. It's a long shot but it could work!" I smiled and decided it was best not to ask if he genuinely believed that, or if he just didn't want to shoot down my idea.

"One condition, though," he said, taking another slurp of coffee. "I'm the one to ask. If he gets angry, then he gets angry with me, not you."

I nodded eagerly. Opposite me, Wendall's nan forked a big slice of kipper into her mouth and smiled again, oblivious to what was taking place.

Gramp scanned the room with a new-found purpose. "Suspect at six o'clock," he said, with a little smile. I glanced over and saw what he was talking about.

Sonny was queuing for the eggs and bacon, dressed in his usual tattered waistcoat and silk cravat. His crop of wild grey hair looked even more dishevelled than usual and he was staring gormlessly into space. He looked like a man with things on his mind. Gramp stood up, his shirt neatly tucked into his chinos. "Now's as good a time as any."

"Now?" I asked, slightly surprised.

Gramp nodded, not taking his eyes off Sonny. "So he can't create a scene." Then he picked a plate from the table and headed over to the queue. I leapt up and hurried after at a safe distance.

Gramp squeezed into the queue next to Sonny and I took up a position a few places down. "Hello, Sonny old boy," he said. "Mind if I cut in with you?"

I peered around a granny to get a better view. Sonny didn't look in the slightest bit happy to see Gramp; he just shrugged and stepped aside to let him in. He looked tired and anxious. He looked like a man with secrets. And I think Gramp sensed the same.

The queue shuffled along. Gramp made small talk about the mountains and Norway and whales. Sonny said nothing in reply. They approached the silver trays of food, and Sonny started loading eggs on to his plate. Gramp copied. Then, as they both stepped towards the hash browns, the line thinned out and Gramp took his opportunity. Sonny reached for the tongs and Gramp went for them at the same time, accidentally-on-purpose grabbing hold of his hand. Sonny looked up in surprise and Gramp whispered something in his ear. Sonny sprang back, a look of shock and horror on his face. He stared at Gramp for a moment, saying nothing. Gramp stared back. Then, as someone in the queue behind them coughed impatiently, he leaned forward and whispered something into Gramp's ear. I could feel the excitement bubble up inside of me, almost ready to pop.

As quickly as I could, I loaded some breakfast items on to my plate, then scurried after Gramp as he retreated to our table.

He sat back down as Wendall stared at him with eyes half worried, half eager for news, the hearing aids still in his hand.

"And…?" I hissed, climbing back into my chair.

Gramp didn't look up. He sliced a piece of bacon with cool-handed restraint, then whispered: "I think your hunch was right. Sonny says he wants to tell us something. Something that has been weighing him down."

"Amazing!" I whispered. "When?"

"After the 10 a.m. bingo session," he said. "We will meet him on deck and he says he'll tell us everything."

"Yes!" I hissed, clenching both fists.

I checked my watch: 8.20 a.m. My whole body pulsed with impatient excitement, like it was Christmas morning or something. I could hardly believe it: just one hundred minutes and a bingo session till we cracked the case!

CHAPTER 21
The Text from Dad

I needed to kill some time before we met Sonny so I headed up to the top deck. It was surprisingly warm in the sun. Hunched figures gathered at the railings trying to glimpse a whale in the still, turquoise waters. The air was warm and crisp and clean.

I took a little seat on a bench in the sunshine towards the rear of the deck, then pulled out my phone and switched it on. The message sign blinked at me – a little tick in the corner urging me to open it. I took a breath and pushed my thumb against it. The message from Dad popped up.

DAD: How are you enjoying the cruise?

He'd sent it sometime yesterday.

I punched the sort of reply I imagined he'd like to hear.

Having a great time. Very quiet and absolutely nothing out of the ordinary happening.

Dad must be at a loose end because he read it immediately.

DAD: How's Gramp?

ME: Awesome!

DAD: Really? I guess he is.

I could feel his lack of conviction even through a message.

DAD: There's DEFINITELY nothing weird happening, is there? I've been worrying about you being out there alone with Gramp.

Weird for a dishcloth salesman or weird for an international master detective holidaying with a load of his old enemies? Because they were two very different answers. It felt strange knowing more about Gramp than Dad – his own son – did.

I thought of Felix's silver slippers and Jemima

the mega-gun and Sonny dressed as a maid and lied through my fingertips: *Nothing weird.*

DAD: How is Norway?

ME: Epic. Lots of mountains. We might see the Northern Lights tomorrow.

DAD: I'd have loved Pops to have done that with me when I was your age. I've always wanted to see the Northern Lights.

He was stalling. I could sense it. I thought about turning my phone off there and then, before he had a chance to say anything else. The little dots indicated he was typing. I grimaced, moved my thumb to the power button, but it was too late.

DAD: We should really talk over the phone. There's some stuff we need to tell you about. Are you free now?

I felt my stomach squeeze into a ball. I was numb. This was it. The Conversation had happened. I'd been powerless to stop it. My future panned out before me. Mum and Dad living apart, me bouncing between them. It wasn't fair. We were a family. Mum and Dad might be completely different from each other but they were like two standing stones holding me up, like a bit of Stonehenge. If they were pulled apart, we'd just be three rocks lying in the dirt.

I couldn't bring myself to type anything. I sat there, my phone cradled in my lap, staring blankly at the horizon.

DAD: Are you still there? Dad was typing something but I couldn't face him saying any more. And I certainly couldn't face speaking over the phone and making it real. The corners of my eyes burning, I didn't wait for the message to land. I punched in the words: *Gotta go, think we're about to spot a whale.* Then I squeezed the off button and watched the screen go black. I let my hands drop into my lap and stared out at the glistening blue sea.

An old lady got excited that she'd seen a whale and everyone gasped. But it was just a log.

I wiped my eyes and pushed The Conversation with Dad deep, deep down. I couldn't make myself any happier. I couldn't make Dad happier. But I could hang out with the one member of my family who wasn't trying to make my life a hundred times harder: Gramp. More than ever, I really, really, really wanted to solve this attempted murder – as if somehow solving it would fix everything. Even though I knew it wouldn't.

I sniffed, stood up and set off to find Wendall. It was nearly bingo time.

CHAPTER 22

Bingo

The bingo machine rattled chaotically, like ping pong balls in a washing machine. It was the only sound in an otherwise deathly silent games room. The hundred-odd pensioners held their breaths, their eyes fixed on the grey-faced captain on stage.

SCHLUUUUUUUUUUUPPPPPP

A violent sucking noise came out of the machine, like a sock going up a vacuum cleaner. A ball was spat out. The captain removed it and squinted at it.

He lifted his mic to his hand and called out: "Forty-two. Run to the loo!"

Markers frantically splodged on cards. Excited chatter filled the room. No one made a call.

This was bingo. And it was taken very, very seriously aboard the *Tom Cruise*.

A deathly silence fell once again, as everyone waited for the next ball.

I let my eyes rove around the dusky, packed games room. It might have been bright sunshine outside, but the portholes were blacked out. The only light came from little lamps on each table and the illumination of a large projector screen behind the captain, which flashed up the bingo numbers. As subtly as I could, I looked from Gramp to Wendall to Perkins to Fists to Felix to Ivan to Sonny and lastly to Ms Ho-Renton, who was arguably taking the bingo more seriously than anyone. She had about twenty cards laid out in front of her and wore some sort of high-tech goggles that she said helped her find the correct numbers. As soon as a ball was called, she worked with lightning speed, using a pen in each hand to mark her cards. It was like watching some sort of weird cowboy sharp-shooter.

While Ms Ho-Renton was focused one hundred per

cent on the bingo, Fists, Felix and Sonny had something else entirely on their minds. The tension between them was thicker than a quadruple Big Mac. Fists and Felix were scowling at Sonny like a couple of attack dogs. He refused to meet their gaze. He looked cowed. Scared, even. Was last night's argument still raging? If so, *what* was it about? Or, even worse, had they found out that Sonny was about to talk to us? It had me on edge.

SCHLUUUUUUUUUUUUPPPPPP

"Sixty-nine! Retirement time!"

I looked down at my card again. No sixty-nine.

I desperately wanted this to be over. With every filthy glance Fists and Felix shot Sonny, I became more and more nervous. What was going on? Were they threatening him? Might it scare him out of confessing? We needed to get him on his own so he could spill the beans.

SCHLUUUUUUUUUUUUPPPPPP

"Thirty-eight! Tripe on a plate!"

Across the table from me, Sonny marked his card. Then he leaned back and inspected it with a strange degree of alarm. From my position on the opposite

side of the table, it looked like he had a bingo row. Ms Ho-Renton, who was sat next to him, leaned over his card.

"Sonny, my dear, you've got bingo!" She didn't let him reply before bellowing, "BINGO! We've got bingo!"

A chorus of excited chatter filled the room and everyone turned towards Sonny.

"No, it wasn't a call," he said, red-faced and sinking into his chair.

Felix looked down his nose contemptuously and muttered, "He is most likely cheating. Always cheating and lying."

"Was it a false call?" asked the captain, cupping his eyes against the dusty glow of the projector beam.

Sonny nodded desperately. "Yes! Carry on."

"It's bingo!" said Ms Ho-Renton. "I can see it with my own goggles!"

Wendall hopped off his chair and circled the table. "Don't worry. I remember all the numbers. I'll tell you if it's bingo!" He stuck his head between Ms Ho-Renton and Sonny and squinted at the card.

The room grew impatient. There was a swell of tutting and muttering.

The captain sensed he was losing the crowd. "Do you need me to check it myself?" he asked, irritably.

"No. No," said Sonny, without looking at the captain. "It's fine. No bingo."

"BINGO!" yelled Wendall. "It's bingo!"

"Right! That's it!" exclaimed the captain, sliding off his stool. "I'm coming over to check!"

"No!" shouted a desperate Sonny. His chin was to his chest and his hand over his eyebrows, almost as if he wanted to hide his face from the captain. What was going on?

"Move aside, everyone! I'm coming through," barked the captain.

Things were reaching fever pitch. Fists stood up furiously, his chair falling backwards on to the floor.

"You are a liar and a cheat!" he spat.

Sonny slid further into his chair. The tension was electric. The hairs on my neck were on end. I could see Gramp watching it all, taking it in, as unsure as me about what, exactly, was happening.

"Shame! Shame!" cried a few muttering tables, peeved at the disruption.

"This is completely unacceptable behaviour!" yelled the captain, cutting a swathe through the dusty projector beam, so that it briefly illuminated his stubbled cheeks. "I demand you all to calm down and tell me if you have bingo!"

As he closed in, Sonny seemed to break. He too leapt up, his face pallid and anxious. "You have to help me," he said, looking at Gramp. "I'm being blackmailed! I can't stand it any longer. You have to help me!"

And suddenly, the room plunged into a power cut – the lamps and projector and bingo machine all cut out. Alarmed chatter filled the room. Chairs scraped. The captain cursed.

Sonny still pleaded through the hubbub: "Theft is one thing ... but attempted murder! I can't keep it to myself any more! It's..."

He cut off.

The lamps flickered. Once. Twice. Snapshots of alarmed faces flashed and disappeared. And then the room burst back into dim light.

Everyone's eyes were fixed on Sonny.

He was still standing. But he was silent; staring down blankly at his bingo card.

Go on. . . I begged him to continue. *Who was it? Who has been blackmailing you? And why?*

"Oh dear Lord!" croaked Ms Ho-Renton, staring at the back of Sonny's jacket.

"Holy macaroni!" said Perkins, raising a hand to his mouth.

Whatever they could see was obscured from my view.

"What is it?" said Gramp, springing to his feet.

But he didn't need to move to get an answer.

Slowly, like a felled tree, Sonny keeled forward, landing on the table with a painful SMACK, his face planting on his bingo card, a patch of red spreading out across his back.

CHAPTER 23
Passenger in Heaven

Gasps and cries and screams filled the room. But our table was stone-cold silent – each and every one of us staring, ashen-faced, at the body lying between us.

I didn't need Perkins to push two fingers into Sonny's neck and check his pulse to know he was dead. Really dead. Then, as he picked up a pair of scissors that lay beside the body, Gramp grabbed his jacket, threw it over Sonny and turned me and Wendall away from the murder scene.

"I think we've found our murder weapon," said Perkins, holding the scissors up to Gramp, who nodded in response.

I desperately scanned the shocked faces around our table, groping for any clue as to who was responsible for stabbing Sonny in the back, seconds before he incriminated Bridget's attempted murderer. But everyone looked as shocked as me.

"*Dios me!*" muttered Felix, making the sign of the cross.

"I don't Adam and Eve it," mumbled Fists, taking his trilby off and pressing it into his chest.

Ivan said nothing. His face was as deadpan as ever. He hadn't even bothered to stand up.

If there were any clues as to who was responsible, I couldn't spot them. Everyone around the table was in the exact position as when the lights had turned off. The nearest person to Sonny was Wendall. But it *obviously* wasn't him.

The captain sprang to life and began waving his hands about like he was shooing a cat off his tomato patch: "Everyone out! Nothing to see!" he shouted.

Chairs squeaked and slippers shuffled as horrified passengers streamed out, hands covering mouths. "Not you lot, though!" barked the captain to our table.

We stood there, like eight naughty children around a smashed vase of flowers, as he marched over. "You lot are giving me a headache!"

He took a deep breath, pressed his chin into his chest and squeezed the bridge of his nose, collecting his thoughts. Finally, he said gingerly: "What are we saying ... slip and fall?" He glanced from face to face in fragile hope.

Gramp gently lifted the jacket to reveal Sonny's back and the captain let out a disappointed "humph". He couldn't brush this one under the carpet.

"You need to call the police," said Gramp. "Or the coast guard. Or whoever deals with murders at sea."

The captain didn't answer. He carried on thinking, like he was desperately searching for a way that he could cover this up again. His eyes landed on the scissors, which Perkins had placed carefully on the table. He frowned and moved in closer, studying their sides, his eyes scanning the embossed letters on the blade. It was the first time I'd noticed them, glinting in the light of the projector, spelling out the word: *Wendall*

I could see an idea resolve itself in the captain's face. "No need to have all that hullaballoo disrupting the cruise," said the captain. "Why, we have the murderer's name right here."

My heart skipped a beat. "What? No! You can't be serious!"

Wendall's face turned a ghostly white.

The captain straightened up and fixed Wendall with a steely gaze. "I am deadly serious. This is very easily explained. I've said it before and I'll say it again: children and cruises don't mix!" He nodded his head, firmly, like he had solved the whole affair. "Case closed. I will have two deckhands escort this young man to his cabin, and safely lock him away until we can hand him over to the Norwegian police."

Wendall stared, unblinking, trying to compute what he had just been accused of. "Pl-pl-please, sir," he said. "It wasn't me, I promise I... My nan will be ever so cross..." He looked around desperately for her, but she had exited with the rest of the passengers.

The captain pulled a walkie-talkie from his pocket and spoke into it. "Two members of staff to the games room. Please escort a suspect to his cabin for solitary confinement."

My chest was tight. My head spun. Of course it wasn't Wendall! He wouldn't hurt an ant! "You have to be joking, Captain!" I cried.

It was Gramp's turn to protest next: "Come now! A twelve-year old boy stabbing an old man in the back?"

Perkins joined in: "This is nonsense, Captain! There's clearly a murderer at large and you are blaming it on this young boy!"

The captain fixed them with a harsh glare: "We have a murder weapon and a murderer. That is enough for me. The passengers will see that justice has been done and everyone can sleep easily." He looked Gramp and Perkins up and down. "This is the second time I've had to warn you to keep your noses out of ship affairs. Three strikes and you are out!"

Ax arrived with another deckhand, ready to escort Wendall to his cabin. He rubbed the back of his neck and opened his eyes wide at the sight of Sonny's body: "Whoa!"

"Take this young man to his cabin, please," said the

captain, waving a hand in Wendall's direction. "And check his pockets first!"

"What have you done, little Windmill?" asked Ax, gently shaking him down and pulling out a folded square of lined paper and his notebook. He handed these to the captain, who gave them a cursory inspection, then threw them down on a nearby table. Even in my horror-struck state, I took the chance to subtly step forward and swipe them off and into my own pocket.

"I haven't done anything, Ax! I swear it! It's a mistake!"

Ax shrugged helplessly. "Captain's orders, I'm afraid, Windmill," he replied, gently taking hold of an arm while the deckhand grabbed the other, guiding him towards the exit.

Watching Wendall being led away was like a dagger in my own heart. I had got him involved in all of this. This was my fault!

Wendall looked back, panic in his eyes.

Ms Ho-Renton shook her

head: "Didn't think he'd have it in him," she croaked.

Felix sucked his teeth: "It is always the ones you least expect, heh?"

I wanted to call out after him. Tell him that I'd clear his name – prove it wasn't him. But doing so would bring the captain's attention on to me. And so far, my stealth had been my greatest weapon. All I could do was watch – my heart like a water balloon ready to burst – and vow to sort out this mess.

The captain brushed his hands together like that was the end of the affair. "Right, let's get this body down to the chiller, eh?"

The captain pushed his sleeves up and reached over to grab Sonny's body. Sonny's glassy eyes gazed across at us, his face lit up by the projector beam. I looked away, turning towards the captain, whose forehead had furrowed into a deep frown. "Hang on a minute! I know this face," he said, peering in closer. "He was … He was the young man who put something in my safe this morning!"

My jaw hit the floor. "He did *what*?"

CHAPTER 24
The Swim Mask

The captain peered into Sonny's face. "Yes. This is him," he muttered. Then he looked up at us and tried to explain himself. "He was dressed as a deckhand! I thought he was just a young crew member. I mean, I was half-asleep, but he was very convincing. He must be a master of disguise!"

"He is," said Felix, with a certainty that I would have argued with if I had the energy.

The captain stood up straight. His eyes darted left and right in thought. He looked suddenly worried. "He asked to put something in the safe…"

"And did you let him?" I asked.

"Yes, of course," replied the captain. "He said it was expensive. I just assumed he was storing a passenger's valuable item for them. . . Why wouldn't I?"

"And was the diamond in there at the time?" asked Perkins.

The captain nodded and stared into the middle distance, the alarm spreading on his face like wildfire. "It was."

"You need to check that safe now!" said Gramp.

The captain didn't waste time. He spun on his heels and ran towards the exit. Gramp, Perkins and I exchanged glances and gave chase.

When he got going, the captain was fast, bowling over stragglers from the bingo hall in the corridor, powering his way to the front of the ship. He pushed open the door to the bridge. It swung back towards us. Gramp wavered momentarily, then shrugged and grabbed it, ushering us both inside before slipping in himself. It was a long, bright room with a huge bank of dials and controls spreading out from the ship's wheel. The huge glass of the front window framed an epic mountain-scape.

The safe was at the rear of the room – a big grey box built into a faded wood-panelled wall. The captain rushed over, punched in some numbers, and pulled the heavy black door open.

He stared at the inside, then tilted his head back and let out a huge sigh of relief. "Thank heavens," he said. "It's still here."

We pulled up behind him and I scanned the safe for the *Gâteau*. "Where?"

He looked momentarily annoyed that we'd followed him in, then his shoulders sagged and I could see he didn't have the energy for an argument. He pointed at a bundle wrapped in blue velvet.

"Can we see it?" said Gramp.

The captain looked at Gramp and, too weary to quarrel, reached a hand in and removed the blue bundle. Then he furrowed his brow, moving it up and down in his palm, as if checking its weight.

"What's wrong?" I asked.

"It ... feels different."

He grabbed the loose end of the blue fabric and pulled it. The bundle spun wildly as it unwound, getting faster and faster as the captain pulled and pulled. Then, with a final yank, the fabric ended and something shiny flew out and plummeted towards the floor. I reacted just in time, ducking low and catching it in both hands. It was heavy and cold to the touch. I stood up, my mouth open in shock as I held it up.

"What the…?" muttered the stunned captain.

I looked from Perkins to Gramp to the captain. We all stared incredulously at it. Snug in my palms, gently reflecting our faces, sat a glass swim mask. Written on the sides in neat blue marker, a single word: *Wendall*

CHAPTER 25

Gotcha!

Perkins, Gramp and I sat in the captain's private office and waited for him to return. It was a claustrophobic room with lots of dark wood that smelled of library books. We were lined up in front of his big leather-topped desk, each of us silently thinking about the events of the morning.

Only Perkins broke the silence: "You don't think it actually *could* have been Wendall, do you?"

Gramp gave him a withering look. "Come on, Perkins, you always take the easy option."

Perkins nodded and struggled to disguise a look of hurt at Gramp's tone.

We'd been in here almost an hour. The captain had ordered a search of both Sonny's and Wendall's rooms, and locked us in here until it was complete. All I could do was worry about Wendall, shut up in his room, accused of murder. I needed something, anything to take my mind off it. I desperately thought of *how* I was going to clear his name. Where had I not yet looked for clues? Suddenly, I remembered that I'd snatched up the contents of Wendall's pockets when the captain had emptied them. Maybe there was a clue among them?

I emptied them on to the captain's desk while Gramp and Perkins talked, inspecting them one by one. I unfolded the small scrap of paper first. It just had a number on it: 540016. I folded it back up and put it on the desk. Then I picked up the biro, opened Wendall's notebook on a fresh page, and decided to write down every single question I could think of to do with the case, and a best-guess answer. So much didn't make sense and I needed to see it written down if I was to understand it.

1. When did the murderer steal the vial?
   When Ms Ho-Renton was in the loo on Day 1.

2. How did the murderer get into the sunroom?
Climbing along the side of the ship?

3. How did they escape?
Climbing along the side of the ship?

4. What was Sonny doing in Bridget's room?
Trying to steal the necklace?

5. Why was he arguing with Felix and Fists?
About the necklace?

6. Who murdered him and why?
Fists/Felix to stop him confessing that he'd stolen the necklace?

7. Why did he have Wendall's mask and why did he put it in the safe?
REALLY don't know...

8. Why are we all on this ship together and who invited us?
REALLY, REALLY don't know...

Then I sat back and inspected it. I didn't have a definite answer to ANYTHING. But through the uncertainty, I could make out one simple thing: Fists and Felix were involved somehow. They had *clearly* had beef with Sonny about something. Were they blackmailing him to steal the necklace? But what were they using to blackmail him?

I showed the list to Gramp and Perkins.

"What's this?" Gramp asked.

"Every question to do with the case that I can think of, and possible answers."

Gramp held it up between them as they read it. Finally, Gramp let it fall to his lap. "You're a chip off the old block, Jesse Hall. I'd have employed you back in the day!"

I gave a little smile. "Thanks." Just yesterday that would have filled me with warmth. But things had moved on from that. It wasn't about me helping Gramp any more, now it was about clearing Wendall's name.

Perkins gave a side glance at Gramp. "What do you think, Sid? The clues are starting to point towards our old friends Felix and Fists." He studied Gramp's face, eager for him to agree.

Gramp nodded and stared pensively at the desk. "Let's talk this through, see how it might have played out. Fists, Felix and Sonny hatch a plan to invite Bridget on this cruise, kill her and steal the *Gâteau*…"

"Yes, yes!" added Perkins. "And Ms Ho-Renton hears about it and comes too!"

"No," said Gramp with a dismissive shake of the head. "They need Ms Ho-Renton's poison to help them murder Bridget, so they *invite* her along…"

That look of barely disguised hurt flickered across his face once again and Perkins nodded. "Yes, that makes sense. And Ivan…?"

"Well, they need someone to blame it all on. Who better than Ivan?" replied Gramp, his eyes twinkling in thought as he stared into the distance, the wheels of his brain whirring. "They steal a vial. Felix scales the side of the ship, poisons her in the sunroom. It's supposed to look like a heart attack or a slip, but the vial doesn't wash away as planned. It doesn't all go to plan – Bridget doesn't die, but she is out of the way, no questions asked. Then all Sonny has to do is sneak into her room, disguised as a maid and steal the *Gâteau*. No one will *ever* know it has been stolen. BUT Bridget must have sensed something was up – she'd already stashed the *Gâteau* in the captain's safe."

I felt a surge of excitement listening to Gramp

play out the crime in his head. He was back on form. Whatever had happened in his room yesterday when he confused me for Dad and Wendall for Gran *must* have been the chicken nugget speaking.

"So they kill Sonny for messing up…?" says Perkins, watching Gramp in the hope that he'd got it right.

"No…" says Gramp, squeezing the bridge of his nose and screwing his eyes shut. He looked like he was thinking hard – trying to focus on his thoughts. The silence lasted so long that Perkins and I exchanged a glance. I began to worry that he'd lost his train of reasoning completely when he let go of his nose and took a breath. "When they discover it is in the safe, Fists and Felix order Sonny to steal it in the morning. Perhaps he is reluctant and they have to give him a talking to – which is what Jesse saw last night. This morning he steals the *Gâteau* dressed as a deckhand. But *still*, something weighs on his mind – perhaps Bridget's attempted murder doesn't sit comfortably with him. He is ready to confess. Fists and Felix find out. They have to stop him. The lights fail during bingo at the perfect moment, one of them grabs a pair of scissors and … BAM."

Gramp fell back into his chair, exhausted.

"Not bad ... not bad at all..." said Perkins, nodding his head, impressed.

Gramp looked deflated – like the whole thing had taken every ounce of energy. But having watched all of that, I could see more clearly than ever that Gramp had been the brains of the operation – the master detective. Perkins was his sounding board, his sidekick. It gave me a thrill to watch them in action, even if it had been a struggle for Gramp.

"There's just one problem..." said Gramp, still thinking. "*Why* would they invite *us* on the cruise? If you're going to rob a bank, you don't ask the police along."

He bristled his moustache and thought. He was right. That question was still hanging over us: why were we all here? Not just the criminals ... but Gramp, Perkins and me? Did their plan somehow involve us as well? I shuddered at the thought. We *had* to stay one step ahead of them.

"Shall we tell the captain our theory?" asked Perkins.

Gramp shook his head. "No, no, no, no, Perkins, my boy. At the moment, this is all conjecture. We need hard evidence. The best we can do is convince him that it couldn't possibly be Wendall. Let's get him off the hook, then go after Fists and Felix."

At that moment, the door swung open and the captain stomped in.

"Nothing!" he said, moodily traversing us and plonking himself into his chair. "Searched Wendall *and* Sonny's room and not a thing! The necklace is nowhere to be found. But I'm sure the police will be able to get that boy to confess where he hid it."

I felt fury rise inside me. I know we were supposed to be *gently* persuading the captain that Wendall was innocent, but I couldn't help myself: "It wasn't Wendall! You don't know him! He's the nicest person I've ever met! He didn't even want to ride the Black Hole when I suggested it!"

I winced. I shouldn't have said that.

The captain looked too tired to berate me. All he could do was raise an eyebrow. "Well, I'm glad you didn't. That thing is the bane of my life. Five of its panels fell out a few years back and it spat six pensioners into the ocean."

I blew out my cheeks. *Thank heavens* we didn't try and ride it.

The captain straightened up in his chair and spoke at us like an angry, exhausted headmaster. "That young boy is guilty, end of discussion. He was standing by the victim. His scissors were the murder weapon. The case is closed. We shall hand him over to the police once we return to a Norwegian town."

None of us said a word of reply. What could we do? Arguing would only anger him further.

"Off you go then!" he said, ushering us out with a dismissive wave. "Oh! But before you do. These items were on the body." He pulled a little bag from his pocket. "You're his friend, perhaps you want to give them to his family or something. Some of them look expensive."

Gramp picked the bag up and peered inside. He pulled out an old handkerchief, then dug a little deeper and extracted a battered metal watch.

"This is yours, Perkins, my boy!" he said, handing it over.

"My watch!" he exclaimed, taking it from Gramp.

The captain leaned back in his chair, put his hands on his belly and gave a slow whistle. "Rolex Submariner. That thing is a collector's item."

Perkins slipped it on his wrist gratefully and muttered: "That nasty little thief, he really would steal anything."

Gramp continued to sift, pulling out a fake goatee and a pair of glasses. He held them up and compared them to Perkins's beard and glasses. "Looks like this was how he got it – dressing up as you and slipping into your room."

Perkins shook his head disbelievingly as Gramp stuck his hand into the bag and retrieved the final item: an empty memo pad.

The captain peered at it with initial interest, then huffed: "It's blank."

Gramp flicked through it, then held it up to the light. "Yes ... but..." He reached across for a pencil on the captain's desk. "May I?" He picked it up before the captain could answer.

Gramp put the pad down and started colouring the page in. As he worked his way from top to bottom, white writing began to appear. "Indents from the page above," explained Gramp.

He reached the top, held it up and showed it to us. It was six numbers:

540016.

I grabbed the scrap of paper from Wendall's pocket and unfurled it, holding it next to the pad. My tummy gave a little flutter. They matched exactly.

The captain scowled. "Where did you get that from?"

I thought for a second about lying, but the words fell out of my mouth before I could make a decision: "Wendall's pocket."

The captain gave a triumphant snort. "Hah! Gotcha!"

"What is it?" I asked.

"The code to the safe! That dead thief friend of yours must have given it to the boy!"

I squeezed my eyes shut and felt sick. We'd achieved the opposite of what we wanted. We'd been trying to persuade the captain that Wendall was innocent, but instead we'd given him more reason to think he was guilty. Someone *must* have framed Wendall. Why else would he have a piece of paper from Sonny's notebook in his pocket? I couldn't believe that I'd got him wrapped up in all of this and now he was being accused of murder.

The captain leaned back in his chair again and looked smug. "Gosh, I'm a great detective. Got an instinct for this kind of thing! You can't teach it! Either you have it or you don't!" he boasted. "Now, I'll have no more mention of murderers running loose on this ship. I consider this case closed."

Then he pulled his captain's hat over his eyes and, with a casual flick of the wrist waved us out of his office. "Case closed, gentlemen. Now scram."

CHAPTER 26

The Case Is Back On

Gramp, Perkins and I stood on deck. The sun was bright, the air was crisp, the mountains rose up like a wall of grey on the shoreline, but inside my head was a tangled, confused mess. I felt racked with guilt and worry over Wendall. The thought of him all alone in his cabin, accused of murder, made me feel sick to the pit of my stomach. I desperately wished I'd never dragged him into all this. But I couldn't wallow in pity. Soon, the captain was going to hand him over to the police. I *had* to get him out of this mess, and quickly.

I gazed out at the mountains, wondering how much time I had. We seemed to be getting further and further away from civilization. I could see the ship was headed for a break in the mountains, a little V-shaped doorway that signalled the start of the fjords. Beyond which, all I could see was forests and rocky peaks. At a guess I had a day – two max – before we were near a town. It *might* be enough.

The deck had filled with passengers while I'd stood there, all snapping away like mad at the scenery. I spotted Ms Ho-Renton among them. She was wearing what looked like a pair of giant green-tinted binoculars strapped to her face, like some sort of homemade night-vision glasses. She was surveying the water, stopping every few seconds to fiddle with a dial on the side of the goggles. After a moment or two, she turned and saw me.

"'Ello, Jesse!" she called, shuffling over. "Seen any whales yet?"

I shook my head. "I've been kind of busy."

"Here, then. Have a go with these." She slipped them off and on to my head. I felt the weight of them pull my face down.

She pressed a couple of buttons on the side and

suddenly it was like I was wearing X-ray specs. I could see straight through the wall into the men's bathroom, where three white silhouettes washed their hands.

"Don't look that way!" she said, turning me towards the ocean.

"Whoa!" I muttered. It was like someone had made the water see-through. I could see below the waves. Silhouetted schools of whales glided through the depths; mothers followed by calves, tails beating in slow, powerful strokes. I glanced closer to the ship, where pods of dolphins sped through the waves breaking off the bow, rolling and riding in the slipstream.

"These are AMAZING!" I said.

"Yeah," she croaked, slipping them from my head and popping them back on. "I invented them to help find a rebel militia in the Vietnamese jungle. But they work just as well for nature watching. Now, if you don't mind me, I've got some fishing to do."

"Fishing?" I asked. But instead of replying, she pulled a pistol from her belt and fired it. A four-pronged silver hook flung out with a rope trailing behind. It arced across the sky and landed with a splosh in the water.

Everyone on deck stared at her in shock.

"Got it!" she cried, pressing a button on the pistol so the rope retracted, hauling a huge plastic tub out of the waves and up on to the ship.

She fished it off her hook and looked at the crowd of stunned faces. "What?" she croaked, defensively. "Plastic is killing these oceans. Just doing my bit."

She was so weird. But I liked how much she didn't care what other people thought. "Erm, enjoy your 'fishing'," I said, backing away and heading back over to Gramp and Perkins while she launched another grappling hook into the water to shocked gasps.

The two of them were leaning on the railings, basking in the sunlight and talking in hushed voices. "Perkins and I were just discussing next steps," said Gramp. "Perkins thinks we should cool it for a bit – not ruffle the captain's feathers. But I say we press on! I've got the scent of these crooks and I intend to give chase!"

That was exactly what I wanted to hear. It was worth risking the captain's fury to clear Wendall's name. And I'd been doing my own thinking about our next move.

"I think we should re-examine the crime scenes," I said. "See if there are any clues we've missed."

Gramp shook his head and chuckled. "Jesse Hall! You really are *my* grandson, aren't you? I was thinking *exactly* the same. We haven't thoroughly investigated either crime scene."

"Great!" I said, with a proud roll of the shoulders. "Sauna first?"

"Absolutely. Perkins, care to join us?"

He looked nervous at our gung-ho attitude. Finally, he said: "I left my trunks at home. Genuinely. You two do this one alone. I'm going to head off so that the captain doesn't think we're scheming together."

Gramp gestured to the stairs. "You ready, young Jesse?"

"Sure," I said, steeling myself for the challenge. I took a step forward, then stopped, another feeling of guilt and sadness washing over me. "There's just one thing I need to do beforehand. Meet you outside your room in ten mins." And with that I headed off to Wendall's cabin.

CHAPTER 27
Stop Asking Questions

I wound my way down through the ship. The bright sunshine was like a magic app filter on the *Tom Cruise*. Suddenly, everything looked, if not newer, then somehow prettier, more characterful. Little copper flecks glistened in the brown rust patches around each porthole. The blue of the dirty carpet had a new intensity to it. The tarnished handrails shone. But the brightness was in contrast to how I felt inside.

I made my way down the stairs, rays of sunshine catching the mirrors with blinding intensity, and into the dingy cabin corridors. There was a knot in my tummy at the thought of Wendall locked up behind one of these doors. I'd got him into all of this mess. I had to tell him we were doing everything we could to clear his name.

I swung around a corner and found Ax guarding Wendall's door, sitting down with his back to the wall, flicking little bits of dirt along the carpet in boredom.

"Jesse, heeeeey," he said, moving as if to get up, but then not bothering.

I looked over my shoulder and checked the coast was clear. "Can I go in and see Wendall?"

He shook his head, his long hair sweeping back and forth across his face. "Sorry, dude. It's locked. I ain't got access."

"What about your skeleton key?"

He shook his head.

"All the key cards have been deactivated for this door, except the captain's."

"You can do that?" I asked, amazed the ship had that kind of technology.

"Yeah!" Ax replied, sounding slightly amazed himself. "All on the main computer. You can do anything. As long as you have someone's cabin number and their ticket barcode, you can deactivate their key card, charge drinks to their room, upgrade their ticket. You can even find people's passport details. Pretty smart stuff, you know." He shrugged and looked up at the peeling wallpaper on the ceiling. "Least, for this ship."

I nodded, turning away from Ax and rapping a quiet knuckle against Wendall's door. Ax looked momentarily alarmed. "I'm supposed to be stopping anyone from talking to him." He glanced up and down the corridor. The coast was clear. "Just quickly, OK?"

"Wendall, it's me – Jesse."

I could hear him hurry over to the door. "Jesse! It wasn't me who murdered Sonny! I promise!" His frightened voice was just the other side.

I pushed my cheek close to the door, placed a palm against it and said: "I know. Of course it wasn't you. We think it was either Fists or Felix or both. And we're going to prove it. Gramp and I. You won't be in there for long, OK? We'll clear your name."

"Thank you!" he said, his voice fragile.

"Stay strong, *little Windmill*," I whispered, using Ax's name for him. He laughed and I felt even sadder and more determined.

I stepped away from the door, said a little thanks to Ax, and made to leave when a brainwave hit me – a brainwave that had been staring me in the face this whole time. I felt like slapping my hand against my forehead. I knew *exactly* how we could find out who'd invited us on this cruise. And it was SO simple. "Did you say you can find out pretty much *anything* with a cabin number and ticket?" I asked.

"Pretty much," he replied.

I dug deep into my pocket, praying that the crumpled ticket would still be in there somewhere. My fingertips felt its folded corners stuffed right at the bottom and I pulled it out triumphantly and handed it to Ax. "Could you find out who bought this? Like, whose credit card was used to buy it?"

Ax shrugged and took the battered ticket off me. "Reckon so. I'd have to sneak on to the computer without getting caught, so it might take me a little while."

"Tell me as SOON as you have," I said. "This could help solve everything!"

And, with a chipper step in my walk, I headed off back down the corridor, pleased with myself for the new lead. Whoever bought that ticket had summoned everyone on this cruise. And whoever had summoned us all on this cruise was clearly behind everything.

I hurried back to my cabin, threw some swimming trunks on and knocked on Gramp's door.

There was no answer so I let myself in.

He was sat on his bed in his Bermuda shorts and T-shirt, staring pensively at a piece of paper in his hand.

"Ready to go to the sauna?" I asked.

"Go where?" he replied, not looking up from the paper.

"The sauna? The games room? To look for any clues we've missed," I said, with a little frown.

"Yes, that's right, Mike," he said, absently.

I felt a hollow, gnawing feeling in my tummy. This was the second time today that he'd lost track of himself. Once when he'd been trying to walk through the sequence of events leading up to Sonny's murder. And now this – calling me by Dad's name. This wasn't the chicken nuggets talking. Gramp wasn't sick any more. So what was going on?

I grabbed his shoulder and moved him to face me. "Gramp! It's me, Jesse! I'm your grandson, remember?" I stared deep into his blue eyes, begging him to snap back. "Dad – Mike – is at home. We're on a cruise together. We're trying to catch a murderer and…"

His glassy expression passed and – like a raincloud moving off the sun – the sparkle returned to his eyes.

"Sorry, Jesse, my boy. Momentarily lost myself there."

He rubbed his eyes and sat in silence, like a man waking up from a daytime nap. Slowly, he gathered his composure. I sat next to him, still feeling on edge.

Finally, he held the note he'd been staring at and said: "Looks like they are on to us." I peered over to read it and my alarm rocketed even higher. It simply said:

Stop asking questions or you'll be next.

He was right. The murderer was on to us. But we couldn't stop now, not when we still had Wendall's name to clear.

"What do you want to do?" I asked.

He folded it and tossed it in the bin. "Carry on," he replied. "We just need to keep our eyes open."

I tried to pull a face that looked confident. We didn't have long to clear Wendall's name and work out who was *really* behind all of this. And I couldn't get distracted – not by Gramp's erratic behaviour and *certainly* not by threatening notes.

CHAPTER 28
The Sauna Revisited

We headed back through the ship and to the pool to inspect the first crime scene. It was practically deserted – everyone must still be on deck enjoying the view. There was only another dopey-looking lifeguard who was playing a game on his phone and didn't notice us enter.

We skirted the loungers, and I paused by the spiral ladder up to the Black Hole. To think: if Wendall and I had ridden it, we would have been spat out into the open ocean. Mum always said my itch got me in trouble – but this time it *really* would have been true.

Gramp made his way into the sunroom and I hurried

after. He was snooping around, looking for clues. He inspected the bucket shower and the window latch while I looked under the sunloungers.

"Nothing," he said, with a disappointed bristle of his moustache.

"Nothing," I replied. "Sauna?"

I grabbed the door. A waft of pine-scented heat hit me like an opened oven and we headed in. The heat prickled my skin. It was a tiny room clad in yellow pine, with nothing but a two-tier slatted bench, a wooden bucket and what looked like an electric radiator with artificial coals on top.

We did the same routine – Gramp searching high and me searching low – while the hot air filled my lungs and beads of sweat formed on my forehead. The space was so small it hardly took us any time at all.

"Nothing," I said, plonking my bum down on the lowest rung of the bench.

"Me neither," said Gramp, settling on to the top tier. I could taste the salty droplets of sweat on my top lip. It was *hot*.

Gramp leaned back and sighed. "Perkins and I used to enjoy one of these a day back in our prime. They had one installed in MI6 HQ during the sixties. It was quite the fashion."

The heat didn't seem to be bothering him. In fact, he seemed to be loving it.

I drew in a breath of hot air that felt alarmingly short of oxygen, and – thinking back to their dynamic in the captain's office – asked: "What was he like, as an assistant?"

Gramp chuckled. "A good man. One of life's triers. Not a natural detective. In fact, he'd often get a lot wrong. But he was organized, he was always on time, and he was a friend. I insisted he stay on as my assistant across all my department moves."

A thought flickered across my brain. "You don't think he could be involved in any way, do you?"

Gramp laughed. "Perkins? No! I've known him since he was not much older than you! He doesn't get mixed up in this kind of thing. Very straight-laced. Always reminded me of your father." He tailed off.

I mopped my brow, soaking my palm. The evidence we'd gathered from the CCTV room felt like a lifetime ago, but of course Gramp was right. We knew Perkins hadn't left his room till after the murder had happened. There was no way it could have been him.

"What about Ivan?" I asked. "He *was* a criminal mastermind, wasn't he? It says in your scrapbook that he called for an amnesty … but that he is an infamous double-crosser."

"Ivan is certainly an enigma," he replied. "He and I had our run-ins. Boat chases through the Everglades. A tank battle in the old Soviet Union. A failed sting on his Luxembourg mansion. He always got away, though. Closest I got to him was the time I pulled him out of a burning tank. But he *still* managed to escape. In fact, it was shortly after that he retired and called for that amnesty. No one believed him to begin with, of course. But the offer was too good to refuse and he's stayed true to his word. I can't see why *he'd* want that necklace either – all that criminal activity has left him with more money than you could possibly dream of."

I shook my head. "It just doesn't make sense. Why would he be here if he wasn't involved somehow?"

Gramp shuffled on his bench as the heat seemed to get thicker – so thick you could practically slice it. "Why are any of us here?" he replied. "That's the mystery."

Drained by the heat, the two of us fell into a silence. I could have left the sauna, but I wanted to show Gramp that I could hack it. This is what he and Perkins used to do. I wanted to show him I was every bit as good an assistant, if not better. In a bid to distract myself I unfurled my phone – which I'd rolled up tight in my towel – to check the time.

I pushed the power button, it loaded up and immediately let out a double beep to signal a new message. It flashed up on screen and my tummy squirmed into a knot.

DAD: Are you there? Mum and I both want to talk to you. It's really important Jesse. Please call us.

The knot tightened and made me feel sick. I knew what this was about. The D.I.V.O.R.C.E. It was suddenly all too real. Maybe it was the heat. Or the case. Or the text. Or all three combined. But I felt it all crushing me at once. A tonne of worry hit me all in one go and I felt the room getting fuzzy around me.

"What's so important that your dad and mum want to interrupt your cruise?" asked Gramp.

I spun around and saw he'd been peeking over my shoulder at the phone.

I put it down on the bench, let out a long sigh and it all came flooding out. "They haven't told me properly yet but Mum and Dad are getting a D.I.V.O.R.C.E." I spelled the word out, still not wanting to say it.

Gramp's eyebrows shot up. "A divorce?"

The sound of the word made me feel ever sicker.

It seemed to have a profound effect on Gramp as well. With a murderer on the loose, a false accusation against a twelve-year-old, a missing ten-million-pound necklace and a walking-stick flamethrower, somehow this was the first time he had looked shocked – stunned, even.

"What? Sarah and Mike are getting divorced. But … but … they were always so happy together."

His eyes dropped down to his lap as the news hit home. "She's always been so good for him," continued Gramp, still staring off in vacant thought. "What happened?"

"I dunno." I took a deep breath and my voice cracked a little as this dark, festering thought became real: "Do you think it's my fault?"

This shocked Gramp back to life. "Not for a second," he said, his steely blue eyes catching me in their laser beam. "Blame anyone you want, Jesse. But *do not* blame yourself. Adults are idiots: they do stupid things. I've spent my career trying to second guess them – and it never gets any easier. You'd think that when people get older, they'd get smarter. But they don't." He reached out and put a hand on my shoulder. "You grow old, you learn more facts, you know how things work – but it doesn't stop you doing dumb stuff." He let go, sighed and looked down at the pine bench. "If you want to blame anyone, blame me. If I'd been around more, if I'd been a bigger part of your dad's life. Who knows – maybe this wouldn't be happening?"

Now it was Gramp's turn to sound upset. I'd never even seen him ruffled. Now he was positively crumpled. I would never blame him. But I could see he blamed himself. Not just for this, but for his whole relationship with Dad.

"Should I call him, do you think?" said Gramp.

I sniffed. "It's not official yet. Dad and Mum want to talk to me but I don't think I can handle it," I said, letting out a controlled breath through the heat. When it came to detective work, Gramp was so assured, so in control – like he always had the answers. But the moment it came to Dad, he suddenly had none.

"It was a bad idea turning my phone on," I said. "I wasn't thinking."

I picked it up to turn it off and it seared my fingers. "YARGH!" I yelled, dropping it like a hot coal. It plummeted down, slipping between the bench's wooden slats and landing with a crack on the floor beneath.

"Dang!" I said, squeezing my eyes shut in frustration. "I'm never going to get that out."

Gramp pushed his eye against a gap. "I can see it," he said. "Maybe there is some way you can crawl under there."

He wrapped his fingers around a slat and pulled, but it didn't budge.

"Hmmmmm," he said, knocking along the bench with his knuckles.

I copied him, knocking every slat, looking for a little door or service hatch. I reached the top tier, and as I banged the closest board to the wall, it gave a little wobble.

"This one's loose!" I said, getting my fingers beneath it and prizing it up. It made a little gap, perhaps thirty centimetres wide, enough for me to squeeze my legs through and lower myself down under the bench.

It was hot and dusty and dark down there – the thin gaps between the boards letting through just a few slivers of light – and barely big enough for me to lie down. Certainly not big enough for me to stand up. I crawled towards my phone.

From my position under there, I could see out through the sauna's glass door to the bucket shower and all the way through to the swimming pool's entrance. My eyes dropped to the floor to search for my phone and I froze. Next to it, imprinted in the thick layer of dust that had built up over the years, was the unmistakeable shape of a handprint. It was bigger than mine – the size of a large man's hand.

It hit me like a gorilla down a flume. Suddenly it all made sense! The killer hadn't climbed in through the window. "Gramp!" I blurted, struggling to get my words out over the rising flood of excitement that was rushing through me. "Whoever killed Bridget was hiding in here the whole time!"

CHAPTER 29
The Note

"So the window latch has been a red herring all along," Gramp said as we raced back to the main deck again, having changed out of our swimming trunks, eager to catch Perkins and share our discovery. The air outside felt crisp on my hot skin. Mountains rose up from either side of the ship; great grey walls that almost seemed to touch the sky.

"It makes perfect sense," I said, breathlessly. "Whoever killed Bridget was *already in* the sunroom when Ax opened it. They must have been hiding there all night, when the sauna was off. When they saw her enter, they rushed out, put the vial in the bucket shower and rushed back in. Then, when we all ran out to get you and the captain, they snuck out."

We searched the deck for Perkins, but he was nowhere to be found. Hot and tired and tingling from the sauna, we plonked down on a bench and stared at a photo I'd taken of the print. It was definitely a man's hand, but its fingers were slim.

"Fists' fingers are much thicker than that. Sonny is missing a finger on that hand. So we're looking at Felix as the most likely candidate." He clicked his fingers and clapped his hands. "Golly I love detective work! It gets the old brain firing again, know what I mean?" He wrapped his knuckles gently on his temple. "I'd forgotten what this feels like. And it feels great."

I smiled, wrapped my arm through Gramp's and rested my head on his shoulder. In spite of everything else going on – D.I.V.O.R.C.E.s and murders and false accusations – it made me unapologetically happy to help Gramp recall his glory years.

"We've still got the other murder scene, the games room, to search. You ready?"

"Ready when you are!" he chimed. But I didn't

want to move immediately. I wanted to sit there with Gramp, my head on his shoulder. Everything about the mountains and the landscape made our problems feel so tiny, like we were two tiny planets spinning in space, and all we had was gravity holding us together. Whatever evil plans were afoot, whatever terrible false accusation had been levelled at Wendall, whatever was happening at home between Mum and Dad, there was one ray of light shining through – Gramp and I had each other.

Gramp checked the corridor was empty, cracked the games room door ajar and slipped through. I followed, gently pushing it shut behind me. The lights were off and the porthole blinds were drawn. Gramp pressed a light switch and the table lights blinked on.

The room was exactly as we had left it – half-finished bingo cards and strewn markers still littered the tables, chairs toppled over backwards, and there was a rumpled indent on our table from where Sonny had fallen.

Gramp surveyed the scene. "We're looking for

anything that is out of the ordinary. You can find clues in the most unlikely of places."

We split up. Gramp headed towards the stage and I began with our table.

It was a long, slow process: crawling around on our hands and knees, looking for anything unusual.

After an age, Gramp sighed and said: "Anything out of the ordinary?"

I shook my head. "Nothing." I plonked down on a chair and couldn't hide my disappointment. We'd gathered clues, but we were *still* missing the one that would bring it all together and tell us who was behind the murders.

I settled back into my chair and felt something press into my bum – it felt like the stiff corner of something buried between the backrest and seat cushion. I stood up hastily and pulled them apart. There was a folded piece of paper stuffed down there. I gripped it between thumb and forefinger and wiggled it free.

"Gramp!" I whispered, and he hurried over as I unfolded it and spread it out on the table, butterflies flapping in my tummy.

It was a biro-written note in blocky handwriting. I read it out loud.

Sid and Jesse are getting suspicious. We need to act as soon as possible. We'll do it on deck. Tomorrow, 9 p.m. We'll make an excuse and invite Sid. Ms Ho-Renton has the gun. Felix has the cake. Sonny refused to cooperate. Can we count on your support? Do not forget – this is why you are here.

Fists

My mouth fell open and the blood drained from my face.

"Cake … that's *Gâteau* in English," I said.

"Exactly what Fists would call it," said Gramp.

I looked around and took stock of where I was sitting.

"This was Ivan's chair at bingo," I muttered. "It's a message from Fists to Ivan. He must have read it and stuffed it down the back of the seat."

I could see the realization move across Gramp's face. "You were right. Ivan *is* involved. They're all involved. This isn't a theft … it's a heist. They're all working together to steal the *Gâteau*. And to kill anyone who gets in the way."

A sense of hollow dread grew within me. "Including..."

Gramp finished my sentence: "...me."

CHAPTER 30

Stop the Heist!

Gramp, Perkins and I stood outside the captain's office. Perkins was still arguing his case, just as he had been for the last hour: "I think this is a silly move. *Why* do we need to tell the captain?"

"Because they are going to try and kill Gramp, and maybe us too!" I said for the hundredth time. "We need help. And this proves Wendall has nothing to do with it!"

Perkins huffed: "It just seems so … risky."

Outside, the sun was beginning to set. Through a porthole I could see the pink-and-orange sky above the mountains, framed like a pretty, round watercolour – a world away from the evil plan taking place on board.

"Look, Perkins, my boy," said Gramp, "if we do nothing, they are going to try and kill me. They have all Ms Ho-Renton's hardware and four criminal brains. We're just two retired detectives and my twelve-year-old son."

"Grandson," I corrected.

"Grandson," corrected Gramp, blinking hard at his error.

"And I'm not retired," said Perkins, with a hint of annoyance. "Not all of us can afford to sit around doing nothing."

If the comment was aimed at Gramp, he missed it completely. "If that bunch want to get me, they will get me!" continued Gramp. "But if we tell the captain, best case scenario: he believes us and we get back-up to spring a trap on Fists and company and catch them red-handed. Worst case scenario, he pulls up at a dock and kicks us off the cruise. Either way, I get to live."

That seemed to cheer Perkins. "Yes, I suppose that *is* the worst that can happen – he kicks us off the cruise."

Gramp rapped on the door and the captain called out: "Come!"

Gramp pushed the door open and we all stepped inside. The captain was inspecting a map, his tie loosened, with what looked like a large whisky on the table. He looked up and grunted disapprovingly. "You three!" he said, his teeth springing out over his bottom lip.

Gramp closed the door behind him. I peered at the map spread out on the captain's table, a little toy boat marking our position. We were high up along the coast of Norway – closing in on where the jagged, freckled tip of the country ended, giving way to an expanse of empty blue water that – I guessed – only ended when you hit the frozen icebergs of the Arctic.

The captain raised an eyebrow and said: "What do you want now?" He took a long sip of whisky. The morning's stubble was now resembling something closer to a beard.

Gramp sucked in a breath, pulled out the note and held it up. "We know who killed Sonny and tried to kill Bridget."

"Right! That's it!" said the captain, jumping to his feet and picking up his phone, an old-fashioned one with a handset connected by coiled cord. "I shall be throwing you off the ship when we get to the next port and you three can make your own way home."

I'd had enough of the captain and his bullying ways. I stepped forward, reached over and pressed the receiver down.

"Read this note first," I said, all the while keeping my hand on the receiver.

The captain looked furious, then when he saw it was a choice between that and prizing my fingers from his telephone, stubbornly scanned the note.

"We found this in the games room. It was written by Fists Harris. It clearly lays out a plot to kill Gramp tomorrow afternoon. *They* tried to kill Bridget to get her necklace. *They* blackmailed Sonny into stealing it from the safe. Then *they* killed him when he was in danger of confessing. Now, they plan to kill Gramp to cover it all up. If they get to him then you will have another murder on your hands – one where your supposed culprit, a twelve-year-old, is locked away in his cabin. How are you going to explain *that* to your bosses?"

The captain looked at me like he'd sucked a lemon

through a dirty sock.

"Either you can throw us off and risk a bunch of murderers prowling your ship for the next four days, or you can help us catch them red-handed. What do you say?"

I let go of the receiver as Gramp whispered. "*Jeez Louise*, Jesse Hall. You are something else."

The captain glowered at us, still gripping the handset. Then he proceeded to punch in a telephone number.

What the?! He was still going to boot us off? After I'd given the best speech of my life!

I went to move forward again but Gramp put his hand on my arm to stop me. "Just give it a moment," he whispered.

"Yup, hello, or how do you say it: *hallo*," said the captain into the handset. "Norwegian coastguard, please." He thought for a second, then added: "And navy."

Then he pressed the handset into his chest and said: "If we're going to do this properly, we'll need back-up."

CRUISE DAY 4: THE NORTHERN LIGHTS

CHAPTER 31

The Sting

The next night and day seemed to go in slow motion. I kept my phone off and desperately avoided Fists, Felix and Ms Ho-Renton. The only time we crossed their path was when Felix approached Gramp at breakfast.

"*Buenos dias*, Sid," he said, with a little bow. "Might you by chance be free for a, erm, meeting with us on top deck at 9 p.m.? Nothing special, nothing special. We were thinking perhaps it would be nice for us to all get together as we have seen so little of each other among the … unfortunate events of this cruise." A wicked grin spread across his face like a snake in the sun.

Gramp forced a polite smile and gave a single

nod: "Of course, Felix."

That was it. The trap was set. Or so they thought. Because we had our own trap to trap their trap. Our trap went like this: Felix and company planned to meet Gramp on the mini-golf course on the top deck. It was the perfect location to ambush him – no one ever used it and its old obstacles meant there were plenty of hiding places.

I had insisted on accompanying Gramp. Yes, it was dangerous. But I wanted to be there to help. We would arrive at 9 p.m. on the dot. The captain would be hiding up by the funnel, with a clear view over the whole course. Above us, a blacked-out helicopter would be circling in the dark of the evening with snipers trained on Fists, Felix and Ms Ho-Renton, in case they tried anything that we weren't expecting. In the waters below, a navy rib boat full of SEALS would be waiting. When Ms Ho-Renton pulled out the gun, the chopper would throw on its floodlights and the navy would scale the side of the ship, ready to catch them red-handed. Perkins offered to patrol the lower decks, making sure all the other passengers stayed down there and reassuring them that the boats and helicopters were nothing more than a standard fire-safety drill.

It was a brilliant counter-trap. There was, however, one little worry nagging at the back of my head: it meant putting Gramp in the line of fire. Predictably, he had insisted on it. In fact, I think he relished the opportunity. It was his chance to be back in the thick of the action. But if our timing was wrong, or Fists and company sprang another surprise … well, it didn't bear thinking about.

The minutes ticked by like hours as the liner trudged north, winding its way through the labyrinth of islands till even the red fishing huts disappeared, then out into the open ocean, where the phone signals died and there was nothing but sea and sky and non-stop water till the end of the world. It was the night we were supposed to see the Northern Lights. I clung to the image of Gramp, Wendall and me watching it together on deck – Fists, Felix and Ms Ho-Renton in handcuffs being carted off to some Norwegian police station.

Noon slowly came and went.

1 p.m. I had a bit of food but wasn't really hungry.

5 p.m. ticked by painfully. We were now in open sea, so I couldn't even distract myself looking at the pretty islands.

7 p.m. The seconds slowed even further.

Then, finally, it was very nearly time: 8.50 p.m.

Gramp and I met as planned at Davy Jones's Bar. My stomach felt like it was on a spin wash and I had a lump the size of Gibraltar in my throat. I spotted him sitting by the window. He was wearing his bright orange cardigan and sipping an espresso; cool as a watermelon, unruffled as a plastic tablecloth. He spotted me across the room and grinned. "Nearly, showtime, huh?" he said, then clapped his hands and clicked his fingers. He was buzzing, like he was about to go on stage at Glastonbury, not be used as bait to ensnare a bunch of evil criminals. "This is what it's all about!" he said, still beaming. "This is the feeling!"

I felt a little stirring of satisfaction in amongst the nerves. I guess I was *sort of* glad he was enjoying himself...

"Ready?" I asked.

He stood up, pressed his cardigan down and, with a big grin, said: "Absolutely."

I nodded and we headed back out of the bar and up

the steps to the top deck. The sea was calm. The sun had set half an hour before. The sky was clear and moonless. It was perfect conditions for the sting, but also strangely eerie – as if there was a stillness haunting the edge of the world. The only sound: a soft flapping coming from the side of the ship. It sounded like a flag blowing in the breeze, but the flagpole was empty.

I took one last breath and said: "Good luck, Gramp."

He smiled and winked. "Real people make their own luck." He'd stolen the quote from *Titanic*, which didn't fill me with confidence.

I checked the funnel. The captain was peeking over the little metal fence that surrounded it, binoculars in hand. He flashed a thumbs up.

In the dark of the evening, the golf course stretched out before us like some spooky funfair. Fists and Felix and Ms Ho-Renton could be hiding out there somewhere. I felt my sweaty palm against Gramp's cool, dry skin.

"Showtime," I whispered. And, as we went to step inside, a nagging feeling that had been lingering in me all day suddenly articulated itself as a thought: if Fists and Felix and co. were behind this, why invite Gramp? Why ask him on the cruise, just to get annoyed and try to kill him? It didn't add up. I had a horrible feeling that we were making a mistake, but I couldn't put my finger on why. It was just nerves, I told myself. I was sure all the greatest detectives went through this on their first sting operation.

We made our way past the first obstacle – a big broken pirate ship. I listened closely. Sure enough, amongst the sound of the waves and the hum of the engine, I could hear the distinctive sounds of a helicopter far up above – a low CHUKKA CHUKKA CHUKKA. It gave me a little burst of comfort.

"Hello?" shouted Gramp, still holding my hand.

Nothing.

We stepped in deeper, creeping around a big octopus. The golf course was like an abandoned forest of statues.

My heart felt like it was beating a thousand times a second.

The CHUKKA CHUKKA CHUKKA got a bit louder.

"Felix? Fists?" shouted Gramp.

Silence.

We skirted around a big cod, now surrounded on all sides by the towering ornaments.

I could hear Gramp's breath: it was slow and composed compared to my crazy-fast heartbeat.

"I'm here!" he called. "Just like you asked!"

Something felt wrong. They were drawing us too far in. Could the captain still see us from the funnel? Did the snipers have a clean shot? This was too risky. I felt a sudden panic. We needed to turn back. I stopped and tugged Gramp's hand just as a loud shout echoed out from behind a giant shark.

"SURPRISE!" yelled Felix, stepping out into view.

I jumped and spun to face him. He had a grin of smug self-satisfaction.

His voice was followed milliseconds later by another. "SURPRISE!" boomed Fists, stepping out from behind a lighthouse, a cardboard box in his hand.

And then, almost simultaneously, the strangled croak of "SURPRISE!" from Ms Ho-Renton. She stepped out from behind the windmill, a pistol in her hand.

This was it. My heart did a double beat as she slowly raised it.

I looked up at the helicopter; where was it? I wanted to run, but Gramp didn't budge. He just stared her down.

"What are you doing, Eileen?"

The gun reached higher and higher until it was almost pointing straight at us.

"NOW!" yelled Gramp. The CHUKKA CHUKKA CHUKKA ripped the sky apart, the turbulence of the blades pounding down like a hurricane, almost forcing me into the ground. Spotlights soaked everything in a blinding white light, casting huge shadows off the towering ornaments.

"DROP THE GUN!" boomed a megaphone above us.

Time seemed to crawl. Ms Ho-Renton didn't pay attention to the voice. She raised the gun further, till it was pointing straight at Gramp.

"I SAID DROP THE GUN!" boomed the megaphone again.

Fists and Felix were staring up in shock – their panicked faces white in the spotlight – but still Ms Ho-Renton didn't stop.

Terror froze my whole body and an ear-splitting

BANG exploded through the air. Suddenly, Ms
Ho-Renton was toppling backwards, the wind rushing
out of her in a large OOOOOFFFFFFFF and pieces
of fabric exploding from her chest.

The snipers! They had got her just in time. "PLACE THE BOX ON THE FLOOR!" boomed the megaphone.

Grappling hooks flew upwards from the invisible depths below, grabbing hold of the railings with a series of loud CLUNKS as the navy began to board.

Fists sort of did what he was told, but not in the way anyone would have liked. He screamed a high-pitched scream, threw the box in the air and scrambled to catch Ms Ho-Renton before she hit the deck.

"BOMB ALERT, BOMB ALERT! TAKE COVER!" screamed the megaphone.

I grabbed Gramp and pulled him desperately through the blinding light and deafening wind towards the only cover I could see – a large fibreglass mermaid – looking desperately over my shoulder at the chaos on deck. The box arced to a peak and then began to fall. Ms Ho-Renton hit the floor before Fists could catch her. On impact she squeezed the trigger and a rocket blasted out of her gun, shooting up towards the helicopter with a loud FZZZZZZZZ leaving a trail of smoke and the stench of gunpowder in its wake. The chopper veered desperately to the side as it screamed past like a red comet.

The box was almost on the floor. I desperately

pulled Gramp but we were too slow. We weren't going to get to safety in time. I grabbed hold of him, almost frozen in terror, and looked up at his face, his hair and moustache billowing in the turbulence. He didn't look scared. He looked … sad. Incredibly, incredibly sad. He just had time to mouth a single word – "Sorry" – before wrapping his arms around me as the box hit the floor. I winced, buried myself in his chest and waited for the…

SPLAT!!!!

A wave of something wet and sloppy hit us, just as the rocket from Ms Ho-Renton's gun exploded above, a vast, beautiful firework that painted the sky with the words:

HAPPY BIRTHDAY

What the??????

I looked in shock at Gramp. His face was covered in cream and sponge. A birthday candle stuck out of his ear. He was equally as stunned.

My brain felt like it had been scrambled and as it was slowly putting itself back together, a new reality dawned. Suddenly, I knew *exactly* why we were all here and I felt completely and utterly stupid. This wasn't an assassination attempt. This wasn't even a heist.

"Gramp…" I said, finally getting the words out. "It's your birthday, isn't it?"

He stared in bewilderment at the dying firework, the writing turning to smoke and drifting off. Finally, he said: "Yes, I think it is."

I looked from Fists, who was cradling Ms Ho-Renton on the floor and crying, to the livid faces of the navy as they returned to their rib, to the astonished gaze of the helicopter crew, to the captain, who had a face of pure, unadulterated rage.

We'd got this wrong.

Really wrong.

And we were in SO much trouble.

CHAPTER 32

The Fallout

"Stand down! Stand down!" screamed the captain into his walkie-talkie. The helicopter pulled upwards and shut down its floodlights. The wind and noise and blinding light disappeared.

On the floor, Fists was screaming: "EILEEN! EILEEN! COME ON EILEEN!"

You sort of wanted to sing along, but it *really* wasn't the time.

He ripped open her blouse to reveal a thick blue jacket underneath, with what looked like a flattened gold bullet on it. Then, with a startled cough, she spluttered into life, turning her weary gaze to Gramp and croaking:

"Happy birthday, Sid. Glad I wore that bulletproof jacket."

"Yes," mumbled Felix, staring in bemusement at the navy and the exploded birthday cake and the very angry captain. *"Feliz cumpleaños*, Sid."

Fists put his head into his hands and sobbed in relief at Ms Ho-Renton's miraculous resurrection. "Happy Doris Day, Sid."

Gramp sucked his moustache and frowned. "Is this … a surprise party?"

Fists nodded without looking up. "It is, mate."

"Gosh…" mumbled Gramp. "Thanks."

The captain had gone the colour of a sunburnt beetroot. "This is what I called the coastguard and navy for?" he yelled, steam practically coming out of his ears. "A surprise birthday party?"

I pulled out the note. "But we found this!" I said, desperately. "Listen!" Then I read it out loud. "Sid and Jesse are getting suspicious. We need to act as soon as possible. We'll do it on deck. Tomorrow, 9 p.m. We'll make an excuse and invite Sid. Ms Ho-Renton has the gun. Felix has the cake. Sonny refused to cooperate. Can we count on your support? Don't forget – this is what you are here for. Fists."

With each sentence, I could feel my confidence in its incriminating content wavering.

"That's right," sighed Fists, labouring to his feet. "That's the note I wrote Ivan, to try and get him to come along. Sonny was being a right grump about it and refusing to come. So was Ivan. I got the birthday cake, Eileen here brought her special firework gun. We were worried that you were on to our little surprise party." He looked over at Gramp, with a look of confusion and despair at how things had turned out. "Eighty years young, Sid! That's some milestone!"

Gramp looked shocked and embarrassed. Not only at how the events had unfolded but, I sensed, at not realizing it was his birthday. "You did all of this for me?" he asked.

"Of course we did," croaked Ms Ho-Renton, still lying down but with her head off the floor, inspecting her bulletproof vest. "It was Perkins's idea – we thought we'd throw you a surprise birthday party on board a cruise, give you a bit of fun pretending it was a big coincidence – have you guessing why we were all in the same place at the same time."

Gramp stared incredulously – grateful, confused and shocked all at once.

The captain had marched down from the funnel and was stomping around waving his arms about like he had eels in his pants. "I should never have listened to you idiots! I can't begin to tell you how much trouble you have caused! When the news comes out that I called out the navy to stop a birthday party ... I will be hung, drawn and quartered!"

I was also still trying to get my head around things. "So you killed Sonny because he didn't want to participate?"

Fists's eyes popped and he looked shocked. "Hurt old Sonny boy? Why would I ever do that? Me and him go back years! We all do!"

"Kill him over a birthday?!" croaked an incredulous Ms Ho-Renton.

"Never in a million years!" cried Felix.

Slowly, the far-reaching implications of this bungled trap began to dawn on me. Not only had we called on the might of the Norwegian navy to shoot an old lady, we were back to square one with our investigation. We might have figured out why we were all here, but we were no closer to solving the murders or the diamond theft or to clearing Wendall's name. We'd been hopeless. Whatever was going on, it clearly didn't involve these three. All their snooping around, all their sly glances, the mystery of why we were here in the first place – it was all for this surprise party. A sense of despair began to overwhelm me.

I muttered under my breath, "We thought you killed Bridget to steal her diamond, then Sonny for nearly confessing ... and were going to kill Gramp for investigating..."

If Fists could look any more shocked, he now did. His cratered face radiated hurt. "Kill Sid? Why would we want to do that? He's the one that put us on the straight and narrow all those years back! If it wasn't for him, I'd be a low-life gangster still, not a famous TV presenter!"

"And I would still be a man who took pleasure in stealing cats," said Felix, his hand over his heart.

"And my weapons would be starting wars, not helping wildlife," said Ms Ho-Renton, putting her head back on the deck and taking some deep breaths.

"We wanted to do something special for you to say a proper thank you after all these years," said Fists.

It was clearly hitting Gramp doubly as hard as me. He was white and stared blankly into space. "I apologize for all of this," he mumbled. "I'm sorry I ruined your surprise party. And I'm sorry you got shot, Eileen."

She raised a single hand to signify the apology was accepted.

"I'm going to, um, head down to my cabin for a bit," he continued. Every ounce of energy had been drained out of him. From the high of thinking he was about to crack a case for the first time in years, he'd slipped into the depths of despair.

"Too right you will!" shouted the captain. "And you will stay there until I throw you off the cruise!" And then he fixed his eyes on me: "And you too! And your friend, Perkins!"

I wanted to follow Gramp but the captain grabbed my elbow. "But not before you've cleaned up this cake, young man!"

Gramp trudged off, his chin against his chest. He looked crushed as he walked away.

"Lordy," whispered Fists. "Sid ain't the detective he used to be."

CHAPTER 33
Wendall in His Cabin

The helicopter disappeared. The navy ribs motored off. Felix, Fists and Ms Ho-Renton retired to the bar. And the captain stormed back to his office.

Leaving just me and a blast zone of cake to scrub clean. When I was finally finished, my hands were raw and my knees were numb. I was under strict instructions from the captain to head straight to my cabin once I'd finished. As I wove my way through the viewing room, I don't think I'd ever felt so lonely in such a crowded space. Practically the whole ship was huddled against the windows, cameras in hand, nattering excitedly as they waited for the Northern Lights. The engine had shut down and we were at anchor. It was like a theatre before the curtain rose. The air was thick with expectation, all eyes on the still, black sky.

I trudged past them, my head hanging low, wishing Gramp, Wendall and I were getting ready to watch the Northern Lights and none of this whole mess had ever, ever happened. I felt numb. There was nothing that I could do to help Wendall once I'd been kicked off the cruise. That made me feel sick with guilt. Then there was the thought of how angry Dad would be with Gramp about everything. He'd been under instructions to look after me, and now we were having to make our own way back from the top of Norway. It was the last thing Mum and Dad needed on top of the D.I.V.O.R.C.E. I traipsed down a flight of stairs, my gloomy reflection looking back at me from the tarnished mirror.

I arrived down on Deck 2. Wendall's deck. I turned to head down again towards my cabin, then stopped. This might be my last chance to say goodbye to him; to tell him that we had failed and to apologize for everything.

I made my way down the corridor and found Ax still

sitting on the floor, his back resting on the wall and his head against his knees. Asleep. I tiptoed past him and gently tapped on the door. "Wendall, it's me."

I heard him scurry over and whisper through the wood. "How did it go?"

The words caught in my throat. My voice broke as I squeezed out one word: "Sorry..."

There was a tiny pause on the other side as he digested the news, and then – in true optimistic Wendall style – he said: "Don't be sad! You tried your best. You know, it's not so bad in here. If this is what prison is going to be like, I really don't mind."

I stifled another sob and protested: "You're not going to prison, OK!" Then added as an afterthought: "And if you are, it's unlikely it will have an ocean view and a dedicated movie channel." He gave a little laugh as I took a deep breath and exhaled, "I'm sorry, Wendall. I'm sorry I got you into all of this. It's all my fault."

"Don't be sorry!" he said. "I don't regret a thing! We had some fun. In fact, it's the best cruise I've ever been on. SO much better than Theatre Club and Science Club and even Murder Mystery Club. Getting into a bit of trouble – proper trouble, not what my nan calls trouble – is epic."

I sniffed. "The *best* cruise you've ever been on? You're joking, right? You've been arrested on suspicion of murder."

I could hear him think. After a moment's pause he said: "That's true. But then I also met you, didn't I? And we are great detectives! Whatever happens to me back in England, they can't take that away from me. We'll always have each other – how good is that?"

I sniffed again and laughed. Then I stood up and placed my palm against the door. "It's not over yet, OK.

The captain isn't throwing us off the ship until later tonight. We've still got a few hours to work things out – one last throw of the dice."

Wendall's energy radiated through the door: "You can do it, Jesse! The answer's there somewhere. And you'll find it. You're the best detective I've ever seen and I can't even tell you how many episodes of *Midsomer Murders* I've watched!"

I wanted to kick the door down and give him a big hug. But I couldn't. Plus, Ax had just woken up.

"Jesse?" he said, rubbing his eyes. "Hey, you're, like, not supposed to be here. I'll get in loads of trouble."

"Don't worry," I said. "I'm just heading off."

I hadn't got far down the corridor when he called after me. "Hey, I nearly forgot! It took me a while, but I found out who bought your ticket."

"Oh yeah?" I said, with a hint of disinterest. Things had moved on since then. It didn't really matter who had bought the ticket now that I knew we were here for Gramp's birthday.

He pulled a scrap of paper from his pocket and handed it to me. I unfurled it and read the spidery handwriting. "What the?" I said, looking up at him.

He shrugged. "Sid Hall. Whoever that is."

I blinked in bewilderment. "But ... that's Gramp."

CHAPTER 34

The Northern Lights

I rapped softly on Gramp's cabin door. I one hundred per cent wasn't supposed to be seeing him. I was supposed to return to my cabin to stay there until the *Tom Cruise* docked and we were escorted off. But I had to know why Gramp's name was on my ticket. It didn't make sense. Unless there was something he wasn't telling me.

"Come in," Gramp called, his voice hollow.

I pushed the door ajar and slipped through. The room was dim – the only light the orange orb of a reading lamp above his bed. He was sat on a chair, staring out of the window. His usual chipper smile was gone, replaced with an aching sadness. On the black horizon, where the sea met the sky, the first flickering of colour began to dance.

"Gramp," I said, holding Ax's note. "There's something you haven't been telling me. You said you didn't know why we were all here. But ... *you* bought my ticket."

He continued staring straight ahead.

"I certainly did buy that ticket," he replied, sighing. "And there is nothing suspicious about it. When mine arrived in the post – Fists or Felix dressed it up as a competition prize, I guess to surprise me – I thought, wouldn't it be fun to take someone?"

"Oh," I replied, surprised how simple the explanation was. "You mean me?"

He shook his head.

"Oh," I said, slightly taken aback. "If not me, then who did you want to take?"

Gramp took a deep breath and looked down, almost embarrassed. "Your father."

"Oh," I said. Of course. That made sense. But then. .. "Why isn't he here?"

Gramp turned to look at me, his blue eyes radiating sadness. "Because I didn't have the courage to ask him. My own son! I didn't... I didn't..." He turned away and looked out the window. "I didn't want him to say 'no' or, worse, feel like he had to say 'yes' but didn't want to come."

I stepped towards Gramp and put my hand on his shoulder. "Dad would never say something like that." Then I added automatically: "He loves you!" But then I started to wander just how true that was. They never spent any time together. Dad always seemed annoyed at Gramp.

"I'm sure he does," said Gramp. "Because you're supposed to love your dad. But not because we've had an amazing father-son relationship. And that's my fault, no one else's. This was supposed to be our chance to spend some proper time together. To make up, in some tiny way, for all the times I missed when he was little." I could see him blink away a tear. "Getting to know you has been the best thing that's happened to me for decades, Jesse. You're just like me. But that's what makes it so easy between us. Your dad and I are different people. He's not brave or daring or inquisitive. But he's kind and he's thoughtful and he's loving. It took me years to see we could be different people. Years longer than it ever should. I wanted to spend a last cruise with him. While I am still me. Before it is too late."

I frowned. "Too late? What do you mean, too late?"

That gnawing feeling I'd pushed down to the bottom of my tummy burst out and a creeping dread snaked through my veins. I had a horrible suspicion what this was about – a suspicion I'd been trying desperately to ignore, a suspicion that Gramp was hiding something from me. Something big.

Gramp pulled a folded-up piece of paper from his pocket and handed it to me. "I wanted to tell you this as well, but I didn't know how. Heart-to-hearts don't come naturally to me."

I unfolded the piece of paper. It was a letter. From a hospital in America. It was dated a few months back, while he was still living out there.

Dear Mr Hall,

Thank you for visiting last week…

I scanned down. There were a lot of words I didn't understand. But three stood out.

I looked up at Gramp, a numbness spreading through my body. "Early-stage dementia."

He looked out the window and nodded slowly.

The forgetting my name, forgetting little things, forgetting his own past: it had all been adding up in a little part of my brain that I hadn't wanted to give voice to. *Dementia*. I knew the word. I knew it affected some people as they got older. But that was all. "What does it mean?"

Gramp turned to me and gently took the letter from my fingers. "Sometimes brains can get sick, just like other parts of your body. When that happens, they slowly stop doing things that would normally come naturally, like remembering names, remembering events, remembering how to do simple, everyday tasks."

A numbness overcame me; my throat closed up. I thought of how he'd behaved when sick with the chicken nuggets. Forgetting who I was. Losing his train of thought. "But brains can get better, can't they?" I croaked.

"Not in this case," he said, shaking his head.

"But it's not going to get any worse, right?" I asked, desperately clutching at straws – willing him to tell me something that would make this all go away, to tell me that this was just an illness that medicine would make better.

He pursed his lips and I immediately knew the answer. I screwed my eyes shut to hold back the tears. "I have sunny days and cloudy days," he continued, his voice soft and calm. "At the moment, the sunny days outweigh the cloudy ones. I have days when I feel as sharp and clear as I did when I was your age. But I have days when I watch myself struggle with simple tasks, like remembering names or where I put something two minutes ago, and there is nothing I can do about it. Sooner or later – maybe months, maybe years – the cloudy days will become more frequent than the sunny ones. Then, eventually, every day will be a cloudy day."

I didn't want to open my eyes. I didn't want to face this horrible new reality. "What ... what will that mean?"

"It means I could forget..." He paused, unsure quite what to say. Then, when he finally spoke, his voice wavered. "I could forget everything – even how to get out of bed or get changed."

When I opened my eyes, the tears had pooled, making everything a blurred mess. "Will you forget me?"

He drew in a breath to steady his voice. "It could take years and years but" – he drew in another breath – "when it is at its worst, there is a chance that I will forget who you are ... but I am sure I will never forget how you make me feel."

The tears broke free and streamed down my face. I didn't for a second think it was this bad. I thought... I thought ... well, I hadn't thought anything because I hadn't wanted to face up to it. But I never for a moment thought that the gramp I had just got to know might forget my name, my face.

I cried and cried as Gramp stood up and wrapped his arms around me, pulling me into his chest. His cardigan smelled of fudge and mothballs.

"There, there," he said, stroking my hair softly.

Eventually, when I'd cried myself out, I sniffed and said: "When are you going to tell Dad?"

Gramp's hug softened and he said: "When we get back, I suppose." Poor Dad, I thought. On top of the D.I.V.O.R.C.E., this was going to hit him for six. "I moved back to spend some time with him – with all of you – before my dementia symptoms get worse. But..." Gramp looked around and I could see he was thinking about the missed opportunity to invite him on this cruise. "I suppose that's not gone too well, so far."

"It's not too late for you and Dad to build bridges!" I said, wiping my nose on my sleeve.

Gramp sat back down and stared pensively out of the window. "Memory's a funny thing. It comes in different forms. There's lots I still remember – your dad being born, marrying your gran. There's other stuff that I simply can't remember, like playing with your dad when he was little, building a sandcastle with him, pushing him on the swings. And what hurts most is that it might never have happened."

"You must have had *some* moments with Dad?" I insisted. "Even if you can't remember them!"

Just then, the sky burst open in colour. Plumes of blue and green swirled across the sky like it was some magical wall at the very end of the world. It was the most beautiful thing I had ever seen.

Gramp beamed as he watched the colours, and a thought passed across his face. "I'd always wanted to take him to the Tower of London. To sail along the Thames. Get an ice cream. Feed bread to the ravens. Have a photo with a Beefeater." His eyes blazed, like he was conjuring a memory from the magic of the sky.

I stared at the Lights and suddenly I could see things clearly. I'd spent all the time on the cruise trying to get Gramp to feel something again by solving a case. But that wasn't the answer. I needed to help him find a way to connect with Dad!

But to do that we had to stop ourselves being thrown off this cruise. We had to return home just as we had planned – sailing into Newcastle not traipsing back from the Arctic Circle via umpteen expensive plane flights. If only I could fix the mess we were in right now, I knew I could fix Dad and Gramp.

I tried to see a path through all this mess. "Gramp,

you can patch things up with Dad, I know you can. And I can help. But if we get thrown off this cruise, it's going to make everything a gazillion times harder. We *have* to stop the captain ditching us at the next port. And to do that, we need to find the murderer, prove that Wendall is innocent, and show that we aren't troublemakers – we're detectives."

The word "detectives" was like a shot in his arm. He looked at me and smiled, his sadness washing away. "OK, young *detective*. What now?"

I didn't know. But like Wendall said: the answer *had* to be in here somewhere. I just needed *something* to help me see it clearly. I ran through all the possible suspects one by one. But time and time again, my mind came back to the same person.

I started to speak out loud as I thought. "There's only one person left who can be behind all of this. It *has* to be Ivan. He didn't want to be part of your surprise party. He doesn't seem to be enjoying himself. I didn't even see him looking at the Northern Lights. The *only* reason he could be here is to steal the *Gâteau*. But if he is a billionaire, why go to all this trouble to steal it?"

"Perhaps he doesn't have a reason," replied Gramp. "He has always done whatever he wants. Rumour has it, when he was growing up in Luxembourg, he blew up his own school just to get out of PE."

The word bounced around my head – *Luxembourg, Luxembourg, Luxembourg*. That was the third time someone had mentioned it on the cruise. Which – no offence to Luxembourg – was about three times more than I'd ever heard it mentioned outside of geography class. A light bulb went ping inside my brain. "Ivan is from Luxembourg?"

Gramp nodded. "That's what our intelligence told us. If memory serves me right" – he squeezed his eyes shut, imploring his brain to retrieve a nugget of information from the fog – "he was the illegitimate son of the Grand Duke … I think. Loved by his father but rejected by his father's wife…"

I didn't let him finish. "THE *GÂTEAU* IS FROM LUXEMBOURG!" I blurted out. "Perkins said so!"

"Of course!" said Gramp, another nugget reappearing through the fog. "So you're saying…"

"That he wanted to steal back the diamond that

Bridget stole from his father!"

"Golly, Jesse, my boy, you could be right!"

That *had* to be it! Ivan had a motive. As a master criminal, he had the capability. He was the only person it could be.

"It was him! It was him all along!" I cried, perhaps a bit too loudly.

Because, no sooner had the words died in the air than a thumping KNOCK KNOCK KNOCK shook the bedroom door. A door that I had left unlocked.

CHAPTER 35
Cracking the Case

I sprang up to turn the lock but before I could reach it, the door creaked open. My heart was pounding. Was it Ivan? Had he heard us? I went to slam it shut, when a long, gangly arm appeared, followed by a long gangly body.

"Perkins!" said Gramp, with a relieved exhale.

I slumped back on the bed with my own big sigh of relief.

He had his hands in the pockets of his linen trousers. His spindly frame filled the door and his eyebrows slanted down in a look of disarming sympathy.

"I've just heard the news from an angry captain,"

said Perkins. "He's throwing us off the cruise tonight."

His eyes darted anxiously back and forth between Gramp and me.

"I'm afraid he is," said Gramp.

Perkins's eyes continued to dart between the two of us. "I could hear you shouting through the door: 'It's him!'" The corners of his eyes tightened. He looked anxious. "Who were you talking about?"

For a second, and I'm not sure why, I held back from telling him. And then I remembered that it was Perkins. "It's Ivan!" I whispered. "We think it's Ivan!" I unloaded my reasoning.

The anxious look dropped from his face and a smile stretched across it. "Well done!" he said. "You are one incredible young detective, Jesse Hall!" He stood upright, like a weight had been lifted off his shoulders, and laughed as he gabbled: "You've driven this investigation, young man. What would we have done without you? I thought Sid and I were losing our touch. I mean, we couldn't even find a pair of Peppa Pig trunks at the start of this cruise!"

No sooner had he said it than something passed

across his eyes: a barely perceptible wince – a flicker of regret – like he'd said something that he shouldn't have. The words latched on to my brain like Velcro, staying there, lingering there, itching for my attention. I thought how Wendall would hate him knowing about his Peppa Pig trunks. Then a bolt of electricity shot up my spine, exploding into my brain like a firework. I couldn't stop the words falling out of my mouth. "How do you know he had Peppa Pig trunks?" I'd certainly never told him. And I know Wendall wouldn't have. The only other person who knew was Gramp.

"Oh," he said, trying to suppress a look of alarm. "I think Sid must have told me."

Perkins and I stared at each other for a nanosecond too long, like two poker players wondering what was in each other's hands. My heart was going faster and faster. Suddenly, all thoughts of Ivan vanished. And far more pressing thoughts came tumbling into my brain. Thoughts that I kicked myself for not having sooner. And rising up through the middle of them – the realization that Perkins must have been deceiving us.

I stared at him as worry lines grew from the

corners of his eyes like roots seeking out water. Now that I thought about it, the ONLY reason he would have let us call the navy to stop a surprise party he *already* knew about was if he wanted to shift blame for the theft and murders on to Felix, Fists and Ms Ho-Renton. Or Ivan. If they'd been shot or captured before the surprise party was revealed, they'd be presumed guilty.

Perkins wasn't our friend. Perkins had been lying to us all along!

The realization was like a bomb going off inside my skull. I stared at him, dumbfounded, as my brain jangled in shock. What were we going to do? Should I confront him now? No, I had to tell Gramp – get his take on it.

The longer I scrambled for what to do, the bigger Perkins's worry lines grew. I realized I couldn't let him know that I was on to him. I gave an elaborate shrug. "OK," I said, with forced breeziness. "He probably told you and forgot all about it!"

He lingered, not wholly satisfied, still looking anxious. Finally, he seemed to force himself to step back from the door: "Well, goodnight then. See you when we dock, I suppose." Then, with a taut smile, he pulled the door shut – his thin, slender hands the last thing to disappear. For the first time, I paid attention to them properly. They were a perfect match for the long elegant print in the dust below the sauna bench.

I listened for his footsteps disappearing down the corridor, my brain firing like a supercomputer solving an impossible equation. I was running through possibilities, checking my workings, reassessing everything I had assumed. Perkins had *let* us call the coastguard on Fists, Felix and Ms Ho-Renton when he knew it was for a surprise party he'd arranged. And he somehow *knew* about Wendall's Peppa Pig trunks when we hadn't told him. How? And why?

I squeezed my eyes shut and other clues began to emerge from the corners of my brain. Perkins's stolen watch. The goatee and glasses in Sonny's pocket. The seasickness tablets. The mask in the safe.

They began connecting and assembling, building into something much bigger: the answer. And it had been staring us in the face all this time.

I felt so stupid we hadn't seen it before. I looked at Gramp and didn't blink. "It's not Ivan," I said, my heart now going faster than a cheetah on a rocket. "It's been Perkins all along."

Gramp looked incredulous. "Perkins? Never! Not young Perkins! You said he had an alibi – he was in his cabin when Bridget was murdered."

"Someone was in his cabin, but it wasn't Perkins," I said, my hands almost trembling. "I think I know who it was."

I pulled out my phone and searched for the video of the CCTV, then scrolled through to when Perkins briefly entered and and then left his room at 7.45 p.m. I paused it and scanned his blurry face, which was looking straight up, almost directly at the camera.

"That's him all right," said Gramp.

"I know," I replied. "That's what I was expecting. But look…" I pointed at his wrist. "He goes in with his watch on … but leaves without it."

"OK…" said Gramp, clearly not following.

I scrolled forward fifteen minutes to where Perkins

returned to his cabin for the final time that evening. His back to the camera, it was hard to make his face out. I scrolled back and watched it again. Then again. And again. And again. It was definitely someone wearing *his* clothes, with his colour hair. But he still didn't show his face.

"What are you looking for?" asked Gramp.

"I'll know it when I see it," I replied, my hands practically trembling. Was this clip about to destroy Perkins's alibi? Or had I got it horribly wrong?

I scrolled forward to 6.15 a.m., just moments after Bridget's murder. Perkins's door opened and he staggered out, almost slightly woozy. He was looking down. His hands were in his pockets. I could see his glasses and his goatee. But I couldn't make out his face. It could be him. But it could be someone that *looked* like him. I felt a little jitter in my tummy. *Have I got this wrong?* He was just about to step off screen and he lifted a hand to scratch his nose…

"THERE!" I shouted, hitting pause. "This shot here. Look at his hand! Look at his hand!"

"Oh my word," mumbled Gramp, putting his hand

over his mouth in surprise. We both stared intently at the fuzzy hand on screen. Rather than Perkins's long, slender fingers, it was small and podgy. And, more importantly, it only had three fingers.

We turned to each other and said, in unison: "Sonny!"

"Perkins wasn't in his room at all that night! It was Sonny!" I said, buzzing like a battery in a beehive.

"Why…?" said Gramp, racking his brain for an answer I already knew.

"To steal his watch!" I thought back to the dinner with Gramp on the first night. "I saw Perkins showing it off to him. He must have been secretly enticing Sonny to don a disguise and come steal it."

"That's exactly the kind of thing Sonny *would* do. But … he didn't leave!" said Gramp, scratching his head. "Why break in somewhere and then go to sleep for the night?"

"He couldn't help it, that's why!" I replied. "Think back to two days ago – what happened when you took one of Perkins's supposed seasickness tablets?"

Gramp remembered and laughed. "Why, I slept

for about eighteen hours!"

"Exactly!" I said. "They weren't seasickness tablets at all! They were sleeping tablets *disguised* as seasickness tablets. It was almost the most brilliant plan. He showed Sonny his priceless watch – and must have hinted that he left it unattended in his room. He *knew* Sonny wouldn't be able to resist breaking in and stealing it. He gave Sonny one of his 'seasickness' tablets immediately before. It kicked in the minute he had broken into the cabin. The CCTV cameras all make it look like Perkins enters the room that evening, and doesn't get up until after the murder. But it was Sonny all along. It was almost the perfect alibi!"

Gramp gave a slow, awestruck nod. "And then he hid in the sauna all night."

"Exactly!" I replied. "When Bridget arrived for her early morning swim and sauna, he slipped the vial in the bucket, hid back in the sauna and made his escape when we rushed to get you."

I could see Gramp was now in the same chain of thought dominoes as me. Another one fell. "For which he'd need a pair of swimming trunks..."

"Yes!" I was so excited I was almost gabbling. "If you remember – he told us that he had forgotten his own trunks. He needed a pair to be able to walk into the sauna without looking suspicious. So when he saw Wendall's swim bag lying on the floor, he must have swiped it. Unfortunately for him, they just happened to be a pair of Peppa Pig trunks."

More dominoes fell in Gramp's brain. "It all makes sense. Perkins must have confronted Sonny about the watch and blackmailed him into helping steal the *Gâteau*. Which explains why they used the mask to switch the necklace..."

"Because Perkins needed to get rid of it, and it was roughly the same size and weight as the *Gâteau*!"

"Which means..." The grim realization hit him between the eyes. "Perkins must have killed Sonny as well."

We both fell into a stunned silence.

Finally, Gramp said: "Why would he do all this? It isn't the Perkins I remember."

"Maybe you misremember him...?" I offered, gently.

Gramp nodded his head to the side, like it was a possibility.

"There must be something in your past... Some clue..." I replied.

"We were so close, for so many years – right until we both retired."

I thought back to a throwaway comment between Fists and Perkins, right back at the start of the cruise, when they'd all met in Davy Jones's Bar. "But he didn't retire – he's still working as a private detective."

"Of course! How could I forget? Well done, Jesse, my boy." He stood up and started pacing. "We need to act before the ship docks. We need proper proof this time. And lots of it! We have the CCTV footage as evidence. But I don't know if that will be enough."

And that's when it hit me. I knew exactly how we could get that evidence.

"Wait here," I said. "Don't go anywhere. I'll be back in five minutes."

CHAPTER 36
The Napkin That Isn't a Napkin

I dashed through the ship, barrelling up the stairs two steps at a time, ducking and weaving through the crowd of passengers slowly dispersing from the windows, cooing and chattering like they were leaving the cinema after watching the best film of all time. Outside, the Lights were fading. I could almost feel their magic weakening. I silently thanked them for helping me see everything clearly for the first time.

I burst out on to deck, near the old outside swimming pool. Panting, I drank in the evening air in big gulps. It tasted fresh, brand new compared to the stuffy air of Gramp's cabin. I scanned the deck and thought back to the night of the captain's drinks reception. I was standing in the exact same spot as Perkins when he'd thrown that napkin overboard.

I grabbed the railings and peered along the outside of the *Tom Cruise*, trying desperately to catch a glimpse of it. But it was obscured among the rigging and lifeboats strapped to the side of the ship.

There was only one thing for it.

I looked down at the sea: it was calm and black like flat cola. Would it kill me if I fell in there? Probably not. Not while the *Tom Cruise* was at anchor. But it wouldn't be any fun. Still, I wanted to give myself the best odds if the worst happened. I looked behind me to a red emergency cabinet, then yanked it open. A pile of deflated life jackets were stacked up inside. I pulled one out and slipped it over my neck. If this went belly up, at least they might fish me out of the water before I got too cold.

I sucked a deep breath into my lungs and told myself: *You can do this. For Gramp. For Wendall. For Peppa Pig. . . OK, maybe not so much Peppa Pig.* Then I grabbed hold of the handrail, threw one leg over it and pulled my other leg behind, until I was hanging off the outside of the railing. I made the mistake of looking down and I could feel the sweat begin to seep out of my palms. It was a sheer drop into the black water.

Slowly at first, and then quicker, I began to shuffle along the railing until I reached its end. Beyond it, hung two lifeboats strapped to the side of the ship in a row.

I let go of the railing with one hand and grabbed hold of the lip of the little boat. Then, pushing off with my feet, I launched myself headfirst, and tumbled in a tangle of limbs into it. I lay there for a second, suspended in a little boat, far up above the dark sea, my shoulder aching where it had connected with a seat.

Amongst the gentle breaking of waves, I could hear it – a gentle flapping coming from further down. I clambered past the rows of seats until I was at the back of the boat. I could pinpoint the noise – it was coming from the bracket that held the next boat to the ship. I moved to get a better view and glimpsed what I was looking for – a blue napkin. Or at least what Perkins had *claimed* was a blue napkin.

I stood up, swallowed hard – my heart practically ripping its way out of my chest – and leapt the small distance between the two boats, landing heavily, the boat swinging with the impact. I pulled myself up, then reached over the side towards the blue fabric, desperately stretching my arm until I could hook the very tip of my index finger around it. It felt smooth and shiny, like nylon. I walked my fingers along it until it was gripped in my palm and then, with a firm yank, pulled it towards me. The fabric came free from the bracket, the momentum toppling me backwards on to the floor of the lifeboat.

I lifted it to my face and there, staring back at me, was exactly what I was expecting: the eternally happy face of Peppa Pig. It was just as I had suspected: Perkins had stolen them so he could walk into the sauna without arousing suspicion – his tiny waist perfectly suited to a twelve-year-old's swimming trunks. Then, thinking Bridget's murder complete, he had tried to get rid of the evidence by throwing them overboard.

I patted them down. There was something small and hard in one of the pockets. I slipped my hand in and felt my fingers wrap around a smooth little object with a sharp end. I pulled it out and stared at the smashed vial sitting in my palm. If there was any doubt that Perkins was the murderer, it evaporated like a puddle in a heatwave.

Perkins had the *Gâteau*. And he'd incapacitated Bridget and killed Sonny to get it. The only thing I didn't know was why? Why would Gramp's trusted assistant steal a ten-million-pound necklace?

We desperately needed to convince the captain not to dock. If Perkins got a chance to disembark, he would disappear and we'd never catch him again. I needed to get Gramp, take all the new evidence to the captain and pray he believed us. After all, what did we have to lose?

Stuffing the trunks up my jumper, I leapt to the first lifeboat, then clambered across and on to the railing, edging along it and back on to the deck, the adrenaline pumping in my ears. I didn't even take my life jacket off as I set off at speed through the ship, hurtling down the stairs.

I ran and ran until my lungs were about to burst and I pulled up outside Gramp's door, panting.

I pushed it open fully and felt my tummy drop. Gramp was nowhere to be seen.

CHAPTER 37
Ms Ho-Renton's Cabin

Panic began to set in. Something was wrong, I could sense it. Gramp wouldn't have left after I'd told him to stay put. I spun on my heels and sprinted back down the corridor. I didn't know where I was going, I just knew that I had to find him.

"GRAMP?" I yelled, hurtling around a corner, my heartbeat pounding in my ears and my lungs burning. "GRAMP?"

I hurtled past a confused old granny, around another corner and almost slammed into Ms Ho-Renton. She was staring at a cabin door and almost jumped out of her skin.

"Jesse!" she croaked.

"Have you seen Gramp?" I said, bending over and sucking in deep breaths.

"Have you seen this mess?" she replied.

I looked up and let out a startled, breathless "Whoa!" Ms Ho-Renton's door was hanging on one hinge. Where its handle had been there was now just splintered wood.

"What happened?" I said, regaining my breath.

"I've been turned over," she muttered. "Someone's been after my stuff."

Inside her cabin, the towers of cases had collapsed into a sprawling, jumbled heap. A handful of them were open and empty.

"What have they taken?"

Ms Ho-Renton inched her way inside and clambered over the black mound of cases and on to her bed. "Let's see." She read a number on the side of the first empty case. "CX45918. That's chloroform for sedating animals." She picked up another one.

"TP41091." She looked to the ceiling as if trying to recall something. "That's a thermal survival suit." Then she turned her attention to the other two, squinting at their serial numbers. "TX12983. That's a jet-powered cruise board – a handheld jet-ski, if you will. And TR39021. That's..." Her eyes widened and she blew out her cheeks in alarm. "... sticky dynamite."

"Sticky dynamite?" I said, with my own little shudder of unease.

"For sticking to things to blow 'em up. Like icebergs or pack ice."

"Or ships?" I added.

"Or ships."

I closed my eyes in despair. "I think I know who has taken your stuff," I said. "And I think I know what they plan to do with it."

She cocked her head. "Pray tell, dearie."

I took a deep breath and told her about Perkins – the CCTV, the sleeping pills, the swimming trunks, and the handprint under the sauna. "He must have realized I was working it all out when he stopped off and said goodnight, then he stole your stuff. And I'm worried he's taken Gramp."

Ms Ho-Renton narrowed her eyes: "The little worm … I never liked him. He was always Sid's useless assistant."

"I think he's planning on fleeing with the *Gâteau* – jumping overboard in the survival suit and jetting off. But not before" – I gave another little shudder – "he gets rid of all the witnesses."

"You mean sink the ship?" asked Ms Ho-Renton, not waiting for a reply. Then she smashed her fist into her palm and squeezed it so hard that the knuckles cracked. "Not on my watch he ain't."

She stood up and grabbed a case buried somewhere near the bottom of the mound. Then, with age-defying strength, she heaved it clear.

"I knew you'd come in handy, my darling," she muttered, turning her back.

"Are you talking to me?" I asked, trying to peer around her as the locks popped open.

"Not you, dearie," she said. Then she turned, her eyes glistening with steely resolution as she cradled her mega-gun in her arms. "Jemima."

She slung the gun up and over her shoulder so that it hung menacingly on her back. Then she fished a bandolier of cartridges from the case and slid it over her neck so that it sat diagonally across her chest. She followed it with a little camouflaged shoulder bag that contained God-knows-what.

"I've brought down six dictators and microchipped a giant squid the size of a football field. This low-life, murdering thief isn't getting away from me."

Then she pulled a beret across her head and stood up, snarling like some sort of terrifying one-granny army. I suddenly sensed what a formidable adversary she must have been for Gramp. Thank heavens she was now on our side.

"Grenade?" she said, popping open a case and offering me one like it was a box of Quality Street.

I pulled a face. "I wouldn't know how to work one."

"Do you mind if I do?"

I shook my head as she took two and clipped them on to her bandolier.

"You can't go after Perkins without any weapons!" she said, eyeing me up incredulously like I'd suggested climbing a hill on an empty stomach. "How about an iddy-biddy gun or two?"

I winced. "I don't know…"

She pulled out a belt and holster. "They're not firearms – just one of my grappling iron guns."

I shrugged. "OK."

She strapped the belt around my waist and pulled a gun out. It was the same gun she'd gone plastic fishing with. "The trigger fires it. This brake button stops the rope. This button retracts the rope." She beamed, then slipped it back into its holster. I could feel their weight against my hips, and they gave me a new strength.

"Right, let's go!" I said, turning to head down the corridor.

"And where *exactly* are we going?" she replied.

"On deck. Surely that's where Perkins intends to jump off?"

Ms Ho-Renton shook her head. "In front of everyone, dearie? Why that would cause quite a scene."

"But how else could he get off the ship?"

She held up a finger to signal that she had an idea,

then turned her back again and rustled amongst the mound of cases. When she spun around, her X-ray goggles were strapped across her face like some super-intense, weaponized scientist. "Let's find out!"

She played with some settings on the side of the goggles, then gazed around gormlessly like people do when they wear VR headsets. I knew what she'd be seeing – a perfect X-ray image of the *Tom Cruise* and all its passengers.

"We've got a bogey," she said, looking through her floor. "Someone is headed through the lower deck corridor, pushing a wheelchair with my cruise board below it ... and someone slumped in the seat."

"That *must* be Perkins!" I exclaimed. "And he HAS got Gramp." I felt my insides knot. "We have to save him!"

Ms Ho-Renton moved her head to the left, as if tracing Perkins's trajectory. "It looks like he's headed to the pool."

I pulled a face and frowned. "The pool?" And then it dawned on me, like a big ray of flume-shaped light. "Oh, jeez. He's headed to the Black Hole!"

CHAPTER 38
Wendall Returns

I scrambled down the corridor, Ms Ho-Renton waddling behind with Jemima strapped to her back. As we reached the end of the hall and prepared to descend the stairs to the pool deck, I looked back at her shattered door and had an idea.

"Wait, we've got one thing we need to do first!" I said, heading upstairs rather than down, vaulting two steps at a time. A granny and grandpa tottered past, barely noticing Ms Ho-Renton labour past with Jemima.

"Where are we headed?" she wheezed.

"To break down some more doors," I replied.

I strode up the final two steps and as I waited for

Ms Ho-Renton to catch up, I heard the unmistakeable *CLUNK CLUNK* of uncomfy footwear.

"Felix!" I said, as he appeared around the corner, chatting idly to Fists.

"Hello, boys!" wheezed Ms Ho-Renton as she hauled herself up the final steps. "Fancy a mission?"

"We were thinking of a nightcap..." said Felix, before raising an inquisitive eyebrow. "But tell me more, *señora*."

"Perkins has kidnapped Gramp," I said, the words flying out in a breakneck stream. "He killed Sonny and he has the *Gâteau* and he is going to sink the ship if we don't find him."

Ms Ho-Renton nodded. "Just trust us on this one: we need to stop him, pronto."

Fists squeezed his knuckles till they cracked. "I never liked him anyway. We should have known he would never have organized a party for Sid if there wasn't something in it for him."

"At your service," said Felix, rolling a limp hand in front of his chest and falling into a flamboyant bow.

"First, we need to get one more person," I said. "Follow

me." And I headed off down the corridor, swinging around a corner to find Ax still sleeping on the dirty carpet.

He opened a single eye and yawned. "All right, Jesse." Then he startled and sat up as Fists, Felix, Ms Ho-Renton and – most disconcerting of all – Jemima appeared around the corner.

"What's going on?" he asked.

"We're here to break out Wendall," I said.

Ax laughed. "Nice one!" Then, when he saw I wasn't laughing, his face dropped. "Like, really?"

A tiny voice sounded from behind the door. "Really?" It was Wendall.

"Stand back from the door!" I shouted. "We're breaking you out!"

"Golly," he said, with the sound of footsteps as he scampered to the back of the room.

"Fists," I said. "Would you mind?"

"Not at all," he replied, rolling up his sleeve. He lumbered up to the door, thrust one hip forward and raised both hands in a boxing stance. Then he looked at Ax and me and flashed us a TV smile. "Let's start changing some changing rooms!" he said, with a little ding of his gold tooth. We both looked puzzled. "That's my catchphrase ... on my show."

"Ohhhhh," we both said in unison as he pulled a fist back and...

WHACK

He punched the door so hard that it flew inwards, the hinges and handle bursting and splintering. Then he rolled his neck and stood back. "I love making home improvements..."

Wendall was pressed against the far wall, his eyes as wide as dustbin lids. "Wow, Mr Harris. You've got one serious punch on you. Are we going to get in lots of trouble for this?" Then he thought about it and added: "Don't answer that; I don't care any more."

I opened my mouth and the words streamed out: "It was Perkins all along! He's kidnapped Gramp and he's about to sink the ship!" Then I stepped forward and gave him a massive hug, squeezing him hard and saying: "We've got a case to close. He's headed to the Black Hole."

Wendall frowned. "The Black Hole? Why would he wanna ride that now?"

Fists sucked in air. "Oooo, that thing's haunted, ain't it?"

Felix shuffled uncomfortably. "I heard it is a gateway to the worst place imaginable."

"You mean PE class?" asked Wendall.

"No," said Felix, leaving a dramatic pause. "A gateway to hell!"

I held my hands up to ask for a bit of perspective. "It's neither, OK! It isn't haunted. It isn't a vortex or a gateway to another dimension. It's just a badly built flume. A badly built flume with some panels missing. Panels that spit you out into the ocean."

"Oooosh," said Fists. "What a way to go."

I could see the realization of what that meant light up in Wendall's eyes. "That means he's not having a nice ride on a waterslide..."

"No," I interjected. "He's about to make his escape!"

CHAPTER 39
The Escape

Every second counted as we barrelled down the corridor towards the pool. Wendall and I led, followed by Fists and Felix, with Ms Ho-Renton waddling at the back. My nerves sloshed with every stride. I just prayed we weren't too late – that Perkins hadn't done something terrible to Gramp. Or equally as bad: already made his escape and planted the dynamite on the side of the boat. I dreaded the terrible hollow bang that told me it had exploded and the *Tom Cruise* was going down.

We swung around another corner. The glass pool doors lay in front of us. We burst through and...

"GRAMP!" I yelled, my heart nearly exploding.

Perkins was at the top of the spiral staircase, in front of the Black Hole, dragging a bound, gagged and woozy Gramp after him. He was clad in the survival suit he'd stolen from Ms Ho-Renton, with the cruise board slung over his back.

"MMJESSME," mumbled Gramp into his gag.

The others careered in, almost crashing into my back.

"Stay back!" snapped Perkins. His usual disarming smile was gone. Instead, his worry lines were deeper than the Suez Canal. "Don't make me do anything you might regret."

He flicked his chin at the Black Hole and it didn't take a mind reader to understand what he meant: stop, or he'd throw Gramp down it.

I flung my arms out to halt everyone as Perkins backed towards the Black Hole. I could see him spinning woozily. A panicked tightness gripped my chest – one tiny push and Gramp would topple backwards down the flume. Perkins bent over, panting from the exertion, then moved his gaze over to us. Even though the worry lines made him look jittery, he had a look of immense self-satisfaction. He took a second to compose himself and, between breaths, shouted: "Well who's the bumbling sidekick now?"

"What are you doing, Clarence?!" yelled Fists.

Perkins looked around as if the answer was obvious. "I'm trying to steal a priceless diamond, what do you think I'm doing?" He looked at Gramp and nodded his head to the side. "Although, I admit: I hadn't exactly planned for it to end like this. I should have made my escape during the birthday party like I was originally planning. It's just hard to make a clean getaway when the ship is surrounded by navy boats."

All five of us were frozen by the door, desperate to race to Gramp's aid but terrified of the consequences.

"It does not have to end like this, Clarence, *mi amigo!*" cried Felix.

"Yes it does!" he bit back, looking annoyed. "And it's all Sid and his stupid grandson's fault! If they hadn't decided to dig into Bridget's 'accident', I'd have the *Gâteau* and nobody would be any the wiser!" He sighed, squeezing the bridge of his nose and screwing his eyes shut. "But now you all know too much and I can't let that happen."

He pulled the cruise board off his back and moved towards the flume. We all glimpsed the stick of dynamite protruding from his pocket.

"This is a bad idea, Perkins!" hollered Fists. He stepped forward but Perkins threw out a flailing arm.

"Not another step forward!" His palm hovered by Gramp's chest. "Or I'll push." Even from this distance, I could see the sweat pouring down his face. I grabbed Fists's arm and pulled him back. If Gramp slid down that flume, bound and gagged, and out into the freezing open ocean, he'd sink like a stone.

I needed to buy time – stop him doing anything stupid. "You can't hurt Gramp!" I shouted. "You said it yourself, he's like a big brother to you!" I was stalling … but I was also fishing. Fishing for whatever was going on inside Perkins's brain – a reason for why he was doing all of this.

Perkins gave Gramp a look that almost passed as affection. "He *was* like a big brother to me." Then the look melted away and was replaced by something altogether colder. "But such a *knowing, patronizing* big brother." He stared intently at Gramp, as if digging through a deep pool of hurt. "When I was young, it didn't matter. But it never stopped. I could never do anything right! I was always his *bumbling assistant*." He spat the words out, like they had festered in darkness inside his brain for far too long.

"He kept you under his wing!" cried Ms Ho-Renton. "You should be grateful!"

Perkins shook his head and stamped his foot, like a stroppy toddler. "He kept me under his wing because it made him look better! But the minute he retired, do you know what he did?" Gramp's eyes were wide in alarm now, as if he knew what was coming. "He didn't recommend me to fill his role, oh no! I wasn't good enough to follow in his footsteps." I thought back to that picture of Perkins at Gramp's retirement party – *that* was why he was looking so sad. Gramp was biting at his gag, trying to speak. "You thought I didn't know, didn't you? Well, I found out! I was given 'early retirement' under some made-up excuse. Given a pitiful pension. I've had to work every day since trying to make ends meet! I've racked up debts like you wouldn't believe!" He patted his top pocket. "This necklace is going to give me the retirement I deserve!"

Gramp finally worked his gag free. "Clarence, dear boy ... I didn't mean to deceive you. It just takes a certain type of person to be a chief inspector!"

Perkins's face folded into a look of pure hurt. It was like he'd been waiting years to let this out. "And I ... wasn't ... that ... person? Not smart enough to fill your shoes? Not smart enough to befriend a load of old crooks? Not smart enough, full stop?"

He fell into a pained silence, drawing in a breath that swelled his chest before letting out a long, loud sigh. It was like he was exhaling the hurt, letting it go. And replacing it with cold vengeance.

"Well, remember this when the ship goes down – I WAS smart enough to plan this whole charade from the very beginning. I WAS smart enough to invite you all for a supposed surprise birthday, just so I could get close to the *Gâteau*. I WAS smart enough to steal Eileen's vial of poison. I WAS smart enough to take out Bridget. I WAS smart enough to steal the necklace. I WAS smart enough to get rid of Sonny when he was about to talk. And I WILL be smart enough to make my get away!"

"You'll be a mass murderer!" shouted Fists.

Perkins nodded and allowed himself a chuckle that would have sounded warm and friendly were it not for the circumstances. "True. But a really *smart* one."

He checked the dynamite tucked inside his suit and picked up his cruise board. "I'm sorry that it has to end like this." As he moved towards the flume, a little thought seemed to go pop in his brain. "I may have bungled your arrests … but you could say that I got you all in the end, no?" He let out another little chuckle that grew and spread like wildfire into an all-consuming laughter, his chest rising and falling in great hearty heaves. It was the same laugh that I'd once found so infectious, but now looked like the laughter of an unhinged man.

I drew in a breath, ready to scream and shout and call him every name under the sun when…

THWACK

An ear-splitting noise exploded behind me, practically bursting out my eardrums. Something green and purple embedded itself in Perkins's cruise board.

I spun around to see Ms Ho-Renton crouched on one knee, Jemima's butt pressed into her shoulder and her barrel pointed at Perkins.

"Drat!" she said, reaching to her bandolier for another dart.

Perkins had staggered backwards and was inspecting the dart protruding from his cruise board with a mixture of shock and horror. He looked up, clocked Ms Ho-Renton reloading Jemima and didn't waste a beat before launching himself towards the Black Hole.

Everything suddenly seemed to slow down.

Perkins dived at full stretch through a gap beside Gramp, disappearing down the tube like a marble being swallowed into a marble run. As he flew past, his trailing leg knocked Gramp – not enough to send him hurtling down, but enough for him to lose his balance. He teetered on the edge – his eyes wide in desperation – as he tried frantically not to topple backwards. But he was fighting a losing battle with gravity.

"NO!" I screamed, tearing at a lung-busting pace towards the staircase, spinning around like a corkscrew as I bounded up them three steps at a time. "Hang in there, Gramp!"

His whole body was tipping, his head now well inside the mouth of the flume as he slowly pivoted backwards. I could see him trying with every ounce of might to use his bound legs as a counterbalance, but all it was doing was slowing the process, not saving him. I just had to get there before he went, before he fell.

I hurtled up the top step. "I've got you!" I yelled as I reached out a hand. I felt it brush against the tip of his trouser leg and scratch at thin air as he finally toppled backwards and slipped into the black insides of the Black Hole. My heart stopped. Every muscle in my body screamed in horror. But I didn't pause to contemplate what I did next. I grabbed my grappling hook gun, braced myself and dived in after him.

CHAPTER 40
Revenge of the Black Hole

I sped through the Black Hole like I'd been sucked into a vacuum cleaner. Everything was pitch dark. All I could hear was the air rushing past my ears. And all I could feel was the burning friction of fibreglass on my bum. My jaw was clenched tight. My heart was in my mouth. And my tummy was somewhere back at the top of the spiral staircase.

I wrapped my finger around the grappling gun trigger, thrust it over my head and squeezed. With a little bang I could feel the hook fire up the flume towards the staircase. The rope spooled out of it as I clasped the gun tight in both hands and prayed for it to catch hold of something.

Down and down I plunged, the gun clutched in my hands, getting faster and faster. Round a bend. Through a corkscrew. Down a drop. Until suddenly I could see the silvery top of Gramp's head just beyond my feet. I almost had him! If I could just reach out my legs and somehow wrap them around him. I stretched and heaved but he was just out of reach. He must have sensed I was there because he lifted his hands above his head. He reached up, grabbed hold of my belt and I had him!

A wave of hope exploded through me but it lasted about a nanosecond before the smooth plastic of the flume disappeared, my belly flew upwards and suddenly we were plummeting through mid-air in a terrifying freefall. The fresh air whipped past my face. The dark, brooding ocean sped towards us. I instinctively knew what had happened: we'd exited through the broken panel.

Without thinking, I squeezed the gun's brake button. A yank exploded down my arm and suddenly we had stopped. The grappling hook had caught on to something! We were swinging like a clock pendulum off the side of the ship, nothing but cool night air between us and the ocean. Below me, Gramp hung desperately from my waistband.

"Hold on!" I yelled.

To the side of us, almost close enough to touch, was the side of the *Tom Cruise*. Above us: a gaping hole yawned in the bottom of the Black Hole. Below us: the faint orange figure of Perkins in his survival suit bobbed in the water. It looked horribly like he was sticking the dynamite on to the side of the ship.

I desperately clung on to the gun, swaying gently in the breeze. I was taking both of our weight, and the pain in my arms grew by the second. Even worse, I could feel my belt slipping down my waist, and Gramp's grip on me weakening.

I yelled again: "Hang on, Gramp!" What for, I wasn't sure. But if he let go he'd plunge into the ocean. With his legs and feet bound, he wouldn't stand a chance.

He was shouting up to me from below, his words fighting against the wind and the waves: "Jesse! I'm

going to drag you down! I'll kill us both!" Then he took a breath and said: "You've made an old man happier than I ever thought I could be! I love you!"

I knew what that meant. I screamed so loud I thought the words were going to tear my throat. "NO! Don't you dare let go! I need you! I know I can fix things – you, Mum, Dad, everything – and I need you more than I've needed anything ever before!"

I felt one of my fingers slip from the gun.

"Better me than both of us!" yelled Gramp, his voice cracking as the reality of what was about to happen grew nearer. "Tell Mike I love him and I'm proud of him and I've always been proud of him and that I wish I was there for what he's going through now!"

I was yelling, yelling as hard as I could: "DON'T, GRAMP! JUST HOLD ON! PLEASE JUST HOLD ON!"

Another two fingers slipped from the gun. My belt slid down to my thighs. This was it. I knew it, Gramp knew it.

"Jesse!" he shouted. I squeezed my eyes shut. Tears stung their sides. I knew this was his goodbye. "I lov—"

Suddenly, a deafening BONG exploded through the night air.

BONG

Then another.

BONG

It was like being in a bell tower. It was coming from the side of the ship. What was going on? With a crash, the side of the ship split open and Fists's fist burst through, rusty metal flying everywhere. I looked across and could see his face peering out. He stuck two hands through, gripped either side of the hole and wrenched it open like it was nothing more than tissue paper.

Light spewed out from the tear in the side of the boat and in the middle of it – no more than a few feet from us – stood Fists, Felix and Wendall.

"TIME TO START CHANGING CHANGING ROOMS!" he yelled. Felix leaned out, Fists holding his other hand to stop him falling.

"Hold on there, *señor*

Sid!" yelled Felix, grabbing hold of Gramp's cardigan and pulling him towards the hole. Gramp managed to place a foot on the ledge and Fists's and Felix's arms were around him, dragging him into the safety of the cruise liner.

"Now you, *señor* Jesse!" said Felix, reaching out towards me, his hand groping in mid-air. All I needed to do was grab hold of it.

I looked down towards the ocean. The orange figure of Perkins was swimming frantically away from the ship. A red light blinked on the hull. That meant only one thing: the dynamite had been armed. I looked at Felix, Fists and Gramp, all of them imploring me to: "Grab hold!"

But I knew we only had a matter of minutes before we'd all be heading to the bottom of the ocean. I had to do something.

I smiled as bravely as I could. "See you in a minute," I said. Then I reached up, pressed the release button on the side of the gun and I was in freefall all over again.

CHAPTER 41

The Ocean

I don't remember much about the fall, just the cold air racing by my cheeks and the feeling that my tummy had somehow exited through the top of my head. I tumbled down, down, down, getting faster and faster until the ocean loomed up at me like some frothing black carpet.

And then I hit the water.

It sucked me down into its pitch-black depths. The chill grabbed hold and knocked the air from my lungs. The cold ached, burrowing inside my brain, crawling inside my bones. I hung there in the black void for a nanosecond – no sight, no sound, no smell. Just me and the cold.

Then, with a silent pop, something inflated around

my neck, and suddenly I was hurtling back towards the surface, breaking free with a desperate gasp; chill, salty, black water streaming up my nose and down my throat. I looked down and said a silent prayer of thanks for the life jacket I'd put on to retrieve Wendall's swimming trunks.

I bobbed and rolled in the gentle waves, taking a moment to get my bearings. Above me, the *Tom Cruise* loomed like a giant metal cliff. Lights spilled out from its portholes, but down here there was nothing but the soft crash of waves breaking. Perkins had swum clear of the boat and was no more than the length of a bus away, looking as if he was preparing to fire up the cruise board and make his escape. But he wasn't my first concern. That was coming from the side of the ship, in a steady stream of BEEPS:

BEEP BEEP BEEP

The sticky dynamite. It was armed and ready to blow. I barely had time to think – I swam as fast as I could towards it, labouring through the numbing water until I was at the side of the ship. The red display screen blinked numbers at me.

28 … 27 … 26…

I was there with seconds to spare.

My heart in my mouth, I reached up, grabbed hold of it and pulled.

25 … 24 … 23…

It was stuck. Stuck firm.

22 … 21 … 20…

I pulled harder. It wouldn't budge.

19 … 18…

I pulled harder still. Nothing. Why!? Why was it stuck so hard?

I heard Perkins's cruise board start up. He was about to get away.

A sense of absolute defeat overwhelmed me.

17 … 16…

The dynamite was about to detonate. It'd blow me to pieces and sink the ship in seconds. There was no way anyone except Perkins would survive.

15 … 14…

I felt like letting the ocean swallow me up. He'd done it. He'd won. He'd stolen the *Gâteau* and was about to kill us all and get away with it.

All I could think of was Mum and Dad and how

devastated they'd be. The family ripped apart. Divorce. Death. A tragic shipping accident. Just like *Titanic*. Just like Dad feared. I felt sick and cold and weak and alone.

In all the pain and depression I allowed myself a little smile. Divorce – I'd said it! Well, thought it, actually. And, what's more – I realized that if I could cope with this, submerged in the Arctic Ocean waiting to get blown into bits by a block of dynamite with no one to even say goodbye, I could deal with Mum and Dad separating. In fact, if that's what it took for them to be happy, then I had to face up to it, just like I was facing up to this bleeping stick of explo—

And that's when I saw it: a little black button on the side of the dynamite. I didn't think before reaching out to press it. Either it was going to detonate it, or it was going to release it. And right then, I had nothing to lose. I pressed a numb finger into it, pulled my head back and…

5 … 4…

With a soft SHLUMP, the suckers released and the dynamite slid off the hull and into my hand.

Barely taking a second to breathe, I turned away from the ship and threw the dynamite as far as I could in the direction of Perkins. It arced through the air, landed with a splash and a gurgle as it sank down into the ocean and...

BOOM

The sound almost broke my eardrums as a huge mountain of water leapt out of the ocean, growing and growing, Perkins riding it like some helpless orange dinghy, before it came crashing down. Huge waves reverberated outwards, pushing me into the side of the hull and rocking the *Tom Cruise* in towering, terrifying sways above me. But she was still afloat!

As the mist and waves cleared, I could see Perkins desperately coughing and spluttering. I could still hear the roar of his cruise board, but it wasn't coming from anywhere near him. He must have lost it in the blast because it was now perhaps ten metres away, powering around in circles like an out-of-control speedboat.

Pausing only to shoot me the filthiest of filthy looks, he began swimming frantically towards it. Splashing desperately in his cumbersome orange survival suit, he was barely making any progress. I knew I could get there first. I moved to start swimming and that's when I realized just how much the cold was sapping me. My teeth chattered. My body was numb. My limbs barely wanted to move. I couldn't have swum if I wanted to.

I reached for my grapple gun with my frozen fingers, pointed it in the direction of Perkins and – using every piece of strength I had left – squeezed the trigger.

The hook fired out and flew across the night sky like a silver cross-shaped comet, its rope trailing in its stead as it flew closer and closer to Perkins and then gripped hold of his survival suit.

It took a moment for him to realize what had

happened and a second longer for me to press the retract button. I sped through the numbing water towards him, like I was water-skiing, until I'd crashed into him and was on top of him like a lilo.

"Get off!" he screamed. "Get off me!"

He pushed and shoved and splashed, but I held firm. He had been struggling to swim before, but with me holding on tight, pushing his body down into the cold water, it was completely impossible. He was going nowhere. And he knew that. He was trapped in the cold sea with me … the cold, numbing, sleepy sea. He reached inside his survival suit for something, but my eyelids drooped shut momentarily. The cold was leaching the last of my strength.

I wasn't freezing any more. The pain had left. A comforting blanket of sleepiness replaced it, drawing me in, urging me to keep my eyes closed … just for a few seconds…

I wanted to believe it … I *could* close my eyes just for a bit and I'd be fine … wouldn't I?

No!

I snapped to. I had to try and stay awake.

Perkins held something glistening out of the water. At first I thought it was a knife. Then it sparkled, the light from the *Tom Cruise* bouncing off it at a thousand gleaming angles. I knew instinctively that it was the *Gâteau*. It was beautiful. Even in the dark, wet, icy water. Even with its point angled towards me.

There was a loud noise rushing in my ears. Was it my brain packing in? I didn't know.

Even in my state, I sensed what Perkins planned to do. He planned to slash my life jacket. I'd sink like an anvil.

The noise grew louder. The sea began to churn.

What was this? The ocean licking its lips... Getting ready to swallow me?

The *Gâteau* shone even brighter, giving out an almost impossible, blinding light.

Perkins's face scowled and snarled, half submerged in the dark water, his orange arm reaching out, gripping the *Gâteau*.

I could just close my eyes and sink below ... it'd be so easy. It'd almost be nice. Like a big black duvet.

My eyelids sagged closed. I thought of Mum and Dad and Gramp and the sea churned and I realized I'd left my bed unmade and would Mum keep it like that for ever and who would get the house and who would look after Gramp and the noise filled every bit of the air and a hand reached down and gripped Perkins's wrist...

A hand? Whose hand?

Then the pieces connected – the noise and the light and the waves. I looked up and a helicopter was hovering just metres above us. A rope hung off it. And on the bottom of it, suspended in a harness, one hand clutching Perkins's wrist, was Ivan Django.

Ah! It all made sense, I thought woozily. Checkmate! Game over. Ivan and Perkins were in it together and now they were going to make their escape. I was about to sink. Their planned had worked perfe—

Ivan wrapped his arm around the rope ladder to free his other hand, then he reached out and clasped a handcuff around Perkins's wrist. The rope retracted on a pulley and Ivan hauled Perkins up towards the chopper. A small, squat body leaned out and grabbed him. It was Ms Ho-Renton! She dragged Perkins inside kicking and screaming.

Ivan's pulley lowered him back down. He fixed me

in his ice-like glare, his lank white hair stuck to his head from the spit and froth of the churning sea. Then he extended a hand.

I reached out an arm that felt like an icicle. Ivan pulled me into the helicopter and on to a seat between Ms Ho-Renton and him. "Get him out of his wet clothes and into a warmth suit!" he yelled. It was the first words I had heard him speak.

Then the chopper rose up vertically. Out of the open door, I could see us turning towards the top of the *Tom Cruise*. Inside, on the floor, Perkins lay face down, his hands cuffed; finally defeated.

We've done it! I thought. *We got him!* And I was alive! I slumped over on to Ms Ho-Renton's lap, the smell of her lavender skirt filling my salty nostrils.

She reached down and prized the *Gâteau* from Perkins's fingers.

"'Ere, Ivan – you want this thing back?" she asked, placing it in his lap.

He gazed down on it, staring into its glistening insides. "Bah. I never liked it much." And with a casual flick of the wrist, he tossed it out the open door and into the black sea.

Wow. I thought, as my eyelids began to sag. Ten million pounds – gone just like that. I thought of *Titanic* and how the seabed must be covered in expensive necklaces. It was the last thought I had before falling into a deep, blissful sleep.

CHAPTER 42

The Day After the Swim Before

Sunlight streamed in on to my face. I was no longer cold. I sensed that immediately, even in my half-asleep state. I was engulfed again, not in freezing water, but in something incredibly snuggly.

I popped an eye open, then another. I was in Gramp's cabin, wrapped up beneath about four blankets. Sunlight streamed in through the window.

Gramp sat in a chair at the end of the bed, his legs crossed as he filled in a puzzle book.

"How long have I been asleep for?" I asked.

He looked up and smiled. "Ooh. About nineteen hours. It took a long time to warm you up."

I sat up in bed and felt awake but weak.

"Perkins?" I asked.

"Locked up. He was taken off board by the Norwegian police late last night."

I gave a weary, relieved nod.

Gramp's blue eyes blazed. "You saved the ship. All by yourself, young man," he said, folding up his puzzle book and placing it neatly on his table. "You're a hero!"

I looked up and smiled.

"You think so?"

"I know so."

He smiled and I smiled back and a warm feeling took hold that melted the last of the cold from my bloodstream.

"Does the captain know what happened?"

Gramp nodded. "He's apologized – in a roundabout way – to Wendall. And obviously ditched plans to throw us off the ship. He knows what you did."

"And the rest of the passengers?" I asked.

Gramp shook his head. "Not a thing."

Probably best it was kept a secret, I thought. There

was *no way* I wanted Mum and Dad to find out that I had ridden a murderous flume into the Arctic Ocean to deactivate some dynamite and arrested a murderer. They'd overreact.

"Feel strong enough for a little stroll?" Gramp asked.

I heaved my weary limbs from the bed. "Sure."

The sunlight streamed in through the viewing room windows, casting long shadows across the faded insides of the *Tom Cruise*. As we turned a corner, I could see where Gramp was leading me. Up ahead, sat in a little cluster, were Felix, Fists, Ms Ho-Renton and Wendall. Above them, hovered Ax holding a drinks tray. He listened, jaw hanging open, as the four of them regaled him with a story. As I moved closer, I could hear what the story was about: last night.

Felix leaned forward, talking quietly but animatedly at Ax. Those that knew the story seemed to be enjoying it all over again. And those that didn't – Ax – looked gobsmacked. "And then *señor* Jesse, he fired this grappling hook and it caught hold..."

"Here he is!" boomed Fists, spotting Gramp and me approach.

They all stood up and started clapping.

Fists stuck two fingers in his mouth and let out a piercing wolf whistle that made a granny spit out her false teeth.

Felix bowed dramatically like I was a king and he was a courtier.

Ms Ho-Renton raised her walking stick like a rifle

salute. It let out a massive *ROOOAARRRRR* as a flame spilled across the ceiling and made us all stagger back a step.

"Gotta stop doing that, Eileen," said Fists, wiping the soot from his cheeks.

Fists pulled me up a chair and I settled in next to Wendall.

He leaned in and said quietly in my ear, "I can't believe you rode the Black Hole without me!" Then we both

laughed. I was so happy that he was free and I was alive. "Now we've got the rest of the cruise to hang out!"

"Yeah, let's just try and avoid any more trouble."

"Aw," said Wendall, smiling to himself. "I was beginning to enjoy trouble."

Chuckling, I looked from Ax to Fists to Felix to Ms Ho-Renton and suddenly the moment of my rescue came flooding back.

"Where's Ivan?" I said, turning around and scanning the rest of the room.

"Gone," said Fists.

"Gone?" I repeated.

"Gone," croaked Ms Ho-Renton. "Back to his ship."

"But, I don't get it ... how did he get a helicopter...?"

Fists leaned back into his chair and interlocked his fingers on his chest. "There's a bit of a jackanory – story – behind that," he said. "Ivan had a debt he owed your gramp. He rescued him from a burning tank once. He swore, in return to one day save Sid's butter knife." Fists paused at everyone's blank looks, then said: "Life. He swore to save Sid's life."

"Now he is a retired master criminal, he has been

following Sid around, hoping very much that he might get an opportunity to repay the debt. It is the only reason he would come on this cruise," said Felix.

Eileen took a long slurp of tea. "He thought he'd settled it in Butlins ten years ago when it looked like Sid was choking on a strawberry lace. Turns out he just had a chesty cough."

"But now he saved your life, young man, he considers the debt paid," said Fists. "So he's gone back home."

"But where did he get a helicopter from?" I asked.

"His ship!" croaked Ms Ho-Renton. "It's been following us a few miles behind, just in case. It's bleedin' *massive*. He kept it on when he disbanded G.E.M.I.N.I. and declared he had gone straight. I went and found him when you fell out of the flume and lickety-split, it flew over, picked us up and we were out searching for you in the water."

Gramp chuckled at the absurdity of it all. "I can't say I remember him swearing that debt, but there you go."

It prompted Felix to purse his lips and put his hand on his heart. "Your gramp, he has told us about his dementia. We had no idea."

"No idea at all," echoed Fists. "So we've decided to

make the most of the time we have together and make this a yearly thing! Long may this continue!"

Ms Ho-Renton and Felix raised their glasses to toast the idea. "Long may it continue!"

Felix kept his glass raised. "And to our friends who didn't have much luck this time around. Bridget … and Sonny."

"Rest in peace, old boy," said Fists, then had a big slurp of his tea.

I sank back in my chair, shoulder to shoulder with Wendall, as the four of them began reminiscing about Sonny and sharing updates about Bridget.

I let my mind wander home. I waited for the usual pang of anxiety, but it didn't arrive. Last night's near-death experience had given me new perspective.

I nudged Wendall's shoulder. "What will your mum and dad say about you suddenly liking trouble?"

"Well, I don't know," he replied. "I don't see them much."

"What do you mean?"

"Well, I don't live with them. I live with my nan. My dad works away on oil rigs and my mum lives with her other family," he explained, as bright and breezy and unbothered as ever.

And that's when my plan came flooding back to me. My plan to fix the final things that needed mending: to fix Dad and Gramp.

"Back in a second," I said, standing up with a new energy. "I've just got to make a call."

Then I pulled out my phone and turned it on. As I headed out on to deck I opened my contacts list and pressed my finger against the word: DAD.

CRUISE DAY 7:
RETURN HOME

CHAPTER 43
Endings and New Beginnings

There's not really much to tell about Day 5 and 6 of the cruise. Except that it was mega fun. We saw some fjords. Wendall won bingo. Felix let me try on his painfully uncomfy shoes. Ms Ho-Renton darted a seagull that stole a doughnut from her. And I hung out with Gramp loads. Just me and him and no murders or stolen diamonds or vengeful former assistants. It was awesome.

I don't want to get all cheesy about it, but sometimes you don't know what's missing from your life until you find it.

As we docked in Newcastle port, Gramp and I

hovered in the same cramped staircase as we'd stood when we first entered the *Tom Cruise*. Wendall and his nan were on the stair behind us, followed by Fists, Felix and Ms Ho-Renton.

"Well," said Gramp, looking from person to person with his blue eyes glistening. "I thought I was getting too old to have any more adventures. But you proved me wrong."

I smiled to myself. *And it's only just beginning,* I wanted to say. But I kept schtum for now.

The door opened and the sound of seagulls and the smell of diesel smoke poured in. Passengers filtered out slowly, bags in hand, until it was our turn. The mountains and fjords and endless ocean were gone, replaced by grey tarmac and car parks. And, at the end of the gangway waving: Mum and Dad. They stood a good two yards apart from each other. I was sad. But not as sad as I thought I'd be. I'd known this was coming, and I'd begun to make my peace with it.

"Jesse!" said Dad, throwing his hands around me.

"Welcome back, darling," said Mum, giving me a tight squeeze.

I'd talked to them both over the phone about the divorce. I knew everything that had been planned out – alternate weeks at Dad's new house and Mum's new house. Life would still go on. A new life, a different life, but one that could be just as good. Who knew – maybe even better if Mum and Dad were happier?

"Hello, Sarah," said Gramp to Mum. She smiled warmly. "Hello, son," he said to Dad, then Gramp pulled him into a hug that momentarily shocked him.

"Er, thanks, Pops," he said. "I've actually got something for you." Then he reached nervously into his back pocket and pulled out a little envelope. A little explosion of joy popped inside me. He'd found them!

"Jesse told me about your dementia and … I'm so sorry, Pops. None of us had the faintest…" Dad's eyes filled with sadness. "But Jesse asked me to look through our old shoeboxes of photos for something."

Gramp took the envelope from him, frowning curiously. Then he flipped it open and slid out a half-dozen old, faded photos. It was a young Gramp and a *very* young Dad – maybe four or five. They were stood outside the Tower of London eating ice creams, looking like they were having the best day ever. I felt like doing a cartwheel. It was the evidence I'd been hoping for!

Gramp stared at them, unblinking. When he finally spoke, his voice wavered. "It did happen…?"

Dad nodded. "It did. And plenty of other times like it."

Gramp blinked away a little tear as he continued to gaze on them. He looked overwhelmed with emotion. It even made me feel like crying. They *had* been a proper father and son. And that was enough to build on.

Dad looked down at the photos. "I know we've not always seen eye to eye, Pops," he said. "But we've still got time…"

Gramp looked up, his eyes glassy with tears.

"So…" Dad left a pause, took a breath and put a hand on Gramp's shoulder. "I – we – want you to come and live with us." Dad used his other hand to pull me into him and I smiled a smile the size of a watermelon slice. "Jesse will be there every other week."

"Will you?" I said. "Please, Gramp?"

Gramp looked from Dad to me. He smiled a smile of the deepest gratitude. "I'd love to."

"Great!" said Dad, genuinely delighted. My heart nearly burst with happiness.

I gave Gramp a massive hug, squeezing him tight. Over his shoulder, I saw Wendall heading towards the train station. He beamed and waved. Fists, Felix and Ms Ho-Renton followed, huge smiles painted across their odd, lovable faces.

"Thank you," whispered Gramp.

I squeezed him even harder.

"Well," said Dad, reaching down and picking up Gramp's bag. "Why don't you come see the new house?" He paused as a thought hit him. "Although, Jesse, I'm afraid Purrito will be living with your mum."

"How come?" I asked.

He pulled a face and shook his head. "It's weird. It's just, well, there's been a spate of cat burglaries around my new house. Very bizarre. We thought it was safer this way."

Gramp, still crouched down, murmured under his breath. "A new cat burglar's in town, hey?"

Dad raised his eyebrows and looked at Gramp. "What's that? What did you say?"

Gramp shook his head. "Nothing." Then he leaned into my ear. "What do you think?"

A smile spread out across my cheeks. "I reckon we can find whoever's responsible and keep Purrito safe."

Gramp smiled and extended a hand. I spat on my palm and shook his hand, which was probably a bit much, but I was in the moment.

Dad looked at us down his nose and said, with suspicion, "You two aren't going to cause me any trouble ... are you?"

We both shook our heads and replied in unison: "Absolutely not."

ACKNOWLEDGEMENTS

The best things come in threes: Hanson, Back to the Future, the 3 Musketeers (the chocolate bar), the Three Musketeers (the swordfighters), and finally my trio of fantastic editors for this book. To Yasmin Morrissey, who believed in the idea from the very beginning (as well as my ability to plot a murder mystery), before disappearing to have the gorgeous Isabella. To Ruth Bennett, who seems to appear like a fairy godmother at certain points in my career, for stepping in and taking the book to the next level with her maestro-like insight. And to Sophie Cashell, who picked it up when Ruth zoomed off to a fantastic new job and brought a whole new energy and intuition. To the whole team at Scholastic for welcoming me into the family these past two years, with special mentions to: Sarah Dutton, Harriet Dunlea, Liam Drane and Lauren Fortune. To my stellar agent Chloe Seager for always believing in and championing my silly-sad stories. To Nathan Reed for capturing the madcap cast of characters so utterly brilliantly. To Mum, for being my loudest cheerleader. To Albie and Agatha, for making me laugh every day. And to Issy, for being the bedrock underpinning everything. Finally, to my grandmother-in-law Jean McCann, who passed away this year and without whom this book wouldn't exist. Her own struggles with dementia – as well as the outlandish but semi-plausible stories of her care-home friend Peter – helped inspire this book and I like to picture her now somewhere sunny, dancing to a Greek accordion.

ABOUT THE AUTHOR

Tom Vaughan is a journalist, television producer, author and all-round good guy. Despite modest success in those four fields, he'd prefer to be remembered as the man who unsuccessfully tried to invent a meal between supper and breakfast, called supfast. He lives in London with his wife and two small unemployed people, also known as his children.

DON'T MISS:

Read on for an excerpt...

CHAPTER 1

Holidaying in a Hollowed-Out Volcano

I'm Billy Benbow. I'm ten years old. And I HATE holidaying in a hollowed-out volcano.

Bet you can't say *that* quickly.

"I hate hollowing in a holiday volcano!"

See? It's super hard.

"I hate hollowdaying in a holly-out volcano!"

Even *I* can't do it. And I've been trying for the past two weeks, pretty much non-stop, to anyone who would listen: my mum, my stepdad . . . his henchmen.

It was the last day of the school holidays, and I was

inside, you guessed it . . . a hollowed-out volcano. That's right: an actual volcano located somewhere off the coast of Hawaii, I think. It's extinct now and pimped up into a gazillion-pound holiday home by my stepdad, Phil. You probably think that sounds really cool, but I hate it more than homework. No: make that doing homework while drinking PholaCola . . . but we'll get to that last bit. Luckily, my best friend, Viv, came to the volcano to keep me company. And he is smart enough to beat any tongue-twister.

"You – hate – holidaying – in – a – hollowed – out – volcano!" he said, his black eyebrows bouncing over his glasses as he pronounced each word.

I screwed my face up and tried one last time: "I HATE hollering in a holy day volcano . . . o . . . o . . . o . . . o!"

The "o" echoed around the volcanic walls of my bedroom, finally dying out with a little squeak in the corner. I admitted defeat and we both fell back into silence on my bed, bored out of our brains. Hollowed-out holiday volcanoes might look cool, but they are boring as hell.

Above us, the brown rock of the volcano wall met the shiny chrome ceiling, and there was a faint smell of egg that was either volcanic gases or Viv's breath.

The silence only ended when Viv slurped down the last drops of PholaCola from his can, then internalized a burp that looked like a grenade going off inside his mouth. His eyes looked panicked, darting side to side as the blast lasted about a month. When it finally finished, he said: "Let's go ask Phil for more PholaCola!" and held the empty can in front of my face. "Maybe he's got a PholaCola swimming pool?"

Viv might be smart, but he has got one weakness: he'll do *anything* for some disgusting PholaCola. Actually, he has two weaknesses: there is also his overactive imagination. Who's ever heard of a swimming pool filled with cola? Not that Viv is a good swimmer anyway. . . *Actually,* he has three weaknesses: his weakness is also a weakness. He is about as strong as a baby vole. Which is what makes him such a target for bullies. Not that I can talk. I'm not sure who gets picked on more: Viv or me. But we'll get to all of that.

I rolled my eyes and fell back further on to my bed.

"Urgh. Do we *have* to? You *know* I hate being around Pheel."

Phil (or *Pheel* as I call him, just to be annoying) is my new stepdad. And if there's one thing I hate more than holidaying in a hollowed-out volcano, it's my stepdad, Pheel.

"Come on, *pleeaaaaasssseee!*" The echo made Viv sound desperate. I looked him up and down as his eyes bulged with another internal burp. The levels of CO_2 in his bloodstream must be close to toxic. If I poked him, he'd probably explode. I don't know why he liked PholaCola so much; it tasted like cough syrup. But then again, I was pretty much the only person in the world who thought that.

I looked around my vast, empty bedroom. Then I looked at Viv's pleading, desperate face. I couldn't resist him, even if he was slowly morphing from a human form into a fizzy gas.

"All right. But let's be quick. Pheel's always so ... annoying."

Viv bounced off my bed and punched the air. We set off across my room. My door slid open with a futuristic *swoosh* and we hopped on the monorail. I pushed a button that said BOARDROOM and we sped off through the volcano-plex.

"How do you not get excited by all of this?" said Viv, craning his neck as we whizzed through a lava tube dripping with giant stalactites. He loves it here. That's because it's like he's inside a giant school project, which is probably a fantasy of his.

I fixed my eyes straight ahead. "Why would I get excited about having to hang out with Pheel?"

Ever since my mum got remarried to Pheel last year, my life has got about five hundred times worse. First, it's like I'm suddenly invisible to Mum. Second, all the kids at school have started to notice me (and that's not a good thing). And third, I have to spend far too much time around fake, smarmy Pheel, doing things like going to his stupid hollowed-out holiday volcano. It might look impressive, but it is *so* boring – just endless rock corridors and locked rooms. Everyone else at school's parents take them to Center Parcs or Disneyland. And, to make it doubly better for them, their parents aren't Pheel.

We whooshed around a corner. Beneath us, a

heatproof window displayed a long drop into the bottomless magma chamber.

"How'd he even *afford* this?" asked Viv, his mouth hanging so far open you could fit a cow in it.

I kept my eyes dead ahead as the monorail lurched right, and replied, "By making billions inventing that disgusting drink you love."

The monorail pulled to a sudden stop, throwing us forwards. "YOU HAVE ARRIVED AT THE BOARDROOM," said a clipped female voice out of a little speaker on the control panel. We were in a long corridor that stretched for what seemed like miles in both directions. Its walls were bare rock face, and long silver ventilation shafts tracked the ceiling. Viv coughed and its echo bounced down, down, down the corridor until it disappeared. In front of us towered a metal door. Thick yellow-and-black striped lines flanked the frame and a red bulb flashed above it. Maybe to say: "DON'T GO IN". Or maybe just to add a nice lighting effect. Who was I to know? More to the point: Who was I to care?

Viv's eyes bulged with a sudden panic. "Can we go in? The red light's on!"

"Dunno, let's find out," I said with a shrug.

"But the red light's flashing! Surely that means 'Don't go in'?" Viv sounded his usual panicky self and he was hiccuping like a cartoon drunk. The last thing he needed was more fizzy drink, but he was his own boss.

"Maybe. Probably. Who cares?" I said, pulling out my key card and bleeping it against the lock, more in hope than expectation. A siren gave off a loud "BARP!" and the same cold female voice sounded from ceiling speakers: "BOARDROOM UNLOCKED. BOARDROOM UNLOCKED."

"Well, what do you know?" I said, shrugging in surprise. Viv's eyes widened and he started sweating heavily. He's my best friend and all – and he is hands down the smartest person I know – but *boy* is he a wimp.

The metal doors glided apart to reveal the cathedral-sized boardroom full of people . . .